JUSTICE FOR THE *Slain*

HAZEL WATSON MYSTERY BOOK TWO

C.A. VARIAN

Copyright © 2022 by C.A. Varian

All rights reserved.

No part of this publication may be reproduced, distributed, or transmitted in any form or by any means, including photocopying, recording, or other electronic or mechanical methods, without the prior written permission of the publisher, except as permitted by U.S. copyright law. For permission requests, contact C.A. Varian https://cavarian.com/

The story, all names, characters, and incidents portrayed in this production are fictitious. No identification with actual persons (living or deceased), places, buildings, and products is intended or should be inferred.

Book Cover by Blurbs, Baubles, and Book covers

Formatting by C.A. Varian

1st edition 2022

To my family, friends, and readers

Thank you for your support!

XOXO,

Cherie

Contents

1. The Threat and the Murdered Man — 3
2. The Lover and the Ex — 15
3. Mysteries and Ecstasy — 27
4. Unwanted Memories — 39
5. Love Lost, Love Found — 53
6. Distractions — 63
7. The New Client — 75
8. The Interview — 89
9. Hurricane Ida — 105
10. The Collage — 121
11. Discovering the Evidence — 135
12. The Transfer — 151
13. The Prison Visit — 165
14. Glimpses — 183
15. The Girl in the Memory — 199
16. Shadow from the Past — 211

17.	Harmony	233
18.	The Stalker	255
19.	The Stakeout	265
20.	The New Target	279
21.	Over the Edge	293
22.	Moving On	309
23.	Epilogue Honey Island Swamp Murders	315
Enjoyed Justice for the Slain?		318
Follow C.A. Varian		319
Also By		321
About the Author		323

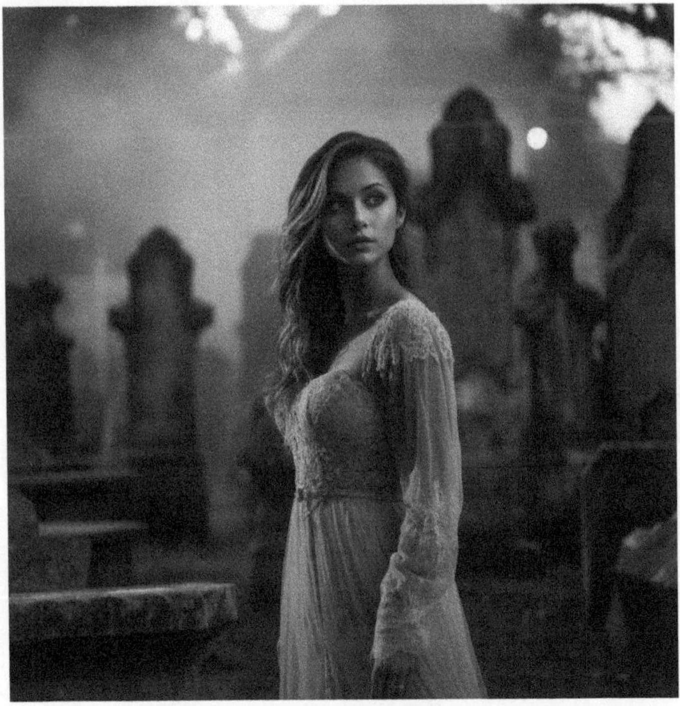

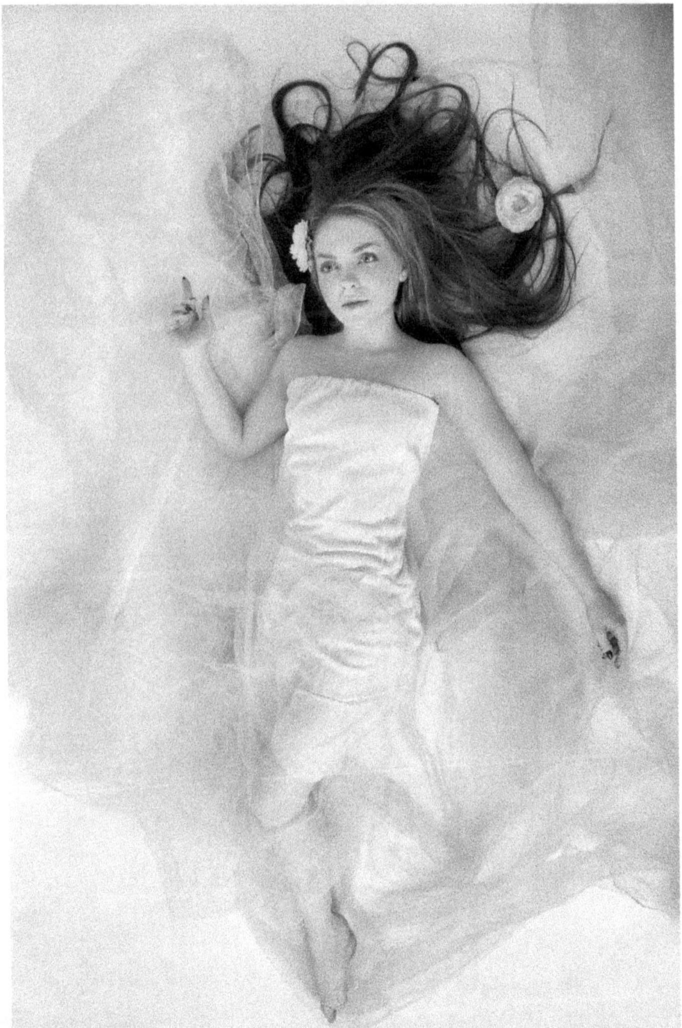

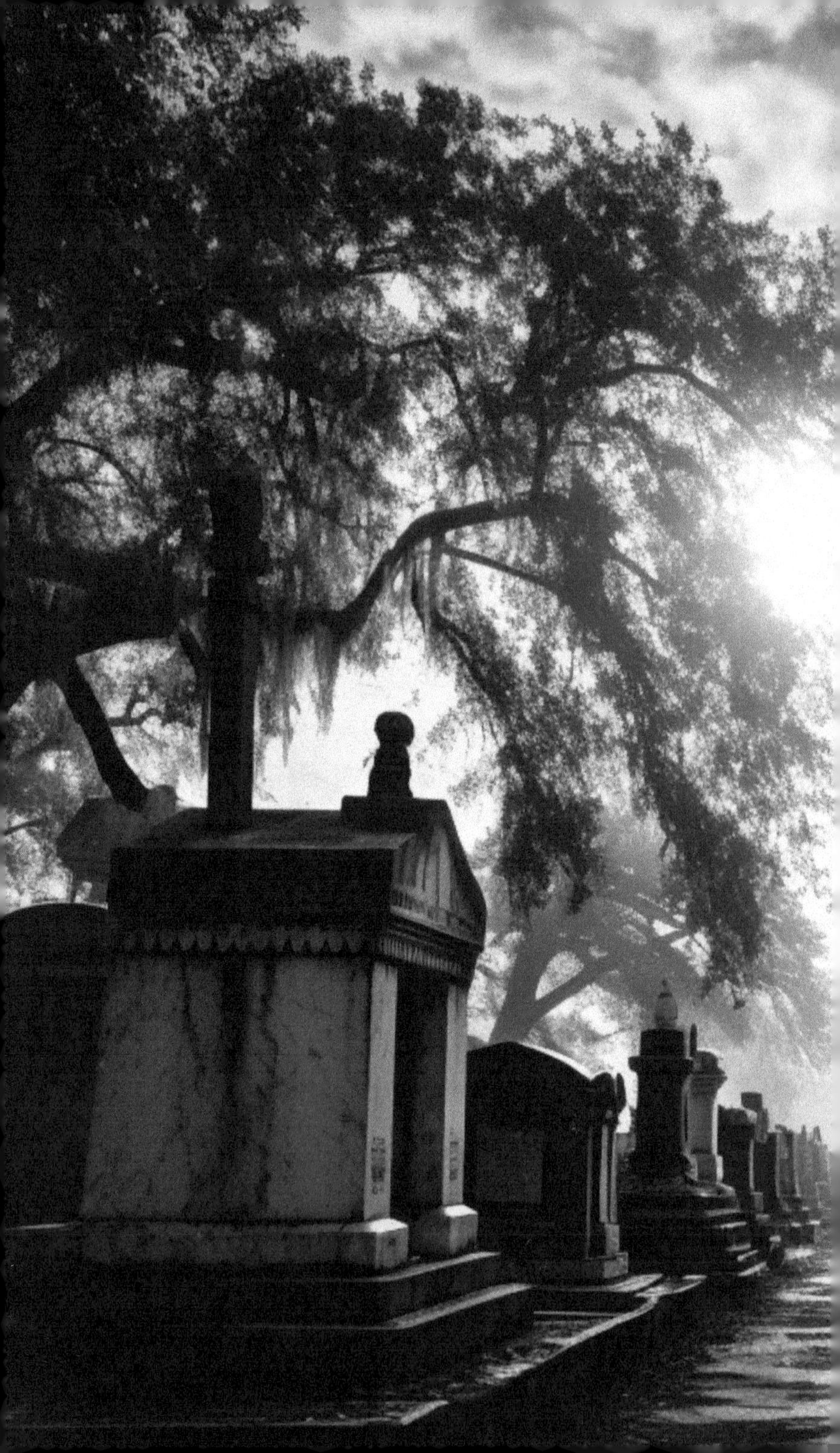

Chapter One
The Threat and the Murdered Man

"*I am a powerful man, and you will pay for ruining me.*" *His voice was a deep growl, but what struck Hazel most was the hatred etched into a face she once knew well.*

That face differed from how she remembered it. His eyes had turned as black as the darkness that surrounded him. A look of evil replaced what was once sophisticated and even handsome. He still wore the wounds he suffered the day he almost took her life.

Unable to move, she laid in utter horror as his battered body floated menacingly over her. She tried to scream, but no sound escaped. But she felt that scream inside her, and knew it must have been showing through her eyes.

She fought back the urge to gag from the smell of rotted flesh that lingered on his breath and gasped as he lowered himself over her, before taking the air from her lungs. She struggled to fight... to choke out a sound.

"You have no control over me!" She sobbed, finally finding the strength to fight the attack, but she only heard a baleful laugh that hit her deep within her bones.

"I'm not going anywhere, Miss Watson. You will see me again."

With a startled gasp, Hazel Watson awoke on the sofa in the comfort of her apartment, her breaths still labored from the trauma of her nightmare. The apartment had grown frigid while she was sleeping, so she rubbed her arms to remove the chill. She glanced around the room for her spectral roommate, but did not see her.

Being a spirit, Candy didn't need sleep, so it wasn't unusual for her to roam the city while Hazel slept. There was plenty to look at in the city of New Orleans, especially at night. Severe weather didn't seem to bother Candy either, so the night's show would not have kept her inside. Meanwhile, the storm had knocked the power out, so Hazel stumbled her way to the kitchen, so she could look for a flashlight. Flashes of lightning temporarily lit her way while sheets of rain beat against the windows.

Finding a flashlight, she walked back to the sofa and sat down, blowing out a breath.

Although the weather outside was torrential, the apartment was fairly quiet, eerily so, leaving her with the burn of dread in her throat.

Setting the flashlight on the coffee table, she resolved to sit there and hope the power would come back on quickly, or that Candy would return to give her company. Tate had gone home after their recent out-of-town trip, because he had an early shift, so she didn't want to call and wake him.

Lying against the armrest, she scrolled through pictures on her phone, hoping the boredom would eventually put her back to sleep.

An unnerving sound startled her upright. She thought she could hear rapid breathing, but the sound was not coming from her. Looking around the room, she only saw darkness. Her chest tightened as her anxiety rose.

"Candy, is that you?" she called out, just in case Candy was somewhere in the apartment, unbeknownst to her.

Holding her breath, she listened quietly, but heard no response. The breath sounds increased in volume, synchronizing with the sound of her own heartbeat in her ears.

Flicking the flashlight on, she stood up from the sofa and faced the direction of the sound. She hoped to see nothing, but gasped when a figure rose from the darkness. A man who appeared to be in his late twenties was bleeding in the corner of her living room, the same man she'd seen in her bathroom before, or at least she thought it was the same man.

Her hand trembled as it gripped the flashlight, watching as he flickered in and out of view. His barely solid presence told her he was not a living man, but a spirit, and judging from the state of his body, he had not died a natural death. He had been murdered.

Approaching him cautiously, the taste of fear rose in her throat, making her mouth dry. Something about him looked familiar, so she wanted to get a better look at him, but he wasn't in a recognizable state. It was too dark, and he was soaking wet, his spectral energy too weak to maintain his presence. He didn't speak, but his eyes followed her movements.

"What's your name? I can help you."

She forced her voice to sound calm, although she was anything but. She may have been helping spirits since she was a child, but it never got any easier when they invaded her personal space. He continued to watch her, but he did not respond.

Maybe he's in shock... Do ghosts experience shock?

Wearing only boxer shorts and socks, his body shivered violently. The stab wounds all over him bled profusely, although he no longer had a corporeal form. There was no question that whoever had stabbed him had fully intended to take his life, and they'd succeeded.

Without warning, Candy rushed past her, pulling the man's spirit into a tight embrace.

"Jake! Who did this to you?" Candy screamed, her tone revealing her pain.

Standing back and trying to gather her thoughts, Hazel watched as Candy frantically tried to calm the bleeding man.

"Candy, who is he?" Her voice had come out more hysterical than she'd intended. Whether Candy did not hear her question, or was prioritizing over it, she didn't know, but there was no response.

The man's teeth continued to chatter as he shivered, his breath shallow but quick. Candy fussed over him, but he didn't speak to her either. Neither of them acknowledged Hazel's question at all.

Watching the scene play out before her, she stood there helplessly, not understanding who the man was, or how Candy knew him. Candy had called him Jake, but the name did not ring a bell for Hazel.

Everything about the moment was confusing and chaotic. Although they both knew it was too late to save him, Candy continued trying to stop his bleeding, the movement of her spectral hands frantic. Without a corporeal form, the blood was an illusion and stopping its flow would not bring him back.

"Hazel! Please grab a towel!" Candy shrieked, never turning away from his face.

Even though Hazel wasn't sure what good it would do, Hazel ran to the bathroom for a towel. The man was already dead, but it didn't matter. Clearly, Candy knew him, and she was close to him, unable to accept that he was dead. Therefore, Hazel had no choice but to go along with her attempts to save him, no matter how futile they were.

Returning to the room with towels in hand, she held them out to Candy, who grabbed one and started trying to dry him off. It didn't work, but Candy still wrapped the towel around his near naked body. She pleaded with him, but he still didn't speak.

"Jake, who did this to you. Here, sit down here," Candy asked, her voice no more than a sob as she shuffled him over to the sofa and guided him down onto it. He obliged. It was clear he was trying to speak back to her, but his teeth were chattering so much that Hazel couldn't make out any words.

"Candy, who is he?"

This time, Candy finally turned to face her, her spectral makeup running down her face from crying. She did not bother to wipe it.

"This is Jake. The guy who I was killed over."

Hazel was taken aback, her heart falling into her stomach from the grief radiating off Candy. "I'm so sorry, but you know that he's..."

Candy nodded, tears still pouring down her cheeks. "Yes, I know. I just wanted to help him." Shaking her head, she rubbed her palms over her eyes.

Hazel approached, wrapping her arms around Candy to calm her, but Candy continued to cry. Having never seen Candy like this before, she didn't know how to help.

"Who would do this to him, Hazel?"

Candy sniffled, wiping at her wet cheeks again.

"I don't understand. I mean... Brad is in prison, so he couldn't have done it. I wish Jake could talk to me."

Candy dropped her sobbing face into her hands, while Jake watched her from the sofa, still not speaking out loud. Sadness twisted his face as his form still flickered. His spectral blood flow had slowed, the crimson beads disappearing once they rolled off his body.

"We may need to give him time, but I'm sure he'll come around. I think he's in shock."

"Yeah…"

Candy trailed off as she moved closer to her slain lover. Kneeling down in front of the sofa, she draped her body over Jake's torso, wrapping her arms around him and letting her sobs pour freely.

Not knowing how to help them, Hazel left the room to get them a blanket. She knew that, as spirits, a blanket would not do them much good, but it just seemed like the right thing to do. When she returned to the living room, she laid the blanket across them, and then left the room to give them privacy.

With one more glance toward her friend, Hazel went into her bedroom and dropped onto her bed, Tate's absence making her heart ache. They had only just begun a romantic relationship, but he was already such a big part of her life. They'd been friends for many years, but now that they were more, she'd grown used to no longer being alone in bed. Seeing Candy cry over her murdered lover only made Hazel miss Tate more.

With Tate being a police officer in a city where murders happened almost every day, she always worried about him when he was at work. The likelihood of him getting injured while at work was pretty high, and she could not even think about what she would do if he got killed on the job. His job was dangerous, and she hated that. She respected what he did. He was a hero, and that made her proud, but it did not make her worry any less.

Glancing at her phone, she thought about calling him, but didn't want to ruin his chance at a good night's sleep. She resolved herself to wait a few hours until he got up for work. He needed all the sleep he could get, so he could be alert on his patrols. Alertness was vital for his safety. His ability to react quickly and correctly could make the difference between life and death.

As she lay in bed, the thought crossed her mind that Jake may have just been murdered, and needed police called to the scene right away, but she had no way to explain how she knew about his death. She didn't want the police to suspect her, and she couldn't tell them she knew about his death with the excuse that his spirit was bleeding on her sofa. It was not a straightforward decision to weigh, but Jake was already gone, so his body would have to wait a few more hours. At least until the one cop who would understand how she knew was available to talk to her.

Hazel was no stranger to getting involved in police business, but her meddling was not always legal. Being a public defender for the city of New Orleans, the predicament was never easy. It was her obligation since birth to help spirits, but she didn't have a choice about whether the spirit needing help was the victim of an unsolved murder. Lately, that was all she had. She never called herself a psychic. The title seemed too commercial, but semantics aside, police departments usually viewed those with claims of abilities like hers with skepticism. This was one of the many reasons she kept her ability to communicate with the dead a secret to all but a few people. Jake may have still been shaken up, but he was newly murdered, so it was only a matter of time before he started demanding justice. Just like all the others, he would probably stalk her until she solved his murder and achieved justice for him. It was the way it almost always went with murder victims, and it was exhausting.

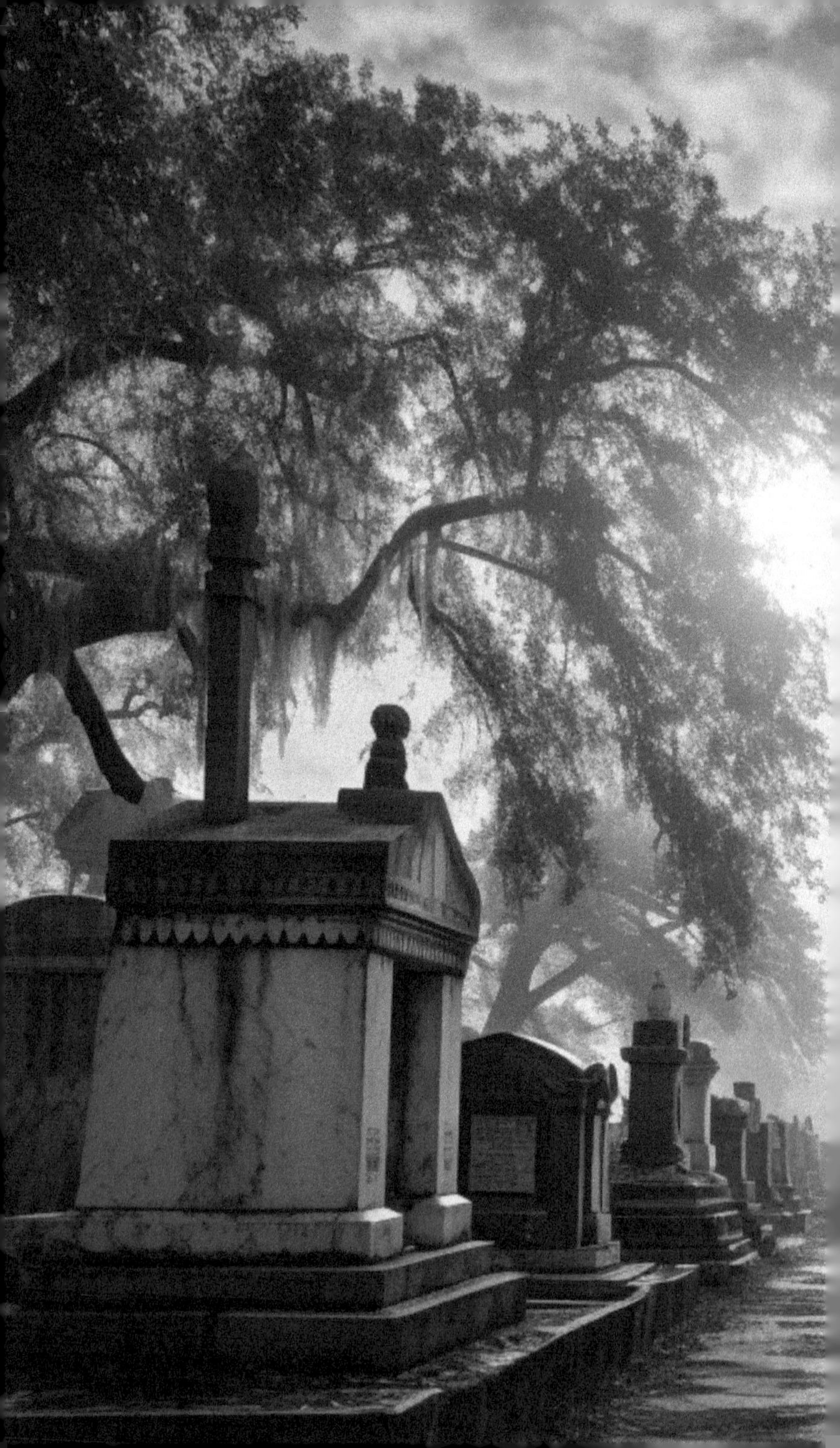

Chapter Two
The Lover and the Ex

Hazel wandered sleepily into the living room at 7 a.m. to find Candy still in the same position as she had left her, draped over the sofa where Jake's spirit had been. One thing had changed, however. Jake was no longer there. She walked up and kneeled down next to the sniffling form, resting her head on Candy's shoulder.

"What happened?"

"I... I... don't know. He was here, and then he was gone."

"How long ago?"

Candy peered around the room, as though trying to find a sign of his presence, or at least evidence that he was not a delusion. She shrugged.

"He tried to talk to me about what happened to him, but he was too shaken. I think. He couldn't stop trembling. I think he ran out of energy, causing him to fade out. He'll be back... He'll be back."

She seemed to be reassuring herself more than anyone else. Hazel gently passed her hand through Candy's fiery red hair, cooing at her sympathetically.

"We'll find out what happened to him, Candy, so don't worry. I'm going to call Tate. I want to make sure Jake wasn't murdered last night. I don't want his body to be lying around somewhere. I need to call and report it. Do you know where he lived?"

For the first time since Hazel had known her, Candy was not even trying to look her best. It was one of her biggest personality traits, never to allow the world to damper her appearance. That was why she worked so hard on her spectral powers right after she died. So, she could change her appearance and look her best, even after death. It was just her thing. She portrayed herself as someone who let nothing get to her. This night, however, she allowed her emotions to flow, as she would have when she was a living woman, and it showed on her face. Her mascara had run down her cheeks and her foundation had become blotchy. She looked up at Hazel with the eyes of a small child who desperately needed help. Her breath hitched.

"I know where he lived... before I died. I'm not sure if he still lived there."

She had spoken in not much more than a whisper. Hazel placed her hand on Candy's cheek.

"You helped me so many times and I'm going to help you now. Don't worry. I'm going to call Tate. Okay? I'll be right back."

Instead of calling from the living room, Hazel returned to her bedroom so she could make the call in private, not wanting to upset Candy more. She could guarantee Candy would not come into her bedroom to listen, but, if she could, she wanted to filter her conversation with Tate as much as necessary. She did not know what Tate would tell her about Jake's death, so she braced for the unknown.

Finding a comfortable position on her bed, Hazel grabbed her cell phone and dialed Tate's number. She did not yet know what she would say to him.

Although he was her boyfriend, she had only recently told him about her abilities. He handled it well, but it was not an easy reality to accept. Most people were not used to the idea of spirits staying in the land of the living, and they rarely took it gracefully when she was forced to tell them. Tate, however, had accepted it without question. But she tried to not fill his mind with her ghosts. She did not want to overwhelm him.

Sounding chipper for 7 a.m., he answered after only the second ring

"Hey, my lady. What's up?"

Hazel's heart fluttered at the sound of his voice. She blushed, but there was no one in her bedroom to see it.

"Hey, babe. I need to ask you a question."

"Um... Okay. What's up?"

She hesitated, as she always did when having to bring up new issues involving spirits.

"Do you know a man named Jake Gautreaux?"

"Do you mean the guy Candy was allegedly murdered over?"

"Yes."

"I know of him. Why? What's going on?"

"His spirit showed up to me in the middle of the night. Looks like he was murdered, but I'm not sure when and he can't seem to speak. So, I'm not sure how, but I guess I may need to report him dead?"

She steadied herself for his response. Thankfully, his voice was compassionate.

"Oh, wow, how is Candy holding up?"

"She's really upset. We haven't been able to talk much yet. How are you going to explain my report? How I know about his death?"

"Oh, I don't need to."

Tate's words confused her.

"What do you mean?"

"Jake was murdered a few weeks ago. I'm sorry I didn't tell you. With everything that was going on with Raymond Waters, it never crossed my mind."

"Damn. Do they know who did it?"

"No. It's still an open case."

"Brad didn't?"

"No. Brad is still in prison. It wasn't him."

"Shit."

"Yea. It's a huge mystery right now. The cops don't seem to have any leads, or at least none they are making public."

Could Brad be innocent? Is Jake's murder related to Candy's? It can't be... can it?

"I just don't understand who would do this, if it wasn't Brad..."

She trailed off as her mind whirled.

"Yeah. It makes you wonder. I'll check on the case notes and see if there are any updates. Let me know if you get anything from Jake. Are we still on for tonight?"

"Definitely, unless something comes up with Candy. Can we stay in though? Just in case?"

"Yeah. That's not a problem. I'm sure she needs you right now."

She and Tate ended their phone call, but she laid on her bed for a few more moments, going through things in her head. With Tate's confirmation that Jake had been murdered weeks earlier, a realization hit her. She had never gotten a good look at him. The visits had always been brief, and he'd never spoken to her, but she now knew without a doubt. Jake was the bleeding man who had showed up outside of her shower twice before. He must have come to the apartment right after he died, probably looking for Candy, but Hazel ignored him. She did not have time for another ghost, so she had ignored him. Now she felt terrible. Guilty.

She returned to the living room to relay Tate's message to Candy, although she was worried about how Candy would take the news. Discovering Jake had been murdered weeks earlier, and that the case was still open, and the murderer still out there, was not something Candy would easily absorb. She would also not take it well that Hazel had seen him twice, but hadn't told her more. Not that it was done intentionally. Candy lectured her repeatedly about being open and sharing her spirit visitations, but she usually brushed them off. She usually swept many of their visits under the rug, always hoping they would not return to haunt her later. Also, until this point, Candy, Hazel, and most other people, believed Candy's murder was committed by her ex-boyfriend, Brad. But with Jake having been murdered as well, it raised whether Brad was responsible at all. But if he was not responsible, who was? Who else could have wanted Candy dead? The thought of anyone wanting her best friend dead made Hazel sick.

Returning to the living room, she found Candy no longer leaning over the sofa, but sitting on it. Her face still showed her emotions more clearly than it ever had before. Her usually flawless makeup was running and smeared. She looked lost. Traumatized. Jake's spirit had not returned. Candy's eyes shot up in anticipation when Hazel entered the room. Sitting next to Candy on the sofa, she pulled her friend in close.

"Well? What did he say?"

Hazel swallowed hard, but her mouth had become so dry that her throat had the texture of cardboard. She tried to find the right words, but being eloquent was not a skill she had, so the words tumbled clumsily out of her mouth.

"Jake has been dead for weeks, but they don't know who did it. Um... also... remember the man I saw in the bathroom, twice, a few weeks ago?"

Candy's eyebrows furrowed as she looked at Hazel with a confused stare. A moment of silence followed, only making Hazel's mouth drier.

"Weeks? Dead for weeks?"

Candy's face dropped back into her hands as fresh tears sparkled down her cheeks. She shook her head slowly, almost like she was trying to shake Hazel's words out of her mind.

"I'm sorry you're having to find out like this, Candy. I'm so sorry."

Hazel squeezed Candy's shoulders and gave her a kiss on the cheek.

"But do you remember about the guy who showed up in our bathroom a few times?"

"Yes. I remember you mentioning the spirit in the bathroom. Was it Jake?"

"I didn't realize at first, because I was so traumatized when I first saw him, and it was dark when he showed up this time, but I'm pretty sure it was him who has been coming to me for a few weeks. Maybe he was looking for you. I'm not sure, but I'm almost positive it was him."

"So, he's been this way for weeks? Shivering and bleeding. He's been lost and looking for me?"

Candy's shoulders shook as she wept. When she raised her head again, she looked horrified. Her eyes searched the room carefully, looking for a sign Jake had returned. Hazel followed her line of sight, but they both had turned up empty. Jake was not there. Candy looked back at Hazel as fresh tears shimmered from her eyes. They sparkled as they rolled down her spectral cheeks.

Hazel's heart broke. She could not do anything more for Candy but be there for her, as a best friend should, but she wanted badly to do more. She wanted to get justice for her, and for Jake.

Fighting the incessant need to shiver from being so close to a spirit, she held her arm around Candy and let her cry. There was not much they could do until Jake returned. If Jake returned. They would eventually have to look into how his murder related to Candy's. They would need to discuss it and try to make connections. For the moment, however, Candy needed to grieve.

Hazel was not sure how much time had passed when she awoke on the sofa, but Candy was still next to her. No longer crying, Candy sat solemnly, her face set with determination. For what, Hazel could only guess.

"Hey," Hazel said softly. "Sorry to fall asleep on you. Has he come back?"

Candy shook her head, but kept her eyes facing forward. Hazel tried to find what she was staring at, but there was nothing there.

"Brad didn't kill me, did he?" Candy spoke, but did not meet Hazel's eyes. Her tone held no inflection.

"I'm not sure. I don't know what to think about this. I guess it's possible he didn't do it."

Turning to look at Hazel, Candy's face was serious. Her blue eyes were wide and her jaw was tight.

"I need to talk to him. I need to know for sure."

Hazel pondered Candy's statement for a moment, unsure how to respond. Candy was a spirit, so the likelihood of Brad being able to see her was slim to none. Hazel opened her mouth to reply, but then closed it again. Candy noticed her hesitation.

"You share messages for spirits all the time, Hazel. I need for you to talk to him for me. I know it would be a gamble. I know it is unlikely he'll even listen to you, but I need you to try."

Although uncomfortable with the suggestion, and feeling backed into a corner, Hazel hesitantly nodded her head. She had never laid eyes on Brad, so she did not know if he would be receptive to hearing a message from Candy from beyond the grave. Hell, she did not even know if she could speak with him at all. She was not his attorney, and he was in prison for murder. There were so many things about the suggestion that made her feel sick to her stomach, but she had to at least try for Candy. After everything Candy had done for her, including saving her life, she owed her everything.

"Okay. We can try."

Candy nodded, wiping her eyes before curling into Hazel's waiting arms.

"What do you want to do for now? Do you want to wait here for Jake?"

"I think so."

They waited in Hazel's apartment all day, but Jake did not return. Candy did not feel like talking, so they spent most of the day watching television. She did not know what Candy had been like in life, but she had turned into a couch potato in death.

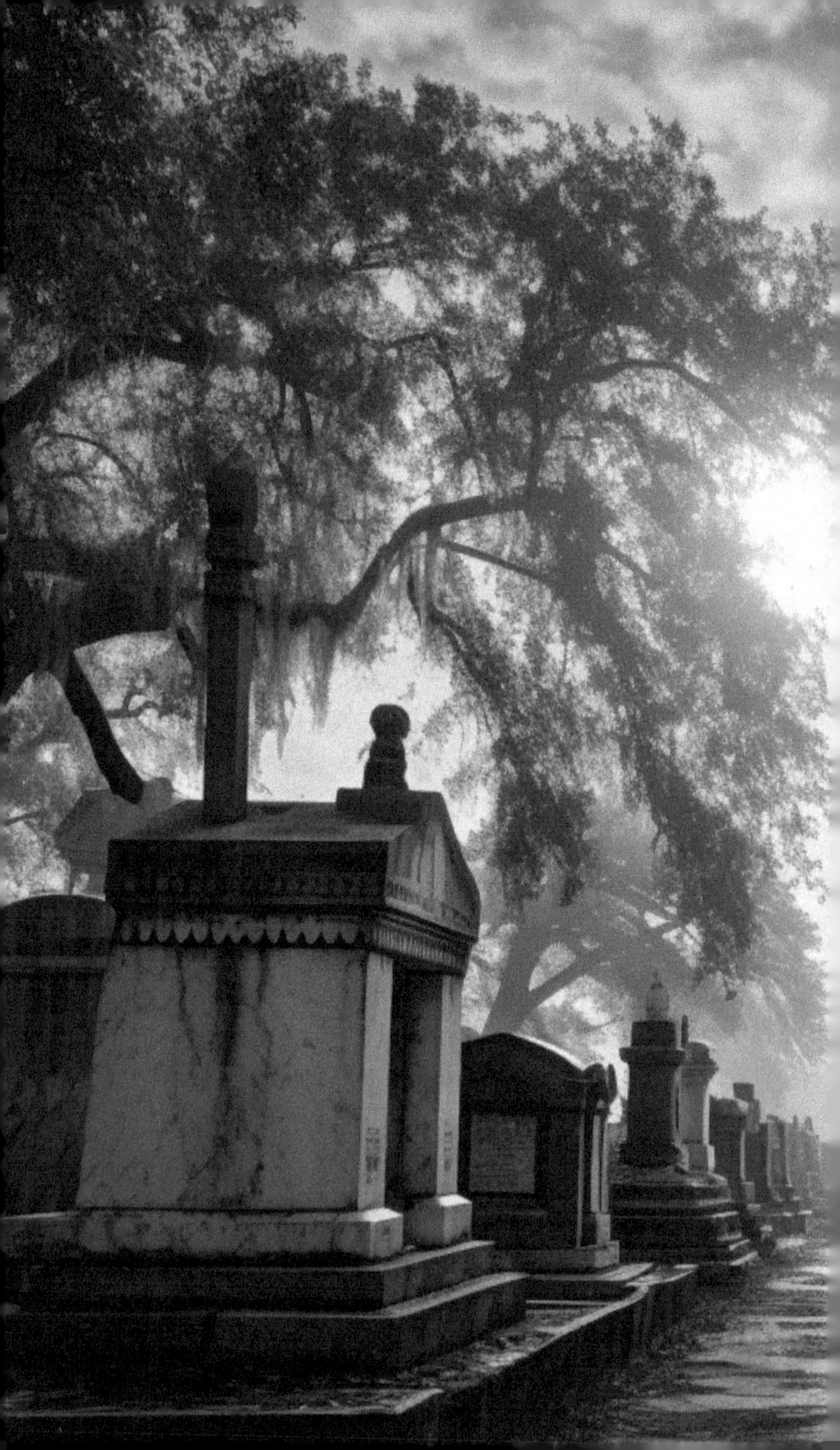

Chapter Three
Mysteries and Ecstasy

A knock on the door made Hazel jump, although she knew who was probably waiting outside. Peeking through the peephole at the top of the door, she could see Tate's smiling face. He was holding up a plastic takeout bag. Seeing him created a ripple of warm energy through her body. She opened the door and jumped forcefully into his arms.

"Hey!"

The morning had been so traumatic. She did not realize how badly she needed to see him until he was standing in front of her.

"Hey to you! Rough day?"

He smiled at her as he wrapped his arm around her waist and they shuffled into the apartment, shutting the humidity outside.

"Is she here?"

Tate looked around the apartment as though he had the sixth sense as well. Hazel followed his line of sight. After his search turned up empty, she pointed at Candy, who looked up to meet her eyes.

"Yeah. She's on the sofa."

"Hey Candy," Tate called out. Although he could not see her, he wanted to acknowledge her presence. Candy flashed a fleeting smile, before turning away to look towards the window.

"She heard you, but she's had a rough day as well."

Tate flashed a sympathetic smile.

"I can't imagine. I'm sorry she had to hear about it in that way. I wish I would have thought to tell you, but it didn't seem relevant then."

"We understand. What's in the bag?"

He smiled, walking to the bag and opening it.

"I grabbed dinner. I figured you were probably hungry."

"You figured right."

Hazel gave him a kiss on the cheek, then dropped into a chair at the table.

"You're too good to me."

He flashed a sheepish smile as he handed a food container to her, along with a utensil packet. Then he pulled his chair next to hers.

"You deserve it."

After eating, they settled onto the sofa next to Candy as he pulled a manilla folder out of his bag and laid the contents onto the coffee table.

"I made a copy of the paperwork in Jake's file. There isn't much to go by, though. The case is still open. They are at a bit of a loss as to who could have done this. Jake was a pretty private guy, so they haven't been able to learn much about his social life."

"Have they spoken to Brad? Maybe he knows something."

"I'm not sure. He's been in prison for a year. Do you really think he would know something?"

Hazel shrugged her shoulders, chancing a glance at Candy, who was focusing on the paperwork across the table.

"Candy wants me to go to the prison and talk to him for her."

Tate glanced up at her. His eyes were wide and his mouth was open. He started to respond, but then bit back his words for a moment.

"I know you disapprove." Hazel said, disturbing Tate's thoughts. "But she's not going to take no for an answer. I already tried. Well, sort of. I owe her everything. If this is what she needs, then I will do it. She deserves to know if he killed her. He might have insight into who it could have been. We need to go back and listen to his testimony and interviews. Maybe there is something the police overlooked."

Tate's face changed, and for the first time in the conversation, he looked open to her idea.

"It's possible. I'm not a detective, so I wasn't a part of his interrogations or trial, but I admit to being curious. I watched her die, so if someone else was to blame, then I would want to know about it. I will say he had to seem guilty enough to end up where he is, even if he didn't actually kill her."

Hazel looked at Candy as she heard Candy's throat clear.

"He was a piece of shit," Candy said. "But he had never been violent to me. I wouldn't have stayed if that would have been the case. I'll admit it was long over between us, although he never accepted it, but I was never one hundred percent on board with the idea that he killed me."

Hazel nodded and then relayed Candy's message to Tate, who nodded as well.

"Okay," he said, "I'm with you. We need to know more, but I beg you to please wait until after I do some research. Please don't act on this information just yet. I'll pull the tapes so we can listen to them first. That way, we can at least have something to go on. Once we know what he originally stated in his interviews, we can compare it to any claims he makes now. Can you at least wait for me? I need to keep you safe."

Hazel chanced a look at Candy before returning her eyes to Tate and nodding her head. She could not repeat the same mistakes that had almost gotten her killed in the past, so she had to let him help her. It was the only way to keep a healthy relationship, unlike what had become of her parents' marriage. He reached out and laced his fingers with hers.

"Good. We will help Candy, but we will do it together. Oh, I didn't even ask if Jake was still here. Is he?"

Hazel scanned the room, just in case Jake had silently returned, unknown to them, and was hiding in the corner.

"No. He faded out shortly after arriving. When you and I were still on the phone. Candy thinks he ran out of energy. He seemed in shock, so we couldn't get anything out of him while he was here. He was in bad shape."

"Do you believe he will return?"

"Hopefully, so we can talk to him. I hope he can tell us what happened to him, or at least tell us who is to blame."

Hazel heard Candy sniffle. She let go of Tate's hand and reached over to comfort her friend. Tate looked a bit confused, but then quickly realized what was going on and his face relaxed.

"I wish I could see her, but I'm so glad you can. She deserves justice. I hope we can do that for her."

"Me too. Do you want to watch a movie or..."?

"Yea," Tate said, sounding relieved. "Let's watch something funny."

They watched two comedies back-to-back. Candy remained on the sofa next to them for a while, but she eventually left the room to give them some privacy. Hazel assured her it was not necessary, but she insisted. It was actually a relief to Hazel because it allowed the energy in the room to lighten. She curled up next to Tate, spending more time kissing him than watching the movie. Her heart ached for Candy. It did. But Tate gave her so much joy, so she had to be a little selfish with him so close to her. She did not want to take his presence for granted, especially after watching Candy grieve for a long-lost love. If there was one thing she had learned over the past few months, it was that life was fleeting and tomorrow was not guaranteed. So, she had to make the best of the days she had.

By the time she and Tate were ready to go to bed, Jake had still yet to return. She could see the worry all over Candy's face, but did not know how to assure her it would be okay.

"I'm going to go out," Candy said, as they turned the television off. "I can't sit here and wait for him anymore."

The idea of Candy leaving, after everything she had been through that day, made Hazel worried, but Candy was a grown woman. Hazel had to let her go.

"Oh, okay. Where are you going to go?"

"I think I'm going to go to his house," she responded with a loud sigh. "I don't know. I just can't sit around and wait. I feel like I need to do something with myself."

"I understand. Just remember how much I love you and come back home if you start to feel overwhelmed. Wake me up if you need to. Okay? I don't mind."

Candy nodded and smiled before wrapping Hazel in an icy hug. Then she vanished from where she stood.

Hazel walked into her bedroom to find that Tate had already jumped into the shower. The reality of being with Tate created a feeling of bliss Hazel could not express with words. All she knew was that she had finally gotten what she wanted for so long and she was not even sure she deserved it.

"Care to join me?" Tate called out as he heard the bedroom door close.

Fighting back her usual urge to shy away from such situations, she bit back her self-doubts to seize the moment that was ahead of her, only to chicken out the minute she walked into the bathroom. Standing in the doorway and staring at the wet shower curtain, she could just barely see Tate's form on the other side. She could not help but smile, knowing he wanted her. He was too good for her. At least that was what she always thought. He did not have the same insecurities she had.

He peeked his head around the shower curtain, causing her to blush. He always seemed to catch her gawking at him with heart-shaped eyes and her tongue hanging out. At least that's how she pictured it.

"Are you coming in?"

"I'll wait my turn. I wouldn't want to kick you out from under the water."

"Suit yourself. I'm almost done."

Before leaving the bathroom, she walked up to the shower and planted a kiss on his lips. His touch sent a shock wave down her body, but she pulled herself away, anyway. If Candy were there, she would have given her a hard time for refusing his invitation into the shower. Actually, she would have probably climbed into the shower with him herself, even though he could not see her. Candy would have also insisted that Hazel wear lingerie, but she grabbed a pair of boxer shorts and a tee shirt instead. Her confidence around Tate had grown, but it was a slow process to change who she had always been. Shy and insecure.

The sound of Tate entering the bedroom after his shower caught her attention, and she could not help but turn around to watch him. Wearing only a towel around his waist, his muscular bare chest still had drips of water that he had yet to dry. Her mouth fell open as she watched the water glisten down his abs and into the towel that barely hung on his hips. Realizing she was probably ogling him as though she had a schoolgirl crush, she turned away quickly. Although the schoolgirl crush was real.

"I'll be right back," she said.

Hiding the heat in her face, she scurried into the bathroom, closing the door behind her.

Thankfully, she had only washed her hair the night before, because she did not want to linger in the shower for too long. It was rare that she and Tate had a night alone, without the presence of Candy, so she did not want to waste their time. Although she got

Candy to vacate the apartment sometimes, she did not expect her to stay away for long, especially not after the events of the morning. She had no warning system for when Candy would return, so she always worried Candy would pop in on something she should not see.

When Hazel got back to the bedroom, Tate was lying on the bed, reading a novel. She lingered in the doorway for a moment, enjoying the view.

He put his book down on his stomach and patting the bed next to him.

"Are you watching me?"

"Probably."

Tossing her laundry into the basket, she climbed onto the bed and curled up next to him.

She and Tate had been friends since college, so it was not as though he was a stranger, but with their new romantic relationship, she still found herself shy. Making moves on him was difficult, although their chemistry was intense, and he was the best lover she had ever had. Her timidity was something she hoped would improve with time. Thankfully, Tate did not have the same reservations, so she did not have to base their intimacy on her own nerve.

Wrapping his arms around her, he pulled her on top of him and into a kiss. She relished the moment. Closing her eyes, she allowed herself to be intoxicated by him, by the smell of his face, by the taste of him. Her body came alive, as though a surge of electricity had flowed from him and into her. With every kiss, every stroke of his body against hers, she fell deeper into ecstasy, and further from the stresses of the rest of the world.

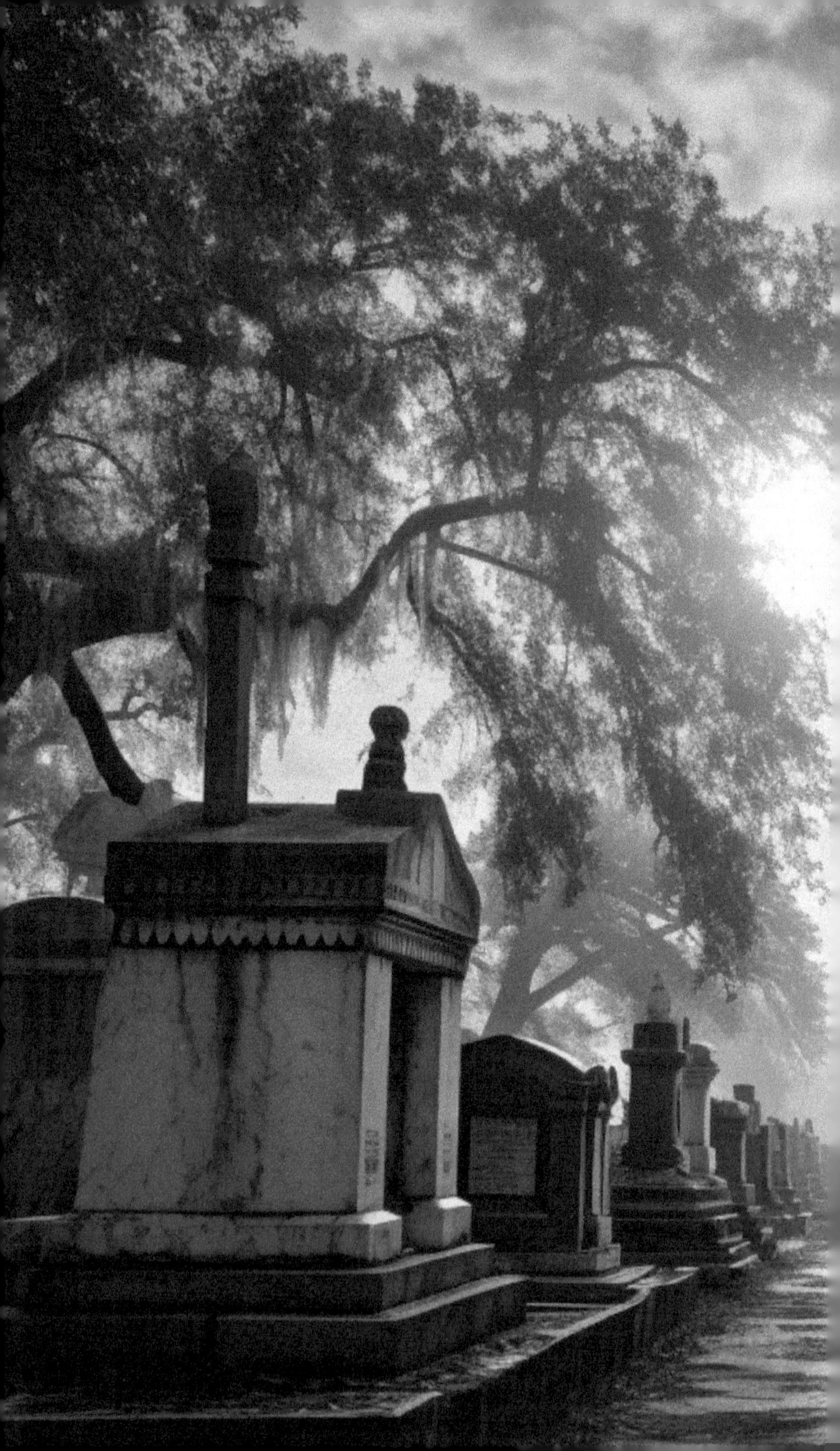

Chapter Four
Unwanted Memories

Sitting on the floor in the corner of the room, I watched as he held onto me, holding pressure over the wounds on my back as the life poured out of me like paint onto the carpet. I knew I was gone, but he still tried diligently to save me. My heart longed to be back there, in my body, so I could tell him thank you, thank you for trying so hard to save me. But it was no use. I couldn't do anything except sit in the room's corner, watching in a blind panic, as the power of my being was stripped from me.

The tears welled up in my eyes, dropping onto my hands in a steady stream. I thought for a moment they looked like little diamonds because of how the reflection of the light added a hint of a sparkle to them. My attention turned back to him as he continued trying to put breath back into my lungs, as he tried to make my heart beat once again. But I knew that nothing he could do was going to bring me back.

My new form felt surprisingly numb, and I hated it. I wanted to feel the good and the bad. I wanted to be alive. I crawled to him, trying to tell him it was okay to let me go but, before I could touch him, he realized the truth for himself. The others moved around him in a frenzy. I knew they were there, but I couldn't stop watching him, the man who gave saving me all that he could. I watched him lean back to sit on his heels, as another man draped a white sheet over me, and then patted him on the shoulder, as if to tell him he had given it his best.

Unable to look at myself in that way for another second, I wiped a tear from my cheek, gave him a kiss on his, and walked into my bedroom. I knew he would never know how much I appreciated him, but I would never forget.

Hazel awoke from a familiar scene; one she had experienced before. This time, however, she opened her eyes to the same man who had appeared in her dream. The first time she had seen Candy's death in a dream, she was surprised that Tate was the police officer who had been called to the incident when Candy was stabbed. Candy hadn't told her until nearly a year after she moved into the apartment where the murder had taken place, but she had seen it.

She gazed at him as he slept peacefully, admiring how his dark eyelashes rested upon his handsome face. Watching him try to save her best friend only made her love him more. Although she had only seen it in a dream, it had been so real to her.

She wondered how she could see the memory at all. When Angela's spirit had reached out to her for help, she always wondered if Angela's memories had gotten transferred to her dreams intentionally or without Angela's knowledge. Unfortunately, Angela crossed over before she thought to ask her. She had seen countless memories from Angela's past. They haunted her sleep for weeks and had only just become less frequent.

On the other hand, she had only seen a few of Candy's memories, although she never confessed that to Candy.

One thing she believed for certain was that Candy was not knowingly sending those memories to her. She would not. Being her best friend, Candy knew how nightmares plagued her sleep and would never intentionally cause more. Candy also knew how much Angela's memories had traumatized her, causing her to lose more sleep than she could afford to lose.

Although Candy was not transferring her memories on purpose, Hazel recognized she would need to tell her. With Candy's murder investigation possibly needing to be reopened, the memory transfers may be something that would become more frequent, so Candy needed to know the truth.

Tate woke up, pulling Hazel out of her thoughts. He rolled over to look at her.

"Good morning. Have you been awake long?"

"Not too long... I had a nightmare, so I wasn't able to go back to sleep."

Tate frowned before pulling her into a hug.

"I'm sorry. I'd hoped I'd be able to keep those away."

"You usually do."

He pulled away so he could look into her eyes. His eyebrows were lowered when he spoke. His voice revealed his concern.

"Does that happen often? Repeated nightmares, I mean."

"Not usually, especially not spirit memories. I rarely see the same memory twice."

"Spirit memory? Memories like you saw with Angela?" His look of concern deepened.

"Yes. I'm not sure how I'm seeing this one, though. I know, for a fact, the spirit is not purposely sending it to me."

"How do you know that?"

"Because it's Candy's memory."

Tate's eyes widened at her admission.

"Candy's memory? From what I know about the relationship between the two of you, Candy wouldn't intentionally give you nightmares. What kind of memory was it?"

He gently caressed her back with his hand. She would have usually closed her eyes and melted into his touch, but conversation prevented that.

"I'm seeing the moments after her death. I only saw them one other time, right after I moved in and met her. I can see you trying to save her while her spirit watched from the room's corner."

Tate's face fell, causing Hazel to feel unsure whether she was right to share what she had seen.

"I'm sorry you had to see that. Did you say her spirit was in the room? She was watching the entire thing go down?"

Hazel nodded her head slowly as the first drops of tears fell from her eyes. He pulled her into another hug.

"That must have been so traumatizing for her, and for you. I'm so sorry. I did everything I could for her. I'm just sorry I couldn't save her. It broke my heart, and I didn't even know her."

"She knows you did everything you could. I can feel her emotions in the memory, and she was grateful to you. Don't apologize. There was nothing else you could have done. She had given up hope before you stopped trying. I promise."

Tate's face looked pained, but he nodded as he squeezed her again.

"Are you going to tell her about the nightmares?"

Hazel bit her lip, thinking about the difficult conversation that would entail.

"Yea, I think I have to. I should probably tell her soon, actually."

He sat up in the bed, reaching for his clothes that had been discarded on the floor.

"There's no time like the present. Would you care for some coffee, love?"

She smiled as she also sat up in the bed.

"Definitely. You're too good to me."

"You deserve it. Let's see if Candy is somewhere around here."

He buttoned his pants and then reached down to help her from the bed. She settled onto shaky legs and then followed him out of the bedroom.

Tate went straight to the coffeepot and got it started, allowing Hazel to search the apartment for Candy. The apartment was small, but she still searched each room, only to find it empty. Unless Candy was not manifesting herself, she was not there. It was a rare occasion for Hazel to wake up and find Candy missing from the apartment. She felt a sense of dread.

"She's not here, but she should be. She's almost always here in the morning. Something is wrong. I can feel it."

Tate, abandoning his search for breakfast, turned to look at her.

"I'm assuming the answer is no, but do you have a way of communicating with each other when she isn't around?"

"Unfortunately, no. I'm not that cool. I have to find her."

Abandoning the coffeepot, he grabbed his keys.

"Okay. Where to?"

Hazel thought for a moment, but she had no idea where Candy could be.

"Well... she said she was going to try to find Jake at his house. Do you know where he lived? I'm not sure if she is still there but we could check."

"Yes. Sounds like a plan."

He made his way to the door before looking her over.

"Do you want to change clothes first?"

Hazel looked down at the boxers and tee shirt she was wearing.

"Um, yeah. I should probably do that. I'll be right back."

Returning with an outfit more suitable to be worn in public, she and Tate left the apartment and headed down to his car. Thankfully, he had driven his personal vehicle to her apartment the night before and not his police cruiser. Her mind was too amiss to drive. She trusted his driving ability way over hers.

Tate carefully pulled onto the highway.

"His house is probably still considered a crime scene, so we will have to sneak in. I don't believe it has twenty-four-hour guards anymore, though. The murder was weeks ago. That should help our chances of getting inside."

She nodded her head, feeling too nervous to carry on a conversation. Thankfully, his place was close to her apartment because she was crawling out of her skin by the time they arrived. Seeing that the house had been left vacant by police, Tate parked on the street in front of it. They hurried to the front door. Peeking in the front window, Hazel could see Candy sitting inside, alone. She tapped lightly on the window, causing Candy to jolt. Her head sprang up to the look out of the glass, clutching at her heart in relief when she saw Hazel.

Hazel motioned to Tate.

"She's inside."

He attempted to open the door, but it was locked. They searched the porch for a key, looking under flowerpots and furniture, but there was not one. Just as she was about to tap on the window again, the door sprang open on its own, revealing Candy's form just inside.

"Hey!" Hazel cried out as she ran inside and wrapped her arms around Candy's frigid form.

"Hey to yourself. What are you doing here?"

"You weren't home this morning. I got worried."

Candy flashed an apologetic smile. Hazel wrapped her in another hug. Her arms were beginning to feel numb from the chill, but she held Candy anyway.

"Oh... sorry. I guess I lost track of time."

"Did you find him? I mean, did he re-materialize?"

Candy shook her head, looking defeated. Spectral tears sparkled down her cheek.

"No. Can you take me to his grave? I need to go there. I need to see it."

Hazel threw her arm over Candy's now shaking shoulder. She had started to sob, causing her form to flicker.

"Absolutely."

Hazel called to Tate, who had remained near the front door, keeping watch.

"Do you know where Jake's grave is?"

"I can find out. Give me a minute," he said, pulling his phone out of his pocket and walking out onto the front porch.

"Did you at least have a good night?" Candy asked, wiping tears off of her cheek.

"Oh, yeah," Hazel muttered as her cheeks turned red. She could feel the heat flood them. No matter how unfortunate her own situation was, Candy would always find the topic of sex as acceptable.

A smile grew on Candy's face.

"Then I demand details later."

She smirked, causing Hazel's cheeks to flush even more.

"We'll see."

Hazel led Candy onto the porch to follow Tate to the car.

"He's in Lake Lawn," Tate said. "So, we have a bit of a drive."

Hazel buckled herself into the front seat.

"Okay. Can we grab breakfast and coffee from a drive-thru on our way?"

"You are speaking my language. I'm starving."

He leaned over to kiss her before putting the car into drive. She could see Candy's amused expression in the review mirror. She stuck out her tongue to lighten the mood, causing Tate to laugh and Candy to return the gesture. She was relieved that, although Candy was going through something traumatic, she still had her sense of humor.

It was hard enough to see Candy in the state she had been in since Jake showed up in their apartment. For someone who always looked runway ready, even after death, she had certainly suffered an undoubtable setback, causing her usually stellar appearance to be less than. Her makeup was still smeared, just as it had been the day before, and she had not used her abilities to change her clothing, a power Hazel still did not understand.

Candy's abilities as a spirit far exceeded what Hazel thought was possible, especially for someone who had not been dead all that long. For Candy, persistence paid off. She did not want to lose her looks after she died, so she spent her first few months alone in her old apartment, working on her abilities. It was an effort that had paid off. But it was also an effort she was putting aside for the time being.

Going through the drive-thru at a coffee shop, she and Tate both ordered a coffee and a breakfast wrap. She was relieved these unexpected events happened on a weekend, and not on a day where she needed to turn up to work. Even Tate had the day off, which was a small miracle. Although she was so used to handling everything on her own, she was growing accustomed to the idea of Tate being involved with her spirit activities, at least those with no easy fix. She never wanted to leave him out of the loop and cause him to worry again. After everything that transpired during her investigation into Angela Spencer's murder, including her being abducted and almost killed, she had learned her lesson in going into such things without his support. She believed that was what had caused her parents' marriage to become troubled, and she was not willing to destroy her own relationship by doing the same thing.

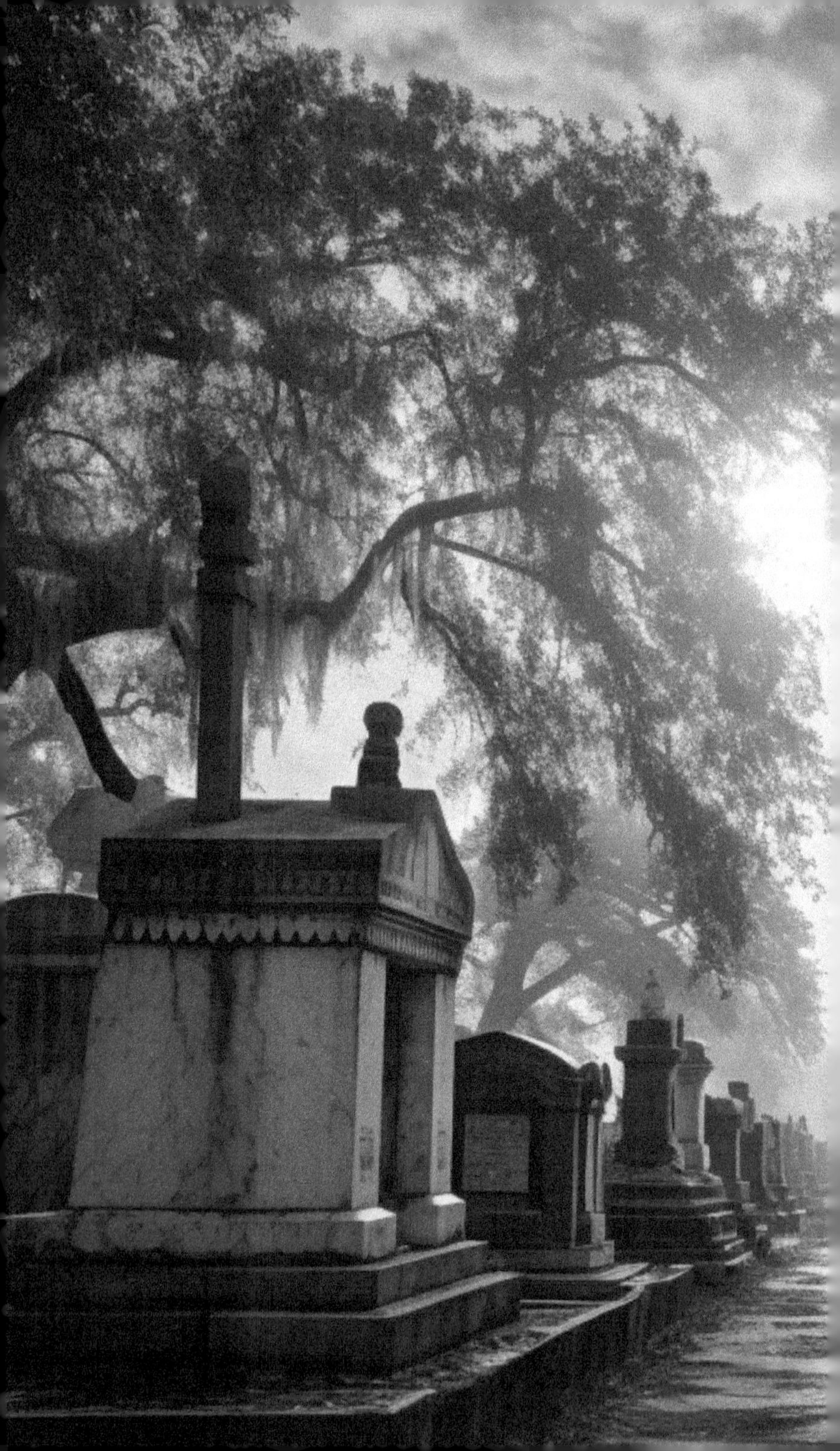

Chapter Five
Love Lost, Love Found

Pulling into the cemetery parking lot, she turned to see that Candy had already floated away from the car and into the gates.

She lifted her chin in the direction of the cemetery entrance before turning to Tate.

"She's already in there."

"Should we go in after her?"

Nodding her head, Hazel opened the door and climbed out of the car. Tate did the same, then walked around to her side of the car and interlaced his fingers between hers. She was not looking forward to going into the cemetery, but Tate's hand in hers made her feel safe.

Ever since she was a child, Hazel had always attracted the dead. Glowing like a beacon to them, she had no way of hiding her abilities. Although most spirits haunted the people and places that were important to them in life, and not the cemetery, she still walked with her eyes down. Making eye contact with them was a sure way to attract them, and she did not have the space in her life to help anyone else.

"He should be straight back and to the left," he said as they began walking towards the gates.

Unlike the major cemeteries in the rest of the city, this cemetery had been less neglected. There were even some fresh flowers among the graves. Many of the crypts had odd shapes. Even some in the shape of a small pyramid loomed before them. As with most cemeteries in South Louisiana, the Lake Lawn Cemetery was filled with above ground tombs and a good deal of underground grave sites that were dug into slightly elevated grounds to prevent the high-water table from destroying them.

Arriving at the back of the cemetery, Hazel let Tate guide her to the location of Jake's grave site only to discover that Candy had beaten them to it. Candy kneeled beside the headstone while her fingers slowly traced over the inscription that had been engraved into it. She was not crying, but Hazel could see she was only a moment away from allowing her emotions to consume her.

Candy turned her eyes in their direction as they approached and let herself fall back on her heels, dropping her hand from the headstone.

"Hey," Hazel said softly. "Are you okay?"

Candy shrugged.

"I don't know. I guess I just didn't want to believe it, but the evidence is right here. He's gone."

Hazel let go of Tate's hand and dropped onto her knees beside Candy

"I can't imagine how hard this must be. I don't know much about the relationship you had with him, but I can tell you cared about him."

Candy's eyes were glassy, and her tears welled up again, pouring down her cheeks. They sparkled in the sun.

"I loved him... I really loved him..."

Hazel reached out and took Candy's hand, ignoring the electric chills that raced up her arm.

"I don't understand. Weren't you with Brad?"

Candy looked away as though she had been caught in a lie and was trying to avoid acknowledging it. Hazel had never dared to ask Candy about her murder, or the events that led to it. Candy had always insisted she did not want to talk about it. Hazel squeezed her gently.

"Candy, it's okay. You can tell me anything."

Candy returned her gaze to Hazel's face, as tears fell freely from her eyes.

"Technically, yes. I was still with Brad. But only because he wouldn't let me go. It had been over for a long time. I was in love with Jake, and he was in love with me. I know he was."

Candy sniffled.

"We got close as I went to him for help with breaking it off with Brad. They were friends, but not as close as people seemed to think. He and Brad were nothing alike. Jake was kind. We didn't intend to fall in love."

She shrugged her shoulders helplessly.

"We just did. He was the one person who saw me for who I was."

"I'm so sorry, Candy. I didn't know."

As they kneeled in front of Jake's grave. His spirit manifested in front of them. However, his form was weak, almost translucent.

"Jake!"

Candy shrieked, springing forward and into the spirit's form, desperately wrapping her arms around him. He looked down at her lovingly. The breathing sounds coming from Jake had calmed, and his body no longer shivered. His change in demeanor, along with the sun pouring light across the sky, allowed Hazel to take in Jake's appearance for the first time.

He was an attractive guy, with a kind appearance. His hair and eyes were both dark, so dark that they were almost black. He wore black-framed glasses, giving him a scholarly appearance. Actually, he had similar boyish good looks to Tate. Although Tate's eyes were a bright grayish blue, they both sported thick dark hair and were both fully capable of growing a thick beard. Although Jake was the only one who seemed to allow his facial hair to reach its potential. His beard was not particularly long, but it was longer than Tate's, who kept his facial hair short when he was dressed in his police uniform.

Hazel had seen pictures of Brad, Candy's ex, who had light hair and eyes, and looked more like a bad boy, so Jake's appearance took her a bit by surprise, but she could see the appeal. If she could have chosen a man for Candy in life, knowing what she now knew, she would have chosen Jake.

"He's here," Hazel whispered to Tate, who could not see the spirits in front of him.

"I'm so sorry," Candy cried to Jake. "I'm so sorry I caused this."

Jake looked down at her, placing his hand on her cheek.

"This isn't your fault," Jake responded. His voice sounded as though it was being transmitted through an old radio station, distant, although so close.

Candy's head sprung up at the sound of Jake's voice, shocked she was hearing him at all. It was the first time he had spoken to them since he appeared after his death weeks ago.

"You... you can talk?" Candy stuttered, looking at him in disbelief.

Hazel approached Jake slowly, stopping only a few feet from where he and Candy stood.

"Do you know who did this to you?" she asked, being careful to keep her voice low.

Her intrusion caught Jake by surprise, causing him to tear his gaze away from Candy and look up at her in confusion.

"Sorry... I'm Candy's friend. We are trying to figure out what happened to you. Do you know who did this to you?"

Jake's shoulders slumped as he shook his head.

"I can't remember anything," he admitted. "My brain feels... disconnected. I try to remember but I can't."

Hazel's hopes were dashed at the thought of Jake losing his memory. She nodded resolutely.

"Maybe it will come to you. Until then, we will keep hoping the police figure it out."

Jake nodded his head before turning to face Candy, who was still wrapped around him. She had stopped crying, but her face was painted with the pain that still plagued her.

Hazel and Tate left the fallen lovers and returned to her apartment. With Jake unable to remember his death, there was not much they could do but wait until his memories came back. Until then, Hazel vowed to stay out of their way and allow them to become reacquainted with each other in their new state of being. Candy promised to return home later that night, but she needed time alone with Jake; which was something Hazel could understand. It did, however, put Hazel into an uncertain situation. Although she felt guilty about Candy never crossing over, she now worried Candy would choose to cross over with Jake and leave her alone. It was a thought she could not fathom. She knew it was selfish. She knew she should be happy for Candy to find peace. But she also knew she was not ready to lose Candy, and she never would be.

"Do you want me to order a pizza, love?" Tate asked as he closed the refrigerator door.

"Sure. I'm sorry. I know I need to get groceries."

"It's okay. You've had a difficult last few weeks. It's perfectly fine for you to take some time away from acting like everything is normal."

She nodded, knowing an empty fridge was not just a phase. It was more rule than exception, something she needed to work on if she wanted to appear domesticated and grown up. Tate would eventually tire of taking care of her, and she did not want to see a day where that would happen, so she needed to learn to be better at taking care of herself. She could not take care of him if she could not take care of herself.

After placing a pizza order, Tate placed his cell phone on the coffee table. Sitting on the sofa, he grabbed the remote and powered the television on. He scrolled to The Weather Channel and then leaned forward with his elbows on his knees, paying close attention as the severe weather alert segment started.

Hazel's summer had already been so tempestuous that she had forgotten all about the fact that hurricane season was in full effect. Both of their expressions turned serious as the meteorologists announced New Orleans was in the direct path of an encroaching hurricane. Her stomach dropped as they were recommended to evacuate in two days in order to be safely out of its way.

She grumbled.

"This sucks. I hate evacuating."

"Maybe you won't have to."

"What do you mean?"

Tate looked at her and smiled.

"Well... I'm not usually able to evacuate since I have to stay on duty. You could stay with me, if you wanted to."

Relief flooded through her. She returned his smile.

"Oh. That sounds great. Will you be staying at your place?"

"It depends. Sometimes they put us up at a hotel near work, but my house isn't in an area that usually floods, so we could end up staying there as well. It just depends on what I'm asked to do, but you can stay with me either way."

"Okay."

She let out a sigh of relief.

"Sounds like a plan."

He grabbed her hand, interlacing their fingers.

"Good. I'd miss you if you left, anyway."

She curled up against him, taking in the scent of his cologne.

"Me too."

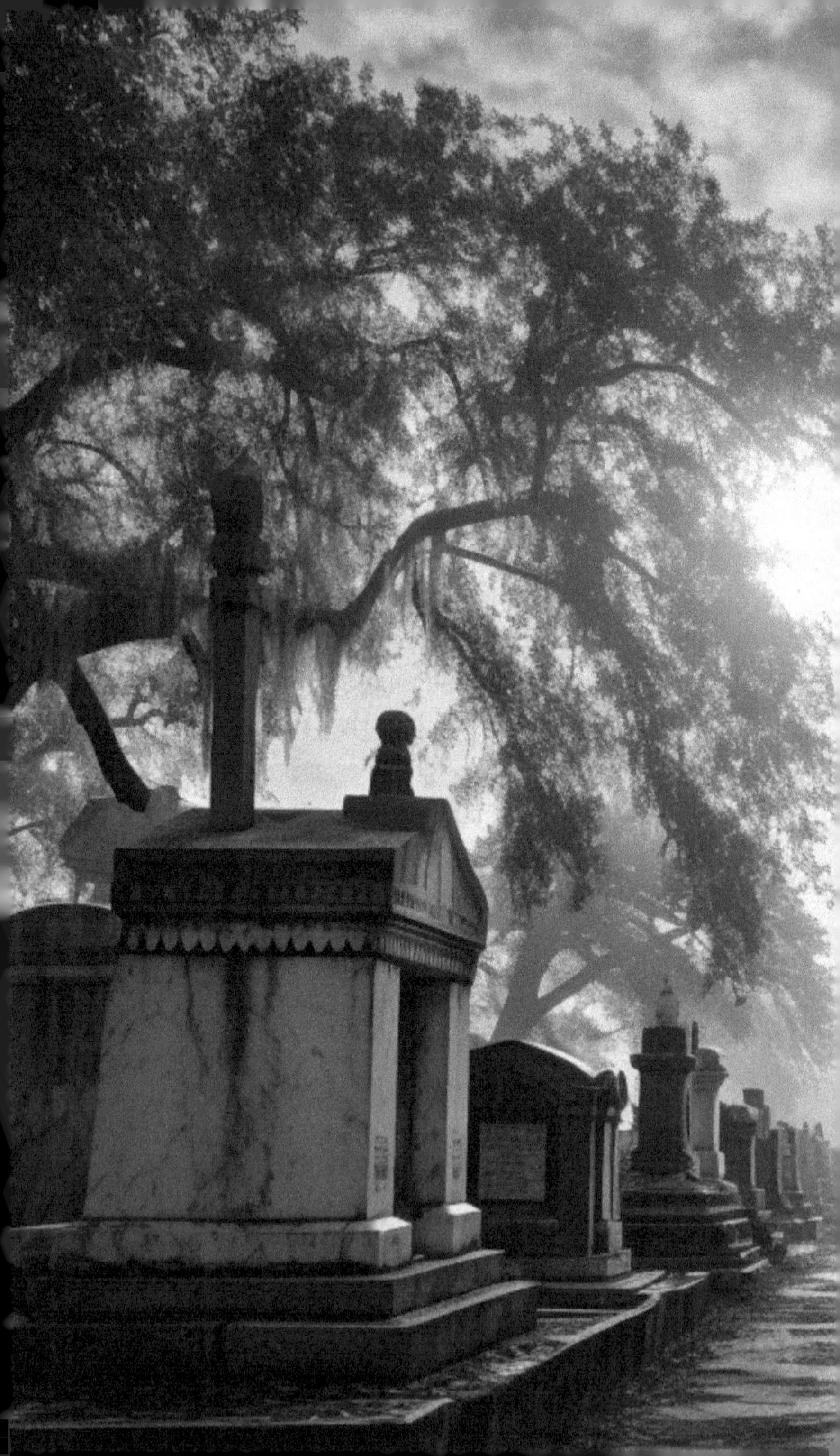

Chapter Six

Distractions

Hours passed before Candy returned to the apartment. When she did, she was alone. She explained that Jake needed to conserve his energy, but he promised to manifest in the apartment at a later time. Her mood seemed to have improved, probably because Jake had finally reappeared and spoken to her. Although she blamed herself for what happened to him, he insisted she was not to blame, which gave Hazel some insight into the person he was.

The incoming storm caused the knot in Hazel's chest to grow, but it released slightly since Tate offered to let her stay with him. She was not naïve and realized staying behind for a storm could be dangerous, and very inconvenient, especially once the power and water went out, but it was still less expensive than an evacuation. She also got to stay with Tate, which made it all worth it. There was also a good possibility Tate had a generator, since he was a responsible adult, unlike her. If he did, they would not have to suffer through the aftermath without some form of electricity. Having barely spent any time at his house, since her apartment was closest to both of their offices, she was actually looking forward to getting the chance to.

"How are you feeling, Candy?" Hazel asked as Candy settle down onto the sofa next to her and Tate.

"Better... Well, better than yesterday, considering. I'm just glad Jake can talk to me, although he doesn't remember much. I need to know what happened to him. I need to know what happened to me. I guess it'll just take time."

Candy's voice got lower as she went on, until it was not much more than a whisper. Hazel reached out to comfort her.

"I know. I do too. Tate's going to check into getting a copy of Brad's interviews so we can listen to them before we try to speak to him. At least we can hear his story beforehand. That should help."

Candy nodded to acknowledge Hazel before flipping the television on and scrolling to her favorite channel. Her demeanor caused Hazel's heart to ache. Her usually snarky and joyful best friend had become withdrawn and depressed. Being convinced Candy needed some space, Hazel grabbed Tate's hand and motioned towards the bedroom with her eyes.

"I guess we will go get showers and stuff," she told Candy as they stood up from the sofa. "We both have work tomorrow. Please come get me if you need me, though. And... if you want... you can come with me to work tomorrow."

Candy's eyes lit up, although she looked at Hazel skeptically.

"You never let me go to work with you."

Hazel pouted

"I know... I'm sorry. I never realized it meant so much to you. But tomorrow is a new day. I can't promise you won't be bored out of your mind, but the offer stands regardless."

Candy smiled, eying Hazel and then Tate before turning her smile into a mischievous smirk.

"I might take you up on that. See you two in the morning. And don't do anything I wouldn't do."

Hazel scrunched up her face and then turned to walk Tate into the bedroom, fully intending to make Candy proud.

As soon as they closed the door, Tate pulled her into a fierce hug. She lingered, allowing herself to sink into his chest as the tension in her body released, like a piece of elastic that had finally snapped against its own pressure.

He pulled away to look into her eyes

"So... are you going to make me shower alone again?"

She hid her face in his chest to hide the flush on her cheeks, shrugging bashfully.

He pulled her face up to meet his.

"Don't be silly... There's no reason for you to be shy with me. Never. Not anymore."

"It's a hard habit to break," she admitted. "I'm trying though."

He wrapped his arm around her shoulder before letting go and heading to the shower.

"I know you are. The door will be unlocked if you change your mind."

Blowing out a deep breath, Hazel went towards the bathroom after him. She realized she needed to get out of her own way, no matter how difficult it was. Knocking gently on the door, she rested her face against it, hoping to build up her courage before he opened it.

Cracking the door open, and wearing nothing but his boxer shorts, Tate grinned at her through the opening.

"What's the password?" he teased.

"Oh," she snickered, "If there's a password, I may have to come back later."

She pretended to be turning to walk away, but he reached his hand through the opening and grabbed her, spinning her around.

"No, you don't. Get in here with me."

She scurried into the bathroom after him, closing the door behind them. Pulling her body against his, he reached around her head, gently taking out her ponytail before kissing her deeply. The kiss disarmed her, relaxed her inhibitions, made her not shy away as he helped her out of her clothes and into the shower. Time seemed to move in slow motion as they stood beneath the warm water in each other's arms. How he rubbed his soapy hands all over her body drove her wild. It was never something she had been brave enough to do before, but with everything that had been going on, all the things that flooded through her mind, this moment was hers to enjoy.

Returning to the bedroom after a long shower with Tate, Hazel plopped onto her bed, dreading the end of the weekend. She knew she would get new clients when she returned to work, which made her admittedly nervous. After her last case with Roy Miller, she needed a quiet client. Perhaps a client who was not haunted by a murder victim would be a good start.

His fist pounded on the door as I cowered behind it, protected only by the lock and the vanity that I had pushed against it. I knew he would get in, but I only had to hold him off long enough for the police to find me. The banging got so loud that all I could do was close my eyes and wait for the inevitable. Tears streamed down my cheeks. I didn't have the strength to fight them, or him.

One second the door was separating us, and the next he was on top of me, hands clinching down on my throat. I choked out sobs of breath while I tried to pry his hands off me, but it was no use. He was too strong.

"I told you I'd be back, Miss Watson."

My breath came in ragged bursts as lights danced in my vision. I struggled against his fingers, that clawed into my neck, thrashing my body violently on the floor. Where was Candy? Where were the screams of the other victims? If this was a memory, then they should be here. I needed to wake up! I closed my eyes and begged for my body to just wake up...

"Hazel. Hazel!"

Tate shook her shoulders gently, trying to wake her.

Her eyes shot open, searching the dark corners of her bedroom for Raymond Waters, but he was not there. Relief poured over her. She looked up at Tate in shock, still not understanding what was happening, still not knowing if she had woken from a spirit episode or a nightmare.

Tate brushed the hair out of her face.

"Are you okay? You were thrashing in your sleep. Another nightmare?"

She shook her head, unsure if she wanted to tell him about her dream just yet. She did not want to worry him if it was only some side effect of post-traumatic stress disorder. She would have to learn to cope with what happened to her, and it would take time.

Tate, still looking at her with concern, laid back down next to her with his arm over her stomach. He watched her eyes with a mixture of concern and adoration.

"I'm okay. I'm sorry to scare you."

"Don't apologize. It's not your fault. Do you want to talk about it?"

"Not yet. I think I'm just reeling from what I went through a few weeks ago. I'll be okay."

"You don't have to hold it all in, Hazel. You have me and Candy. You're not going through this on your own."

"I know, but for now, I've got to go to work. Will I see you later?"

"Yea, I can catch up with you after my shift."

"Okay. I look forward to it then."

She gave him a kiss and climbed out of the bed.

He smirked, slightly tugging her back down and stealing another kiss.

Grabbing a blouse and a pair of slacks, Hazel made her way to the bathroom to get dressed while Tate made his way to the kitchen to brew their coffee. She loved the mornings when she woke up to him in her bed. Although it was a new experience, it was one she could certainly get used to. His presence almost made her feel more settled, like she was doing something right with her life. The relationship was new, but their friendship was not, and she could not see her life without him in it as they were now.

Dressed for success, or something along those lines, she made her way into the living room to find Tate sitting at the kitchen table with a cup of coffee, and Candy sprawled out on the sofa, minding her own business.

"I wish you could just communicate with each other," Hazel said to the room at large. "Good morning, Candy."

Tate looked up at her, a bit startled, as though he had forgotten she had a roommate. Not that it was a normal occurrence for someone to knowingly share their home with a spirit. He looked around to see Candy, as he had done many times before, but he always turned up empty.

"Morning, sunshine," chirped Candy, flashing more of a smile than Hazel expected to see from her after the last few days. Hazel could not help but to smile back at her.

"You look well. I'm glad you're in a good mood today. Any reason?"

"I get to go to work with you, remember? You didn't change your mind, did you?"

"No, not at all."

Hazel waved her hand nonchalantly.

"As long as you don't make me look crazy in front of my clients."

"I'll be on my best behavior."

She drew an air halo over her head with an innocent look on her face, but Hazel was not fooled.

"Breakfast?" Tate asked as he slid a cup of coffee in front of her and set a bowl of oatmeal down onto the table for himself.

"I'll just have some toast, but I've got it," she said as she walked over to the counter and dropped two pieces of bread into the toaster.

When they parted ways after breakfast, Tate heading to work and Hazel doing the same, she felt a mixture of joy and sadness. She was joyful about her own love life, but she could not ignore the heartbreaking events of the past few days. She did her best to compartmentalize the two conflicting emotions. She did not want to seem insensitive to Candy's plight.

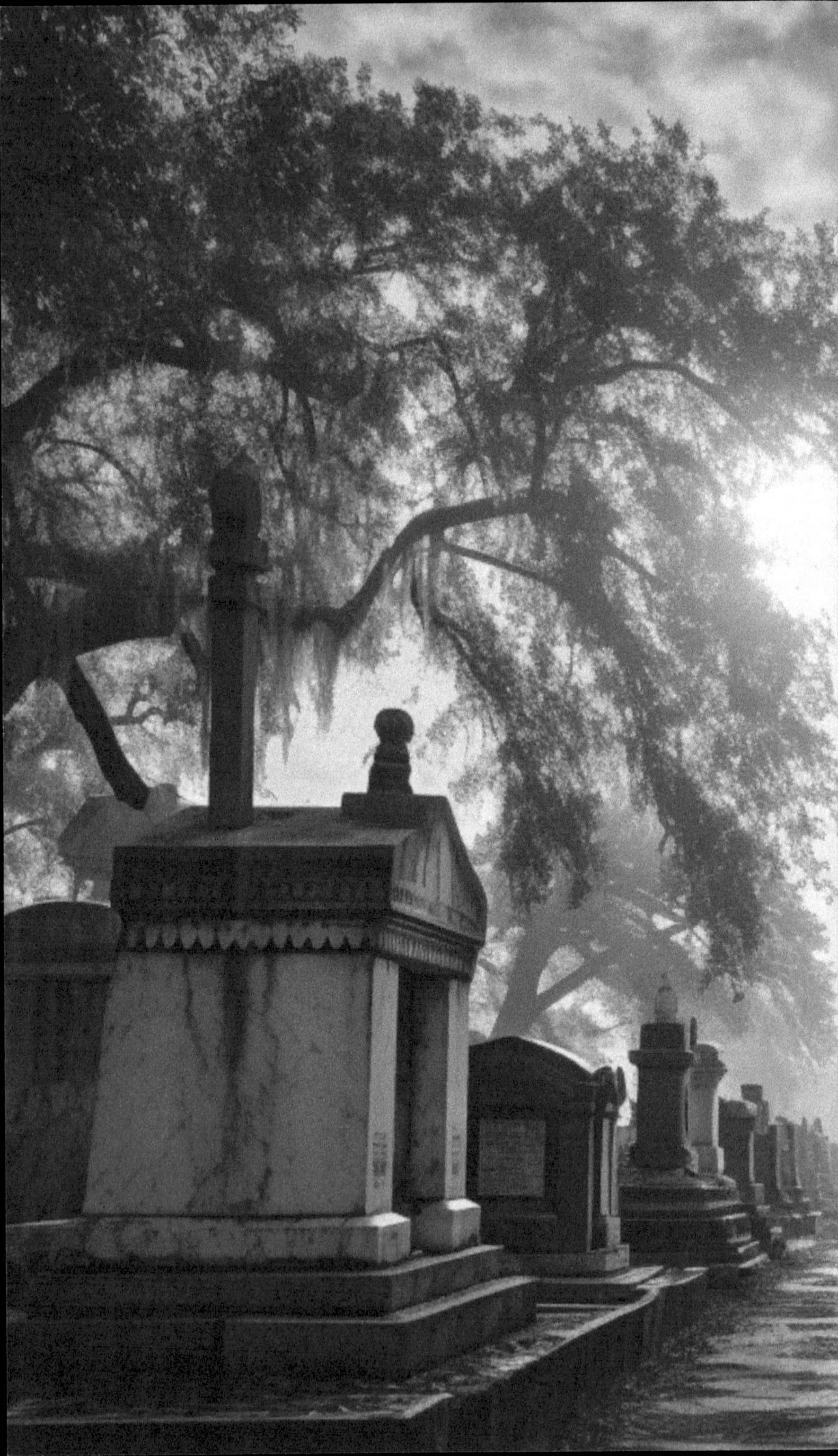

Chapter Seven
The New Client

Heading to her office with Candy in tow was not the norm. Actually, she usually refused to let Candy join her at work because of how distracting she could be. But, considering everything Candy had been going through, she was looking for any way to lift her spirits. Usually, her friend was not one to sit quietly and allow Hazel to work, often causing her to look like an insane person when she would talk to the space in front of her, where no visible person stood. Today, that did not matter. Today, she needed to make Candy her priority. Hazel pulled into a parking spot in downtown New Orleans.

"I'm not sure what's on my agenda for today. So, I will need for you to be flexible if I have to meet with anyone. Maybe you can get to know some of the resident spirits in my office. There are a few who you may find entertaining."

"It'll be all good, doll. I just appreciate you letting me tag along. I won't disrupt your day."

Nodding, Hazel pulled her keys out of the ignition and got out of the car to pay the meter. She was infamous for getting parking tickets, so she promised Tate that she would try harder to not do so. He could only get her out of so many before she would need to pay the fines.

Walking into the public defender's office after everything she had been through with Raymond Waters brought a mixture of feelings. Part of her was excited to move on with her life, but the other part of her was afraid of what a new client would bring.

Her last client, Roy Miller, was haunted by a murder victim, which got her entangled in a case that almost got her killed. The spirit of the murder victim, Angela, had attached to her almost instantly, haunting her in public, private, and even in her dreams, trying to get Hazel to solve her disappearance and murder.

Although Hazel was born to help spirits, having them show up to her obsessively, especially in her own apartment, was not something she would ever get used to. She longed for some sense of privacy from the spirits, at least in her own home, but discovered, after meeting with a Voodoo priestess, that keeping out good spirits would keep out her roommate as well. So, her options to keep her home private were limited.

Arriving in her office, Hazel found client files already on her desk. One was for a client named Hayley Babin, who had been arrested for a hit and run. The file showed no one was injured in the accident, so she was glad it should at least be a straightforward case to resolve. The second file in her stack caused her body to feel cold. Her breath to shutter. The file was for an appeal and the client was Brad Chiasson, Candy's ex.

What were the odds that his file would end up on her desk? She stared at the folder, almost as though she were waiting for the name on it to change, but it did not. Candy, noticing the look on Hazel's face, moved closer to her and peered over her shoulder before letting out a gasp. Candy dropped into the chair next to her as though she had a corporeal form and her legs had given out. Her hands were cupped over her mouth and her were eyes wide.

"What does this mean?" Candy asked.

Hazel shook her head slowly, pondering the question, but feeling unprepared to respond.

"Maybe Brad saw Jake's murder as a reason to file for his appeal, but I'm not sure. I'm going to have to talk to someone about this. I'll be right back."

Hazel shuffled out of the room.

Approaching the secretary's desk with the file in hand, she cleared her throat to attract the attention of the elderly secretary, who seemed lost in her own world. Looking up at Hazel, over bifocals that had dropped to the tip of her nose, the secretary, Mrs. Anne, slightly drew up the side of her mouth into more of a smirk than a smile.

"Can I help you, Miss Watson?"

"Yes. Sorry to bother you, Mrs. Anne, but I was curious about this client. Was he assigned to me?"

Appearing to not be in the mood for questions, the elderly woman looked at Hazel as though she was speaking gibberish, before responding.

"Was the file on your desk, Miss Watson?"

Hazel, surprised, looked at the file as though she was not sure of the answer, like it had magically appeared in her hands.

"Miss Watson," Mrs. Anne called out as her impatience with Hazel's lack of response grew.

"Yes, ma'am," Hazel responded, finally finding her voice.

Anne clicked her tongue and then eyed the file indignantly.

"Then I would assume the client has been assigned to you. Wouldn't you?"

Finding no words to respond, Hazel flashed a weak smile at the secretary before hurrying back to her office, where Candy had waited patiently.

"Well, what did she say?" Candy asked before Hazel could fully enter the room. Although Hazel waited to respond until the door had been closed.

"Looks like he's mine," she muttered, "although the old bat couldn't be bothered to help me. An easy client. That's what I need right now. This is not what I need. I swear they are trying to kill me, or run me off."

Candy pursed her lips as she sat momentarily in thought.

"I know he isn't your ideal client, and I understand you don't need so much stress in your life right now, but it may be a good thing for you to represent him. At least, that way, we can know exactly what is going on in my murder investigation and we will have access to him."

Hazel's eyes shot up to meet Candy's. She was not feeling as positive.

"I know. You're right. It's just intimidating. The stakes are high, but it's not like anyone in my office knows my connection to you. I mean, what if he is guilty? What if your murder and Jake's murder aren't related? I don't want to help him if he did it. I can't even imagine being in the same room with him, if that's the case. I know you want me to talk to him for you, but even that makes me nervous. Ugh, our office must be super overwhelmed for them to give me a case like this. I can't imagine I'm qualified enough for something like this."

Candy wrapped her hand around Hazel's.

"I know it is a big deal. I expect only what you can do, but I don't think you're giving yourself enough credit. You were amazing with Roy's case. I mean, it was unorthodox how you solved it. I can't deny that, but you solved it."

"I almost got killed."

Candy gently squeezed Hazel's hand.

"Yes... but you didn't get killed. You're still here and you're stronger for it. You're not a normal attorney, but that doesn't mean you're a bad attorney. You just have different ways of getting the information you need. At least, with Brad's case, you won't have a murder victim who haunts you in your sleep."

Hazel nearly choked as her insides twisted into a vise. She had yet to tell Candy about the memories that had been flooding into her nightmares, the memories that were inadvertently coming from Candy. She realized she could not put it off anymore.

"About that..." She hesitated. "There's something I've been meaning to tell you."

Candy's face dropped, and she eyed Hazel warily.

"What?"

"Well, it's about you haunting me in my sleep. I've been meaning to tell you, but I didn't want to worry you."

Candy closed her eyes, pinching the bridge of her nose for a few awkward moments. She must have been praying for patience.

"How long?" she asked, with her eyes still closed.

For a moment, Hazel debated lying and telling Candy that it had only just started, but she quickly realized lying would be a bad idea. She needed to tell Candy the truth.

"The first few times happened right when we met," she admitted, causing Candy's eyes to widen in alarm.

"Wait a minute," Candy snapped, her patience clearly gone. "Are you telling me this has been happening for a year and you never thought to mention it to me?"

Hazel had never seen Candy look so angry. She swallowed hard against something bitter.

"Not exactly. It's not like that, Candy."

Hazel wanted to crawl into a hole and hide.

"I promise. It only happened twice when I first moved into our apartment."

Hazel paused, trying to plan her next words carefully but then railed through the entire plan. Words poured out of her indiscriminately.

"I didn't tell you because I didn't want to upset you. The memories were pretty traumatic, and we didn't know each other that well. I tried to forget about them, but it happened to me again a few days ago. I was going to tell you but, with everything going on with Jake, I didn't want to cause you anymore heartache."

Candy's face softened, and she looked towards the window. Hazel sat quietly, too afraid to stir her up anymore. Candy finally turned to look Hazel in her eyes, making her shrink.

"You should have told me."

Her words held finality. She was not accepting any more excuses. Hazel's tears fell as visions of those memories flooded back into her mind, visions she had never wanted to see. Watching Candy get stabbed and crawl to the table to dial the emergency services had traumatized her. Candy's spirit, sitting in the corner of the living room, watching in horror as Tate tried to save her had broken Hazel's heart. She rubbed her eyes with her fists, trying to force the visions out of her mind, but it did not work. They kept spinning through her head, triggering emotions she had been trying to hold in.

Candy wrapped spectral arms around her, enveloping her in a cool embrace, trying to force calming energy into her that seemed to meet an unscalable barrier of misery.

"Shh," Candy whispered. "It's okay, love. It's okay. Calm down."

Candy continued hugging Hazel and rubbing her icy hands up and down Hazel's back as Hazel tried to steady her now shallow breaths.

"I wasn't trying to hide it from you, Candy, I swear. I was trying to protect you."

Candy nodded her head but did not respond, making Hazel feel worse, making her feel like she was not forgiven.

"I want to know what memories you are seeing," Candy finally said, her tone resolute. Her message final and not leaving any room for Hazel to back pedal.

Wiping her eyes and grabbing tissue for her nose, Hazel nodded and looked up at Candy, searching for forgiveness in her eyes, but she could not read them.

"I saw when it happened," she muttered, barely over a whisper.

Candy looked confused.

"When what happened? Be more specific."

"I saw when he killed you... Well, when someone killed you. I saw it from your eyes, so I didn't see them since you didn't see them, but I saw you... die."

She braced herself as her eyes betrayed her, as the memory played through her head again, tormenting her. The memory she never wanted to see, that she was never meant to see, continued to haunt her consciousness, no matter how much she tried to stop it.

Candy cradled Hazel's face.

"I'm sorry you had to see that. It isn't fair for you to have to see that. I'm not sure how you are seeing this memory. I would stop it if I could. Have you seen any others?"

Hazel nodded again, sniffing loudly as Candy still touched her face. She could see Candy's own sadness building up as the memory of her death played in her own head. It was the one thing Hazel had been trying to prevent by not telling her about the visions in the first place.

"I saw Tate try to save you, while your spirit watched."

Hazel broke down again, dropping her face into her hands.

"Damn. I'm so sorry," Candy said. Her own voice faltering. "I'm so sorry."

"It's not your fault. It just sucks. The whole thing sucks."

Candy passed her fingers through her long red hair.

"Tell me about it. There's not much we can do to change what happened to me, or Jake, but we need to find out who's responsible. We need justice."

"Yea. We do."

"Then we need a plan, not that they ever work."

Hazel chuckled, grabbing her phone to text Tate. He'd want to know about her new client, and not the one who was charged with the hit and run.

He called her within five minutes of getting the text and expressed his concerns with her taking on Brad's appeal. Although he realized she had no choice. Court cases had been fought, and lost, over the workload of New Orleans' public defenders. So, if she was given a client, she had no choice but to take them.

But Candy was right. Although Brad would not be the lowest stress client, getting close to him was necessary to figuring out if he killed Candy, and representing him as his attorney gave her the most access to him. Now, whether she did her best to get him free, that depended on if she thought he was guilty. It may have been her obligation to look out for her clients' best interest, but he would never be her priority, not when Candy was involved.

"Let's go," Hazel said to Candy as she put her phone in her bag. "I need to stop at the records department to check out copies of Brad's file, but I've had enough of this day. I'll listen to the recordings in the comfort of my home. My hit-and-run client can wait until tomorrow to meet with me. I need to look through her paperwork too."

"Following you, boss."

Candy saluted Hazel, and they walked out of her office.

Deciding it was not worth the extra traffic, Hazel opted to walk to where the records were kept before going back to her car. It was not like she could not use the exercise. The older she got, the less she could handle physical exercise before panting like she was twenty years older. By the time she finished walking those four blocks in the blistering heat, she regretted that decision.

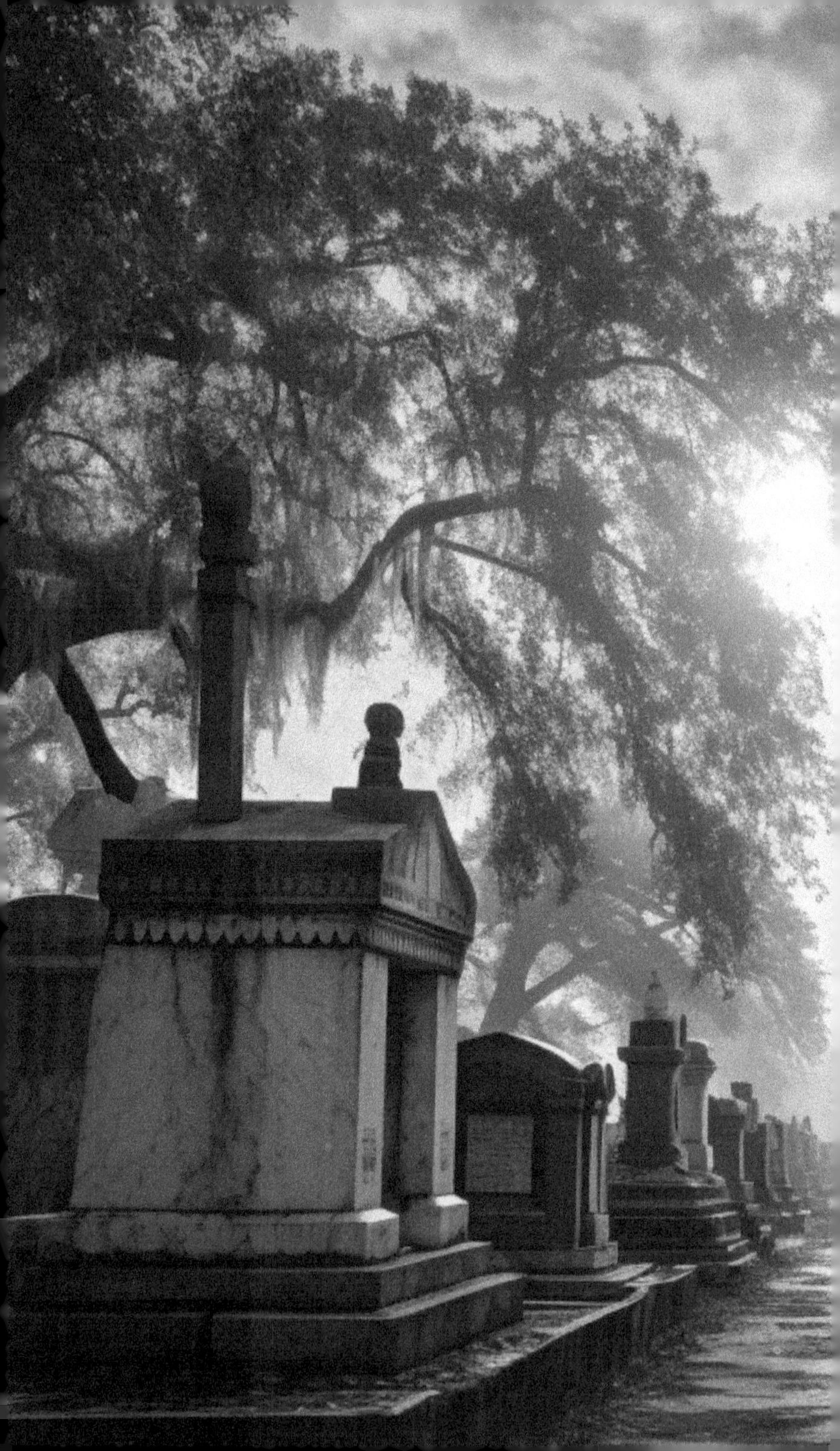

Chapter Eight
The Interview

Returning home with the court records in hand, Hazel sat down on the sofa with Brad's stack first. Candy settled in beside her. The folder was thick, containing not only trial transcripts but also written testimony, interviews, pictures, reports, and diagrams. There was also a box that contained a recording device with several tapes of recorded testimony. With Candy sitting next to her, she opted to not look at the pictures just yet. She had learned her lesson about a year prior with Mary, the young spirit from Loyola University's Marquette Hall. While helping Mary to cross over, she had accidentally opened autopsy photos of Mary's body in front of her spirit. Hazel's guilt had never fully recovered. She did not want to do the same to Candy. She did not want Candy to see herself like that. It was bad enough she saw memories of Candy's death in her dreams. She didn't want to dredge them up for Candy as well.

"So," Candy asked eagerly. "What's first?"

"Maybe the interviews? Written, or recorded?"

Candy pulled her hand to her chin and rubbed it thoughtfully. Hazel intended to leave the decision to her, since it was her murder, so she sat quietly and waited.

"Maybe recorded? They would have done the recorded interviews first, right?"

"Probably. Well... if he cooperated."

Opening the box and flipping through the cassettes, Hazel pulled out the one dated on the day after Candy's murder and dropped it into the player. A few moments of static sounded before she heard the stern, clear voice of the interviewing detective.

"Detective Colt Ford and Detective Tyrone Mangus interviewing Brad Chiasson on September 29, 2020. This interview will be recorded," Agent Ford began. "Hey, Brad. How's it going, buddy? Are they treating you alright? Have a seat."

"Hey, Brad," said Detective Mangus.

The sound of multiple chairs scraped across the floor before a slightly lower voice cut in.

"I just got done throwing up..." muttered Brad, barely intelligible.

"Alright," continued Detective Ford, who was clearly leading the interview. "Can we get you water or something else to drink?"

"I had one... they just... uh... took it from me when I got up and...," Brad stammered.

"Would you like us to see about getting you some water?" Detective Mangus interrupted, cutting off Brad's rambling.

"No. I think I'm okay."

"Well, if you need anything during this interview, something to drink or whatever, we'll provide that," Detective Mangus said. "Do you understand?"

"Okay, yeah. I haven't had anything to eat still, but..."

"Would you like something to eat?" Detective Ford interjected.

"Nah, I don't. Especially not now. I don't think I can handle that. I mean, they've offered plenty of it. I turned it down, but..."

"So, they've been pretty nice to you?" asked Detective Ford.

"Yeah."

"Good."

"Brad, do you know where you are?" asked Detective Ford.

Brad cleared his throat.

"Yes. I'm... I'm in... police department?"

"New Orleans Police Department, yes," stated Detective Ford. "The reason we are asking you this is that we want to be sure that you know what you are doing. You know that by talking to us... we want to be sure, since we have not seen you for the last few hours, everybody's treated you right."

"Okay. I just started feeling sick about the last half an hour ago or so. This is all just getting to me."

"Are you drunk?" asked Detective Mangus.

"I have some like acid reflux and stuff from the, you know, nervousness and everything," Brad explained.

"But you feel okay about talking to us?"

"Yeah, okay..."

"Now you remember Tyrone Mangus?"

"Yeah."

"And I'm Colt Ford, and you recognize us as two New Orleans police detectives?"

"Yeah."

"And we met you briefly last night?"

"Yeah."

"We just need to make sure that you understand your rights, so we're going to have to read them to you."

"Okay."

"You must understand your rights before we ask you questions," Detective Ford explained. "You have the right to remain silent. Anything you say can and will be used against you in a court or other proceedings. You have the right to talk to a lawyer for advice before we question you, and to have him or her with you during questioning. If you cannot afford a lawyer, a lawyer will be funded for you. If you decide to answer questions now without a lawyer present, you will still have the right to stop the questioning anytime. You also may stop the questioning anytime until you talk to a lawyer. Is there any part of that you want to go over again, or is there anything that is not clear to you?"

"Uh, I think it's alright," Brad acknowledged.

Hazel paused the tape and looked at Candy.

"I can't believe he's talking at all," she said incredulously.

"I know. And he said that he thew up. I wonder why."

"Who knows? I would say guilty conscience, but we don't know if he is guilty. So maybe he's worried? Keep going?"

Candy nodded her head and then leaned back on the sofa, stretching her spectral legs out onto the coffee table. Hazel turned the tape back on.

Detective Ford continued.

"Okay, and do you know today's date?"

"I'm tired right now. I'm... uh... I think it's the twenty-ninth," Brad said with uncertainty.

"Yes, it's still the twenty-ninth."

Detective Mangus' voice unexpectantly cut into the interview, causing Hazel to jump.

"Do you know why you are here, Brad?"

Brad went quiet for a moment. His breathing sounded labored. After a few minutes, his breaths became more ragged, and he sobbed loudly. It took a few minutes for him to choke out a response, for him to explain why he was in the room with two detectives, answering questions about a murder.

"I... I didn't hurt her."

"Hurt who?" Detective Ford asked, although he knew the answer.

"My girlfriend, Candy," Brad cried. "They said something happened to her... when they picked me up from my apartment. They accused me... but I didn't do anything to her."

Brad's sobbing intensified. Hazel looked at Candy and saw her eyes had also filled with sparkling spectral tears. Hazel clicked the power button off on the recorder.

"That's enough for now. This is too overwhelming."

"No," Candy insisted, her voice stern. "I want to hear it."

Unsure if continuing to listen to the interview was the best idea for either of their mental health, but supporting Candy's decision regardless, Hazel turned the recording back on. She was secretly hoping Brad would refuse to speak any longer and ask for an attorney so she could spare Candy some of the heartache from hearing anymore. As the recorder crackled back to life, Hazel leaned, with her elbows on her knees, as close to the device as she could, ready to press the power button the minute the conversation got too upsetting for the woman curled up next to her. Brad was still crying and breathing raggedly. Therefore, it did not seem the detectives were getting very far with their questioning. Being an attorney, Hazel was still shocked Brad had yet to ask for an attorney before answering anymore questions.

"Who do you think hurt her, Mr. Chiasson?" Detective Ford asked, his tone even and unprovoking.

Brad's voice hitched as he sobbed.

"I... I don't know, but I didn't do it. I think I should ask for a lawyer."

The room went quiet, as it should have. It would have violated Brad's constitutional rights for the detectives to continue on with their questioning once Brad asked for an attorney. The interview was over, and Hazel breathed a sigh of relief.

"Very well," Detective Mangus said. If he was disappointed, he didn't want Brad to know. "Will you be hiring one yourself, or do you need a public defender to be provided for you?"

"Uh... I think I will need help with that. Lawyers are expensive, aren't they?"

"They can be. We will set up that request for you, Mr. Chiasson. Until then, someone will come to get you and you will be placed back into holding."

"Yes, sir," Brad replied before the recording went silent.

Hazel gave up on Brad's case file after listening to his first interview with Candy. Her insides were wound up like a coiled snake, ready to strike out at any moment, and plunge her into a downward spiral of emotion and self-doubt. Her old friend.

For the moment, she was alone. Candy had left the apartment to look for Jake, so she asked that Hazel not listen to any more tapes until they could do so together. Where Jake's spirit was, Hazel could not say. All that was clear was he did not seem to have control over where and when he manifested, but Candy could not just sit around and wait for him. She had probably gone to Jake's apartment or to the cemetery.

Hazel took some time to review the file for her other client, Hayley Babin, the hit-and-run driver, and then made her way into the shower before Tate arrived after his shift. Pulling on her oversized pajamas and shaking out her damp hair, she made her way to the living room, plopping onto the sofa and scrolling through the channels until she found The Weather Channel. With everything that had been going on, Jake's murder and Brad's appeal, she had almost forgotten the incoming hurricane that was sure to throw her current rat's nest of a life into a frenzy.

Just as she was dwelling on the hurricane map displayed on the television screen, a delightful four-part knock sounded on her door. Tate's signature knock. Hopping off of the sofa, she sprinted to the front door, only taking a second to check the peephole before throwing the door open and yanking him inside by his shirt.

He skittered forward, falling purposely onto her lips and wrapping his arms lovingly around her waist.

"Hey!"

Hazel pulled away and smiled before meeting his lips with hers again.

He chuckled, lifting her under her arms and carrying her to the sofa.

"You missed me?"

"Yes, today was stressful."

He hugged her, pulling her head into his neck.

"Awe well certainly cuddles can help that. They release endorphins, you know."

She grinned, closing her eyes and sinking into his arms on the sofa. The moment of tranquility was short-lived as the breaking news music began on the television, showing that there was a new hurricane update. Pulling one of his arms from around her body, Tate turned the television volume just slightly louder. She begrudgingly opened her eyes, narrowing them in on the television as though it could feel her anger at its audacity to spoil her moment of bliss.

Tate gently caressed her arm, but his eyebrows were furrowed as he stared unblinking at the television. She knew he was deep in thought. The meteorologist warned the storm may become a major hurricane. The implications of which could be severe for New Orleans, but she held her comments until he returned his focus to her. Thankfully, the broadcast went to a commercial break only a few minutes later. She could release the breath she had been holding. As though she had exhaled louder than she realized, Tate turned to look at her.

"You can say that again," he said, reaching out to wrap his arm back around her.

"What are you thinking?"

"Well, this thing is moving faster than I expected, so we will need to come up with a plan."

"Yea... Do you still want me to stay with you?"

He looked at her with one eyebrow arched before allowing a grin to crawl across his face.

"I wouldn't have it any other way. Let me send out a few texts and find out what the plan is for me, so you and I can figure out our own plan. Do you want to order food for us from the sandwich shop down the street? It's my treat."

"Yeah, sounds great."

She pulled out her phone to place the order while he sent text messages to his superiors, trying to get a better idea of his orders during the storm.

After talking with his office, and having their own conversation over soup and a sandwich, they decided they would move to Tate's house the next day and then they would be moved to a hotel near his office on the following morning. Because of the impending storm, court had been canceled for the rest of the week, which was a relief to Hazel, because she needed more time to go through her client files and prepare. The storm was severe enough that the prisoners were actually being moved to another facility outside of the city, so she could not meet with Brad, anyway. Although handling Brad's appeal filled her with dread, knowing she had extra time to prepare made it easier for her to breathe. Not that any amount of time was enough.

When they made their way to bed that night, she was worried about the aftermath of the storm, but she wasn't as worried as she would have been if she would have to evacuate on her own. She would be with Tate, and he would keep her safe.

Jake kneeled onto the wet grass in front of a beautifully engraved headstone. The inscription was long, but perfectly Candy.

Candy Townsend

Born June 17, 1996

Died September 28, 2019

My heart was an inferno,

a raging fire that couldn't be contained.

A flame that lit up the world,

burning with fierce intensity.

A passion that could never be quenched,

a spirit that could never be broken.

A reminder to all that life is too short.

to not make the most of it.

Setting a single red rose in front of the slab, Jake wiped tears from his cheek. He traced trembling fingers along each letter as he held his eyes closed.

"I'll always remember you. I'd give anything to kiss you again."

He spoke sweet nothings to the cold stone, not realizing Candy's spirit had manifested before him. He trembled when she reached out to touch his arm. Her own eyes were glassy from the spectral tears that were threatening to flow.

"I'll always remember you too," she said. Tears sparkled down her cheeks as she spoke in a voice silent to Jake. "Nothing can ever take that away. Not even death."

Awakening that morning, fresh tears fell from Hazel's eyes. She never knew much about Candy's relationship with Jake, but she now realized just how much they had loved each other. It was heartbreaking. She knew how much she loved Tate. The thought of losing him was enough to put her into mourning.

She had promised to tell Candy about her spirit memories, but she chose to keep this one to herself. So, tucking her broken heart behind one of her many walls, Hazel resumed her day.

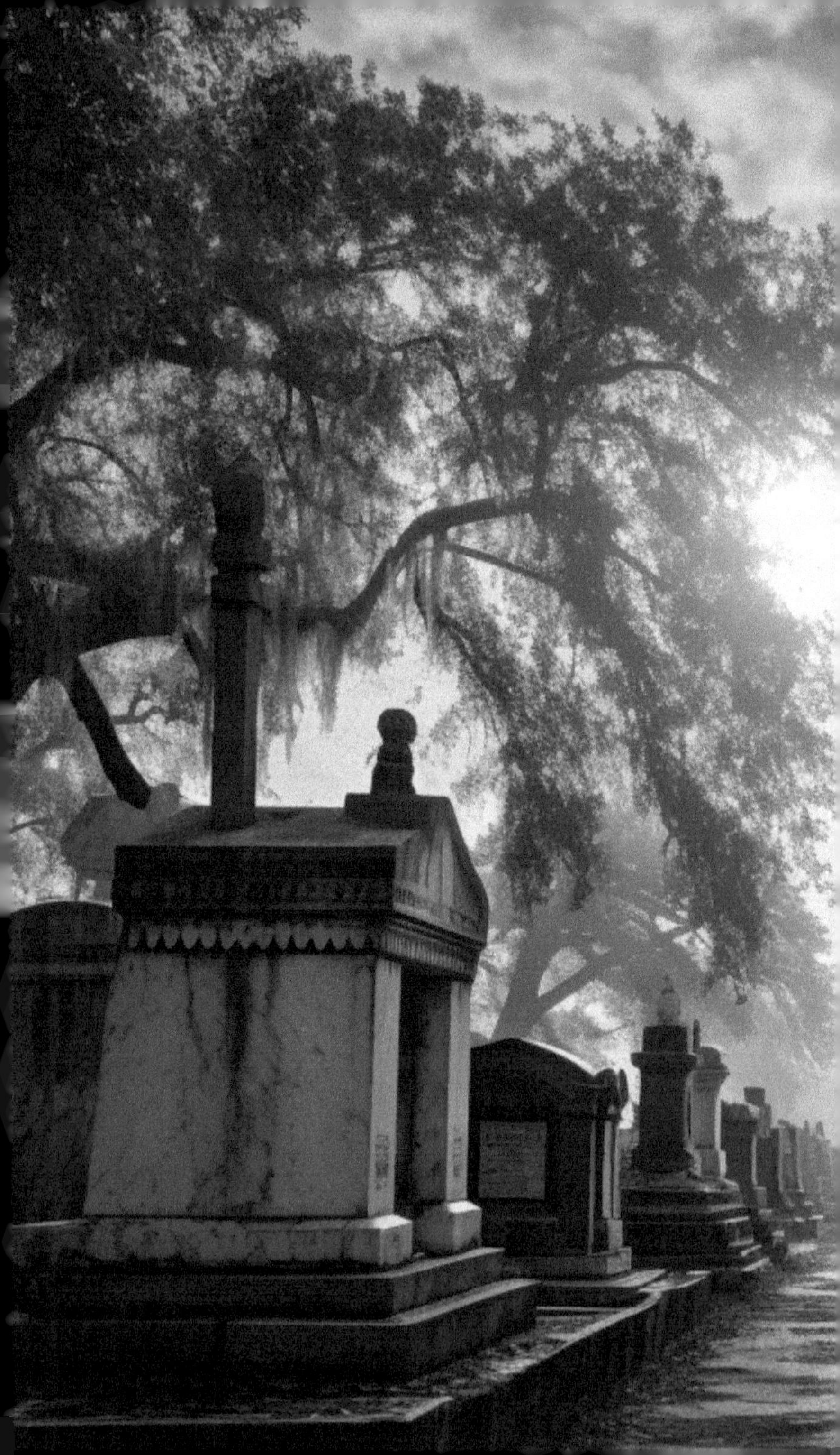

Chapter Nine
Hurricane Ida

Packing up the pathetic quantity of long-life food and bottled water she had in her cabinets, Hazel threw her backpack over her shoulder and rolled her suitcase out of her apartment's front door, giving it one more appraising look before heading to her car. A category three hurricane was barreling across the Gulf of Mexico in a race to her location, and it was unlikely the city would be spared the worst of it. Although there was no way to know exactly how badly they would be affected. She would stay at Tate's house for the night, but the police department had hotel rooms for them to move into first thing in the morning. She had Candy in-tow, however, with Candy and Jake reconnecting in spirit form, and being virtually unaffected by weather, it was unlikely Candy would stick around for the entire time.

With everything that had been going on, Hazel would normally want Candy nearby, but she and Tate would be staying in a hotel room, and that would be a pretty small space for the three of them. Candy's personality, on an average day, was bigger than that.

Hazel had only been to Tate's house a few times, since they usually stayed the night at her apartment closer to the city and their jobs. Following the directions on her GPS, she made it to his house in just under twenty minutes. He worked in the city, but his house was in a suburb on the west side of downtown.

Although his commute was heinous during rush hour traffic, she could see the appeal. He got so much more for his money in the suburbs than she got for hers in the city. It would be a huge change for her to ever consider moving so far away from work, but she would definitely consider it to live with Tate.

His house was in an established neighborhood not far from the Mississippi River, a place that would house mostly small families. It was made of brick and had the typical three bedrooms and two bathrooms, with a small fenced-in yard around back and a modest grassy area in the front.

Candy faded out as Hazel closed in on Tate's house, allowing them to have some time alone. Tate was in the front yard when she pulled into the driveway, and he motioned for her to park her car in his garage.

Dressed in a tank top and shorts, he appeared to be doing yard work, which was not unusual with a storm coming. She could not help but stare at his muscles as they unknowingly peeked through his shirt. He approached her door and opened it for her, reaching in his hand to help her out.

"Welcome."

She took his hand and clambered out of the car, less gracefully than she would have wanted.

"Thanks! What are you up to?"

He wiped the sweat from his forehead with a handkerchief and then bent over to kiss her. She could still taste the sweat on his lips, but she did not mind.

"I just finished mowing the grass and picking up random stuff around the yard. How was your drive?"

"It was good, not too much traffic. Should I bring the food in?"

"You brought food?"

"Oh, I grabbed whatever long-life food I had, but it wasn't much, unfortunately."

"Oh, thanks for thinking of that. Let me grab it and put it in my car and we will take it with us tomorrow. I don't think we will need it for tonight. I was going to order delivery if you're hungry. Let's head inside because I need a shower before my stench causes you to jump right back in your car and drive away."

She laughed, standing on her tippy toes to plant a kiss on his cheek.

"Nonsense! You don't stink, not that I would tell you if you did."

Chuckling and grabbing her bags, Tate led their way into his house through the entrance from the garage, closing the door behind them.

"I'm going to order something for us to eat and then I'll jump in the shower. Make yourself comfortable."

He gave her one more kiss before walking to his bedroom. She stood in the doorway for a moment, unsure of what to do with herself, but decided to go into the living room and put on the news. Surely, he would want an update when he got out of the shower. Placing her satchel down beside her, she pulled out Brad's case file and began to rifle through the contents.

Finding the trial transcripts, she began going through the testimony, trying to see if anything stood out to her. She was not expecting any bombshells, just the mention of a name. If Brad had blamed someone else, or made an excuse that had not yet made the news, she hoped to find it. Disappointed, however, she discovered Brad had not testified at his trial, so she would be unable to compare his testimony to anything he would tell her in confidence.

Between the lack of cooperation in his initial interview, due to him asking for an attorney, and his refusal to testify in his trial, she would have no claims of his to compare. No way to know if his story had changed. She could not blame him for not testifying. Actually, it was probably what his attorney had advised him to do. It just left her at a loss now that she was supposed to fight an appeal for him, and secretly discover who killed Candy in his place. The only story it appeared she would be getting out of him would be the one she got when she went to interview him. That and the one decided on by the prosecutor.

Just as she was beginning to feel herself fluster, Tate walked out of his bedroom wearing only a pair of shorts and a sheepish grin, and her entire attention went to soaking in the view. She did not know what she had done in a past life to deserve him, but damn, she was grateful. He caught her staring and his smile widened.

"Are you staring at me?"

"Maybe."

Throwing his towel in the hamper, he sat next to her on the sofa, sneaking his arm around her shoulders as though he were a teenager in a movie theater. She could not help but giggle and lean in closer. Grabbing the remote control from the coffee table, he turned the television louder so he could hear the update more clearly. They sat in silence for the entirety of the update. Only until the doorbell rang and he paused the television so he could speak to the delivery person.

Returning with a bag in hand, he waved Hazel to the kitchen, where they sat down at his kitchen island so they could eat their Thai dinner.

"So, what do you think about this storm?" Hazel asked as she handed him a packet of utensils from the plastic bag. "Are you worried?"

"I'm always a bit worried about these. It's already expected to be a category two, which can inflict quite a bit of damage. I just hope it doesn't disrupt life in the city for too long. That's happened enough in recent years."

"Agree. I hope our houses fare okay and I'm hoping the prisoners don't stay evacuated for too long either, because I do not want to have to drive an hour to speak with Brad. I don't want to speak with him at all, honestly, but it doesn't look like I have a choice."

Tate reached out and held her hand.

"I know. I'm sorry you are being put in this position. I can't imagine it will be easy to represent him, but at least it'll get you close to Candy's case. It's better than snooping around in a police investigation you don't belong in and chancing getting in trouble. Like you usually do."

He shot her a side-eyed glance and then broke into a smile. She stuck out her tongue before taking a big bite of her dinner and pretending he hadn't called her out for something she was guilty of. He knew, better than anyone, just how much she meddled in cases, even if they weren't her cases. Doing so had almost gotten her killed only recently. So, staying in her own lane was not the worst decision she could make.

After dinner, Hazel took a shower while Tate resumed packing food and supplies for their evacuation into the storm's path. Although counterintuitive, he had to stay close to the police department, so they were being put into a relatively safe location nearby. They intended to head into the city first thing in the morning to beat the worst of the weather, so they needed to turn in to bed early.

Candy returned to Tate's house, just before they went to bed, standing in the kitchen until Hazel happened upon her, to not walk in on anything she was not supposed to. Since she did not know where they would be staying for the storm, she and Hazel had agreed to meet up that night so she could follow them to their new location. After getting Candy settled in the living room, including putting her murder mysteries on the television, Hazel rejoined Tate in the bedroom so they could try to get some sleep.

Staying in the city while an expected category two storm barreled towards them was unnerving. There would undoubtedly be destruction. Hazel just hoped her apartment would be left in a livable condition because looking for another place in the city was out of the question for the time being.

The police department had put all the duty officers in a hotel near the precinct, one that had a generator and the ability to withstand stronger storms. It would still be an uncomfortable situation because she would likely be stuck there for days, if not longer, but it was better than being stuck in another city without Tate.

The sound of shattering glass startled her awake. Her eyes opened sleepily. She could feel a haze over her consciousness that barely seemed to dissipate with waking. She knew she had been drugged, but she didn't know with what. The room was small. A shed, she thought. Grime covered the windows, barely allowing light through the spaces between the bars. Shards of glass from a fallen mirror were strewn across the floor. She was alone.

Her captor had left her there with a cup of water and a sandwich laid on a paper plate by her feet.

Her hands and feet weren't bound, but there were enough locks on the door to ensure she didn't go anywhere. She felt too numb to cry. Maybe it was a side effect of the drugs, or maybe it was because there was no escape. She knew that without a doubt. He wouldn't have left her there if she had a way out.

Hazel woke from another nightmare, but she discounted it to her post-traumatic stress disorder. At least she hoped that was all it was. She did not recognize the scene. It was not one she had been through herself, and she knew it was not anything Candy had been through, so surely her mind had created it. She could not fathom a mental invasion from another spirit, one she had yet to encounter.

She and Tate got to the hotel first thing in the morning, just as the outer bands of the storm were moving onto the Louisiana coast. With sustained winds of one hundred and ten miles per hour, Hurricane Ida was not a storm they wanted to be stuck in. Since Tate was a police officer, he would still be required to leave the hotel and go to his office, once it was safe, but he was not part of the crew who would stay in the office during the worst of the storm. She was glad not to be forced to sit in the hotel room alone.

The room was small, with a queen bed and a kitchenette, but clean. The hotel had a generator, as well as an independent water purification system, so their stay promised to be relatively comfortable, although the weather outside was promised to be vicious.

They had emptied the refrigerator and freezer in Tate's house into ice chests and lugged them up to their room. Tate's house would undoubtedly lose electricity during the storm, so leaving the food in his refrigerator and freezer would have allowed it to rot. This way, they would have food to eat during the storm, although Hazel was no better at cooking than she was when they had met, so she hoped Tate had an idea for what he wanted to use the ingredients for. They also had brought up suitcases containing long-life food from his house and the bags of food she had brought from hers. It was a change from their usual takeout, but she was glad to let Tate save his money since he always paid for their food orders.

Tate left for his office shortly after they unloaded their luggage at the hotel, leaving Hazel and Candy to organize it all in the small space. After refilling the ice in the ice chests and putting her and Tate's clothes into the hotel room's dresser drawers, she and Candy both flopped onto the bed and switched on the television to get a storm update.

"Any luck in getting Jake to remember what happened to him?"

Candy sighed.

"Not really... It's been hard enough keeping him materialized. He's still too weak to stay around for very long. Our conversations are surface level when we are able to talk. He remembers how we felt about each other, but he barely even remembers the time we spent together before I died."

Candy's eyes turned from Hazel's face to the floor, as she fiddled with the hem of her dress, smoothing it out although it was already smooth.

"I'm so sorry. That's got to be hard. Maybe it'll come in time?"

"Maybe. I wish there was a way to jog his memory, like you did with Angela... but I know you didn't initiate those visions. Not that I want anyone else haunting your dreams. I just wish there was a way to find out what happened to him... and to me."

Hazel reached out and grabbed Candy's hand, squeezing it gently.

"I would allow him to haunt my dreams if it helped me to figure out what happened to you, to both of you. I don't know how Angela sent those memories to me, or how you've been doing it, but I wish I did. I know it would be a helpful tool in solving this case, and I'd do anything to make that happen."

Candy looked up at her and smiled, but her eyes were glassy, barely hiding her actual emotions that boiled just below the surface.

A knock sounded at the door as Tate returned from the precinct, just after six hours of the walls seeming to close in on her. Setting a pizza down on the small table near the door, he scooped Hazel up in a hug, and Candy fizzled out of sight to conserve her energy and give them privacy.

"Pizza? They were open?"

"For now, but not for long. Everything should shut down as the storm closes in on the city. It won't be long before things get really hazardous out there. Some areas have already lost power."

Hazel walked over to the window and peered down to the street below. There weren't many people out anymore, causing the area surrounding the hotel to look deserted. The wind and rain came in waves, hitting the window on a near horizontal plane. The nearby businesses all had their windows boarded up with plywood, or had their metal shudders pulled down, reminding her of an apocalyptic scene from a movie. An unexpected blast of wind caught her by surprise, causing her to back away from the window and sit back down on the bed.

"I'm just glad we will have power. Although I'm sure we will lose cable soon. Then we won't have any idea what's going on with the weather, especially if our cellular service goes out."

He pulled her face into his hands and kissed her passionately. She let herself fall under his spell, lying the rest of the way down and rolling into his arms.

"How will we survive the night?"

"Will you protect me?"

"Always."

Forgetting about the storm outside, or the growling in her stomach, she became intoxicated by his scent, electrified by his touch. The rest of the world did not matter. They made love as the storm pelted the window, intensifying the electricity she already felt flowing from his body and into hers.

By the time she pulled herself away from Tate and gave into hunger, the pizza was already cold, but they ate it anyway. It would be the last takeout food they could eat until the city could pull itself back together after the storm. It would likely be cereal and milk, or canned food, for the next few days, if not longer.

The rain slammed against the window in violent torrents. The wind howled and whistled as its force met the resistance against the walls and windows of the buildings. It was not long before the cable shut off and she and Tate were forced to find a way to entertain themselves. Ways that did not include watching the weather broadcast in abject horror while the storm came on land with the wrath of a scorned woman. Ida may have only been a category two storm by the time it was to hit the city, bordering on category three, but that was much more powerful than the non-hurricane affected world realized. Settling into bed that night, it was impossible to avoid worrying about what state the city would be in when light broke, but Hazel let the storm lull her to sleep, leaving those concerns for when she could do something about it.

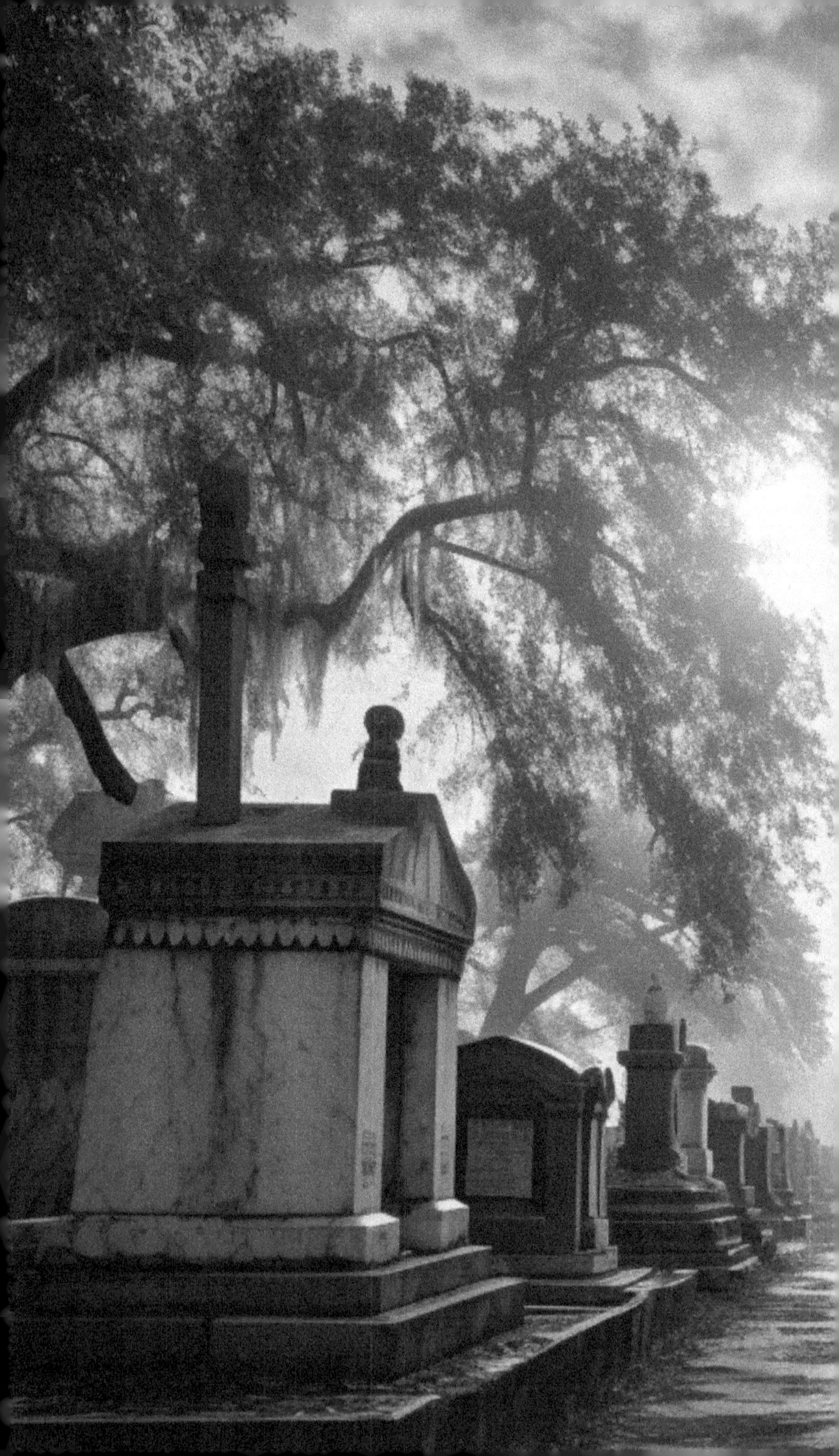

Chapter Ten
The Collage

Doors. One. Two. Three. Four. Five. Six. Walking down the dark hallway, all Hazel could see were the identical doors that lined the walls. She didn't recognize where she was, nor was there any sign on the doors as to where they led. Too scared to walk into the unknown, she slid with her back against the wall until her butt landed gently on the floor. She was utterly alone. The hallway was long and eerily quiet. The only light came from a flickering bulb halfway down the hall between two of them. Realizing she was sleeping, Hazel scrolled through her brain, trying to make any connections that would tell her if she was in a memory instead of a dream, but she could not decide. There were not enough indications to show either way, but it was not one of her own memories.

"Candy? Tate?"

She called out, desperately hoping she would be heard, but only her voice echoed back to her, causing her to feel incredibly isolated.

Tap. Tap. Tap. The noises down the hall started off light and irregular, but they became more clear, more predictable, the harder she focused on them.

"Hello?"

She called out again, but a fluttering echo of her call returned to her as though it was riding on the wind, filling any space it found.

Tap. Tap. Tap. The noises got louder. Hazel stunted her breathing and tried to discern where it was coming from. Slowly lifting herself off the floor and onto crouched feet, she leaned against the door closest to her, touching her ear to the surface.

No sound came from the first door, but she could still hear the rhythmic tapping, as though it was coming from everywhere, all at once.

Making her way to the end of the hall, after listening outside of four doors, she reached the door above which the flickering lightbulb stood watch. She placed her ear against the cool wood, just as she had several times before. But this time, instead of hearing nothing, three loud bands sounded from the other side.

The knocks were so hard against the door that she jerked away from it violently. She could feel the wood vibrate as they rang out. Something was inside.

Tiptoeing back to the door, she hesitantly placed her ear against it once more, hoping whatever was on the other side wouldn't startle her again. The tapping noise had quieted down and was replaced by the sound of shuffling. Taking a deep breath and blowing it out slow enough to calm her racing heart, Hazel tried the doorknob, but it was locked.

She could hear the sliding of feet across the floor. She could hear something digging around and making noise, but she could not hear any voices. Taking her chances that whatever was inside wouldn't harm her, she lightly tapped on the door, then stood back and waited to see who was on the other side.

She heard a click, and the door slowly creaked open, revealing the contents of the room. From what she could see, it appeared to be an old hotel room, or maybe a bedroom. The room was completely devoid of any character or warmth. To her surprise, there didn't seem to be anyone inside, but she still believed it was safer to linger in the hallway instead of barging in. She did not see anyone from her vantage point, but it did not mean someone could not be hiding behind the opened door, or just out of sight, waiting to strike her the minute she crossed the threshold.

"Hello?" she whispered, scanning the opening with wide eyes, before looking up and down the hall for movement, but there was none. There was nothing but absolute stillness. The tapping and shuffling had stopped. All she could hear was the beat of her own heart.

Although she could not see anyone, the room looked lived in. Clothes were piled on the floor, and a half empty water bottle sat on the side table. The bed was unmade, and mismatched blankets hung off it carelessly. The room smelled like a dusty old basement, as though no one had cleaned it for a while, or even opened the door or a window. The lightbulbs in the lamp and light fixtures were weak, causing the light in the room to appear sepia like an old picture.

With her neck stretched out to get a better look, Hazel peered in through the doorway. A forceful push came from behind her in the hallway, causing her to fall forward onto her hands and knees. Gathering herself after the tumble, she looked into the hallway for the person responsible for her fall, but there was nothing but emptiness. With eyes wide, she looked around to see she was now inside the room, the one place she had not intended to go.

Staying on her hands and knees, Hazel crawled to the wall on the side of the door and sat back on her heels. Her mind whirled and her heart raced. She knew she was dreaming, but she had been stuck in the strange place for so long that part of her wondered if she would ever wake up. Digging within herself, trying to build up courage, she lifted herself onto shaky legs, insistent on checking out the room since she was now inside of it. She continued to repeat in her head that it was just a dream, and she would be safe, even if she decided to walk around. There was a reason she was seeing the room, and she intended to figure out what the reason was before wakefulness pulled her out of it.

Still not seeing another soul, living or dead, nor another exit from the room, Hazel decided that closing herself into the space would be the safest choice. Whatever had pushed her into the room, although unseen, was in the hallway. She would prefer to be far away from it.

Grabbing the door and swinging it away from the wall, the scene behind the door came into view, causing a horrid gasp to escape her lips. Behind the door, in a chaotic mess, was an eclectic collection of photographs, newspaper articles, and random scribbling. Hazel scanned the items in disbelief. Her heart fell as she came across a picture of Candy. Actually, she saw several pictures of Candy.

Digital pictures, computer printouts, and even her obituary were scattered across the door. Some had roughly drawn Xs scrawled across Candy's beautiful face. Hazel's hands shook as she reached out to touch a silky lock of red hair hanging from the door that was tied with a ribbon. She recoiled as soon as her fingers grazed it and vomited violently. It was human hair. She knew it. And from the fiery red color, it had to be Candy's.

"What in the hell is this?"

She gasped, wiping vomit from her lips and looking back up at the display in dismay. It looked like the collection of a psychopathic stalker... but who?

Studying the items once again, she scanned them for clues, for anything that could tell her who had made them, but her eyes only came across one other picture before she was startled awake... Jake.

"Hazel. Hazel."

She awoke to Tate petting the hair out of her face as he looked down at her with his eyebrows lowered, obvious concern etched across his face. She felt slightly sick to her stomach and took a moment to calm herself from the trauma of her nightmare before acknowledging his plea.

The hotel room looked so similar to the one from her dream that it startled her, even with Tate's warm presence. Her eyes shot straight towards the door, expecting to see the collection of pictures and papers attached to the wood. To her relief, the back of the door was empty. Tate kissed her on the cheek, and she realized she had yet to address him since waking up. Catching his glance, she forced out a smile, although she still felt shaken.

"Hey. Good morning. I'm sorry. What happened?"

"Don't be sorry. You were having a nightmare. I was just trying to bring you out of it."

"Oh. Thanks. I was actually."

Trying to squeeze his body between Hazel and her pillow, Tate scooted her until she was leaning on his lap. He ran his fingers through her hair, calming her nerves with each pass. She let her eyes fall closed while he doted on her.

"Is the storm over?"

"The worst of it. It's still windy outside, and the cable is still out. I've been in touch with work, and it sounds like there is a lot of damage and the electricity will be out in the area for a while."

"Damn. That sucks. So, I'm assuming my apartment will be without power?"

"Yep, but you know you can stay with me. Don't stress about it. Mine is out right now too, but I doubt mine stays out as long. I have a generator until it's back on. We will be comfortable."

"Are you sure you don't mind? I don't want to intrude."

Tate looked down at her as though she had lost her mind, arching an eyebrow dramatically and making her giggle.

"Are you being serious? Of course, I don't mind. I mean, I know we just got involved like this, but it doesn't matter. This relationship hasn't moved too fast for me, and I doubt it ever will. You staying with me while your apartment has no electricity isn't going to change that. I stay at your apartment all the time, anyway. Never worry that you're intruding."

She allowed his words to sink into her brain, infiltrating the ever-present doubt that had plagued her life since she was a child. Before she could respond, he leaned over and kissed her, taking her words and her breath away.

"Now, what was in that nightmare that had you so shaken up? It took a while to wake you up. I was getting worried."

"Honestly, I'm not completely sure what was going on. I remember being scared and trapped in a room, but I didn't see anyone else."

She paused, fighting the nausea rising within her gut.

"I saw pictures of Candy attached to the back of a door in one of those collages you normally see on a crime television show, one usually created by a psychopath. I remember there being random pictures and newspaper clippings, oh, and scribbled notes, all haphazardly stuck together. I wasn't able to figure out who created it, or why I was seeing it. It was just... freaky."

The vision of the collection flooded back into her mind, churning her stomach and turning her blood cold. She tried to shake it away. Looking back into Tate's eyes, she struggled to find a comforting place to rest her mind.

"That sounds terrible. I wish there was something I could do to help you stop those types of dreams from coming to you."

He slid his body down until he was lying next to her, with his arms still wrapped solidly around her. She snuggled into his embrace, willing his touch to take the memories away.

"Do you think it was a spirit memory?"

She remembered debating the same question in her dream. It was one thing she remembered clearly, but she did not know the answer. If it was a spirit memory, she did not know whose memory it could have been.

"I'm honestly not sure. It was so specific to Candy. I feel like it must have been a memory, but I don't think it was hers, and I haven't seen Jake in days. It could have been my mind playing tricks on me. I really don't know. I have a hard time being able to tell when I'm in the dream. Even when I experience a memory, I usually see it from their eyes, so I still can't typically tell who the memory belongs to, unless I recognize the situation."

"Do you think the collage exists? I mean, do you think the killer created it or something?"

Subconsciously, Hazel had already considered this, but Tate pointing it out caused it to become a more likely scenario in her head. This only got her more startled by the experience in her nightmare, because she did not understand how she could have seen something that belonged to the killer... unless Jake or Candy actually knew them. She did not know of any other way she would have been able to see the scene at the back of the door unless the owner of the memory had seen it as well. She only had one option, and that was to talk to Candy about it.

"Gosh, I hope not. Whoever created that is sick. There was a lock of Candy's hair!"

She felt the bile rise in her throat just thinking about touching the hair in her nightmare and vomiting when realizing what it was. She tried to push the image out of her head. She had touched Candy's hair many times, but she never thought about the fact that it was not Candy's real hair, because Candy was a spirit. Candy always appeared solid to her, like she had a corporeal form, but it was not the same. It was not until she touched the hair that she realized the hair she had been touching for a year was not Candy's real hair. It was a manifestation of what Candy used to be, but it would never feel as real as the piece of hair that was hanging on the back of that door. The worst part was she did not know if that piece of hair had been cut from Candy's head before or after she died, and the thought sickened her.

"A lock of her hair? Like someone cut it off and kept it, like a keepsake?"

She nodded as her tears welled up in her eyes. Poor Candy. She didn't know she was all over someone's wall like that, stalked and studied, and Hazel did not know how to tell her. Candy had been through so much already. The thought of adding one more thing to her only made Hazel feel sicker.

"Hey, it's okay, love. Don't cry. We don't have to talk about this anymore. We will do everything we can to find justice for Candy."

He rubbed her back while she did her best to dry up her tears. There was not anything she could do to bring Candy back, or Jake, but it still made her feel like shit. She did not feel strong enough to handle everything that was being thrown her way, but she had to try, even if she had to fake it.

"It's just hard. Things were just looking up, and then this shit happened with Jake and it's like the entire puzzle flew off of the table and onto the floor, and now I have to pick up the pieces and sort it out again."

"Everything didn't land on the floor, though. We didn't. You have me. You don't have to sort everything out by yourself. For now, let me get something for you to eat. Are you hungry?"

"Yeah, but let me help you. I feel like I need to move my limbs before they fall off."

"Okay. Let's get you up then."

Tate hopped off the bed first, before reaching down and pulling Hazel up in one swift motion. She rocked before gaining her balance, his hug steadying her.

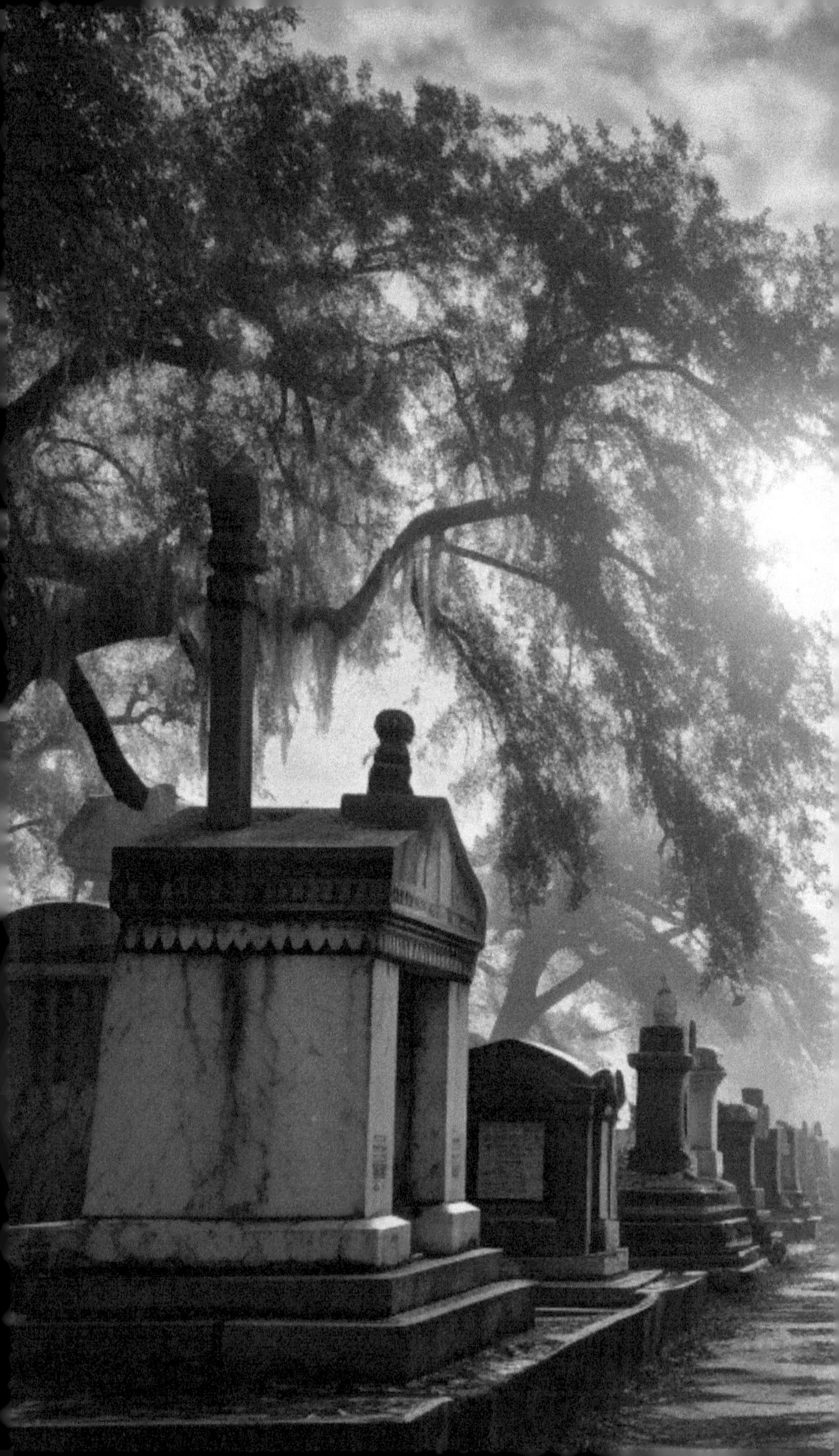

Chapter Eleven

Discovering the Evidence

Ignoring the destruction of the city outside, they spent their day in the small hotel room together, playing games and cuddling. With no television to distract them, to show them the devastation firsthand, they had no other options but to focus on each other.

When it came time for Tate's shift that evening, she was dreading being away from him. But Candy knew he would go to work that night, so Hazel would not be alone for long. Candy would return, and Hazel would have to tell her about the traumatizing nightmare, and the montage on the back of the hotel room door that suggested Candy was targeted for longer than she realized. She was more than targeted. She was the object of a psychopathic obsession, but they were no closer to figuring out who the creator was.

Just as Hazel settled down onto the bed with a book and a bowl of cereal, Candy manifested right next to her, nearly causing her to spill milk all over the place.

"Shit! Candy, you scared the hell out of me."

"Sorry, doll. I was hoping I had the time right. If not, I may have popped up right on top of lover boy, which I admit was kind of my plan."

Hazel reached out and swatted at Candy, forcing the meanest face she could muster, but Candy popped in and out of view, so Hazel hit the pillow instead.

"Well, I'm glad to see you're yourself today, but don't be landing on my man."

"Oh, relax, doll. He wouldn't even know."

"I would."

Hazel scrunched her nose, but Candy, undeterred, winked.

"So why are you in such a good mood?"

"I saw Jake today, albeit not for that long, but I'm just glad I got to see him at all. He was more mentally present today. He still doesn't remember what happened to him, but he remembers me. I had forgotten how much I enjoyed spending time with him. It's not the same, sure, but it's something."

"That's great news Candy! I mean, what happened to him sucks, but I guess this is the best outcome."

Candy's smile faltered, but only slightly.

"I thought our love died with me, but it didn't. It's still there. None of us can live forever, and we can't have another chance at being together in that way, but he can still touch my world. I'll probably love him forever and seeing him again has reignited that."

"Who knew you could be such a poet."

"Oh hush. So, I've been to the apartment, and everything is in good shape. We just don't have electricity, but I'm assuming you figured that out already?"

"Yea. Tate told me this morning."

"So, what are you going to do?"

"He invited me to stay with him until it's back on."

"Ooh! Are you turning into a wifey on me? I'm so proud! Okay, I'll walk in your wedding but I'm picking the dress. No peach! I'm not wearing peach!"

"Shut up!"

Hazel tried to swat Candy again, but she missed again.

"Why are you so violent today? Gosh."

"Why are you messing with me so much today? Oh wait, that's my life."

"So..."

Candy hesitated, as her tone shifted. "It may ruin my chipper mood, but do you want to go through more of Brad's case file? I know you have some extra time with the storm and all, but you don't have forever."

"Yea. We should do that. I want to look at the evidence. I'm curious what all was used to prosecute him. It sounds like the case was completely circumstantial. I'm wondering if there is evidence that was missed, or at least ignored, if it didn't fit their mold. Also, there's something I need to tell you... before we go off too much in another direction."

Candy's face fell into a look of concern, only making Hazel's hesitation heighten. She braced for the onslaught of emotions she was sure to feel flow off of Candy when she told her of her harrowing ordeal.

"What is it? What happened?"

"It may be nothing, but it may be something. I'm not sure."

"Well, get on with it. You're making me more nervous by not just spitting it out."

"Sorry. It's the dream I had last night; well, it was really a nightmare."

"Was it someone's memory?"

"I'm not sure. I think so, but I don't think it was yours."

Candy blew out a deep spectral breath.

"Okay... Let's hear it."

"I was in a hotel or something, but I don't know if the place matters, because me being here could have influenced my surroundings. I didn't see anyone, but I definitely heard a presence, even felt one. Anyway, what matters is what was in one of the rooms."

"One of the hotel rooms?"

"Yes. One of the doors opened and..."

"And what? What happened? What did you see?"

Hazel's throat tightened through her chest until it became hard to breathe. The visions of the door flew into her mind, swirling around until she almost vomited all over again.

"I'm sorry. I just don't want to have to tell you. It's just too awful."

Candy reached out and rubbed Hazel's arm, sending cool, calming energy into her body that barely scratched the surface of her anxiety.

"It's okay, doll. I've seen plenty of awful in my time on this earth, but you need to tell me. Don't bear this burden on your own."

Nodding and wiping the first of many tears from her eyes, Hazel told Candy about everything she saw in that room, even the lock of hair.

By the time she was finished explaining the scene in the best detail she could, Candy's eyes were as big as saucers, and her mouth hung open. She sputtered word fragments, but the right words did not seem to come. Hazel knew exactly how that felt. She was just as speechless, and slightly sick, but she was glad to have told Candy. She could not afford to keep anymore secrets from her.

"That's... that's crazy. I just don't understand. And you said you didn't see anyone? No sign of who created it?"

"No. None. I heard someone before the door opened. I even saw their shadow shuffling across the room. But, by the time the door opened, they were gone."

Candy nodded grimly, pinching the bridge of her nose and closing her eyes, as Hazel stared into oblivion, unsure of what to do or say next.

"And you saw a picture of Jake mixed in with the pictures of me?"

"Yes. I saw one picture of him, although there could have been more. I was pretty upset after noticing the hair, and Tate had started trying to wake me, so I was no longer one hundred percent focused."

"Right. Okay."

Candy leaned back on the bed. Her eyebrows furrowed as though she were thinking intently about something. Hazel took the spot next to her, laying back as well. She remained quiet, unwilling to disrupt Candy's thoughts, and unsure of what else she could say.

Candy remained quiet for a while, so long that Hazel had almost fallen asleep by the time she spoke again. The sound of Candy's voice startled her and she jolted awake.

"Did Jake's picture have an X drawn across it?"

Taking a moment, she processed the question. Closing her eyes, she tried to repaint the picture of the door in her mind, although the sight of it made the metallic taste return to her mouth. After a few moments, she saw it clearly, and the realization hit her like a bullet.

"No!"

She responded with more excitement than she had intended, but softened her tone before continuing.

"His picture did not have an X across it. Do you think that means he wasn't dead yet? Do you think this could have been his memory?"

"So, my pictures were crossed out, but his wasn't?"

"Yes. That's what I saw. Also, his picture looked like it had been cut, and maybe the original had him next to someone else. It almost looked like they had cut the other person out before nailing it to the door."

"Interesting. I think it's possible this was his memory, although I'm not sure how you would have seen it. I mean, he's barely come around you... unless he's been around but hasn't been able to manifest..."

Hazel's heart fell into her stomach. Jake was a nice guy, a really nice guy, but the idea he could be hanging around without her knowing was unsettling, even if he did not have any control over it.

"Would you be able to ask him about it? About the dream I mean... and about where he goes when he's not... visible."

Candy thought for a second, swirling a curl of her hair, which only made Hazel's stomach lurch more. She imagined the lock of hair nailed to the psycho-collage on the back of that door.

"I can ask him, but I can't guarantee he will remember. It would be really helpful if we could figure out how these memories are transferring. Then we might figure out how to start it... maybe even transfer specific memories. I know it's a long shot. Too bad we never thought to ask Angela before she crossed over. I mean,

I know I've transferred some memories to you, but I have zero idea how."

"We could do some experimentation," Hazel suggested, although she had no idea what she meant by it. "I don't know what that would look like, but it wouldn't hurt to try. Maybe, if you and I could figure out how to do it, then we could try it with Jake. I don't know if I'll ever see that scene again, and I can admit I never want to, but I think I need to. I need to see who created it. I think it's safe to say its creator is your murderer, and Jake's."

"Yea. I wouldn't know the first thing to try, but I agree we should. We don't have anything to lose. Wow. This situation just gets more and more disturbing."

"Tell me about it."

"Okay. Let's dig through Brad's file. I think, more than ever, we need to learn more about what the police found out about my murder. Do you think Tate could bring you a copy of the files on Jake's murder? I know it's an open investigation, but isn't it relevant to your current case?"

"Not completely. He can probably get copies of some of the stuff, but not all of it. I'll ask him though. I know he will share what he can."

"Okay, good. I don't want anyone to get into trouble, but the more information we can get, the better. So, what should we look at in Brad's file? I don't want to listen to anymore recordings though, at least not today. I don't think my nerves can take it."

"I'm with you. No... I want to look through the evidence notes and stuff."

Hazel climbed off of the bed and began digging through her satchel, pulling out the large brown folder that contained the paperwork portion of Brad's file. With the file in hand, she returned to the bed and took her spot next to Candy.

She flipped through the folder until she came across the evidence list and accompanying notes, separating it from the pack and setting the rest aside.

"I know they did not convict him on DNA. I'm assuming there was some of his DNA in your apartment, since you two had been dating, but not in any way that would have proven him to be guilty. It's really sad because I'm curious if evidence was overlooked to fit their narrative."

"You really think that's possible?"

"Oh, I know it's possible. It's happened before. You probably see that all the time on your murder mysteries."

"Yea, you're right. I just never considered it having happened in my case. That would be unfortunate."

"It would be. You deserve better."

Candy reached over and squeezed Hazel's shoulder, giving her just enough assurance to keep digging in the paperwork in her lap.

Most of the evidence paperwork reinforced what she already knew about the case. There was no DNA evidence left in Candy's apartment that was considered out of the ordinary. At least not in the apartment. The forensic team had pulled several fingerprints off of the doorknobs throughout the building, including on the stairwell, even in the elevator. However, with several people living in the complex, and even more people thought to be visitors, they weren't able to narrow their investigation in on anyone who could have been a suspect.

"What are you thinking?"

Candy leaned over to get a closer look at the documents.

"I think they overlooked something. I think the killer left some evidence, unintentionally, of course. Too bad the building doesn't have cameras."

"Yea. Cameras would have been helpful. How would we figure out what they left behind? If the investigators missed it, I mean."

Frustrated, Hazel shuffled the documents back into a single stack, setting them aside to remove them from her sight.

"I don't know. I think our best chance lies in Jake's memory. If he saw that crazy collage of pictures, then he must know who created it. I know he doesn't remember right now, but maybe his memory will come back. Or maybe we can accomplish the memory transfer. I don't know, but I think he is the key to figuring this out."

"I don't know if his memory will come back, but I agree with you that the truth is in there somewhere. I'll keep trying… we will keep trying. But not tonight. After what you went through last night, I'd rather you have a night with no nightmares or memories. If that is even possible. When will Tate be back?"

Hazel glanced at her cellular phone to check the time, before setting it back down on her lap.

"He's supposed to be getting off in an hour. I'll probably jump in the shower soon, so it can be free for when he gets back. It's so weird to not have any television in here, and I can't access any news or anything with my phone because there's no internet service working, not even with my data. I feel like we are in a dark zone or something."

"Girl... I'd be finding plenty to do if I were stuck in this room with that man. I hope you're doing the same."

Feeling the flush spread, Hazel held up her hand to block her face, before peeking one eye through her fingers and sticking out her tongue at Candy.

"I'm sure you would."

Candy patted Hazel on the shoulder, pasting a prideful look across her face.

"I know I've taught you well. Momma is proud. Anyway... I guess I should get out of here so you can shower. This room isn't big enough for the three of us, not that you're into that. I'm going to go back to the apartment and hope Jake turns up. If he does, I'll talk to him. Any idea how long the two of you will be here before you go back to his house?"

"I'm not sure. I can ask Tate later tonight. I can tell you then if you want to come back later. I'd imagine we will only be here for a few days. Once we are out of here, I'll need to make a plan to interview Brad."

"Okay. I'll check back with you guys. If you aren't here, I'll go to his house. I'll find you."

Candy reached around, giving Hazel a hug, before disappearing where she sat, leaving only a chill in her place. Hazel sat for a moment before getting off the bed and making her way into the shower.

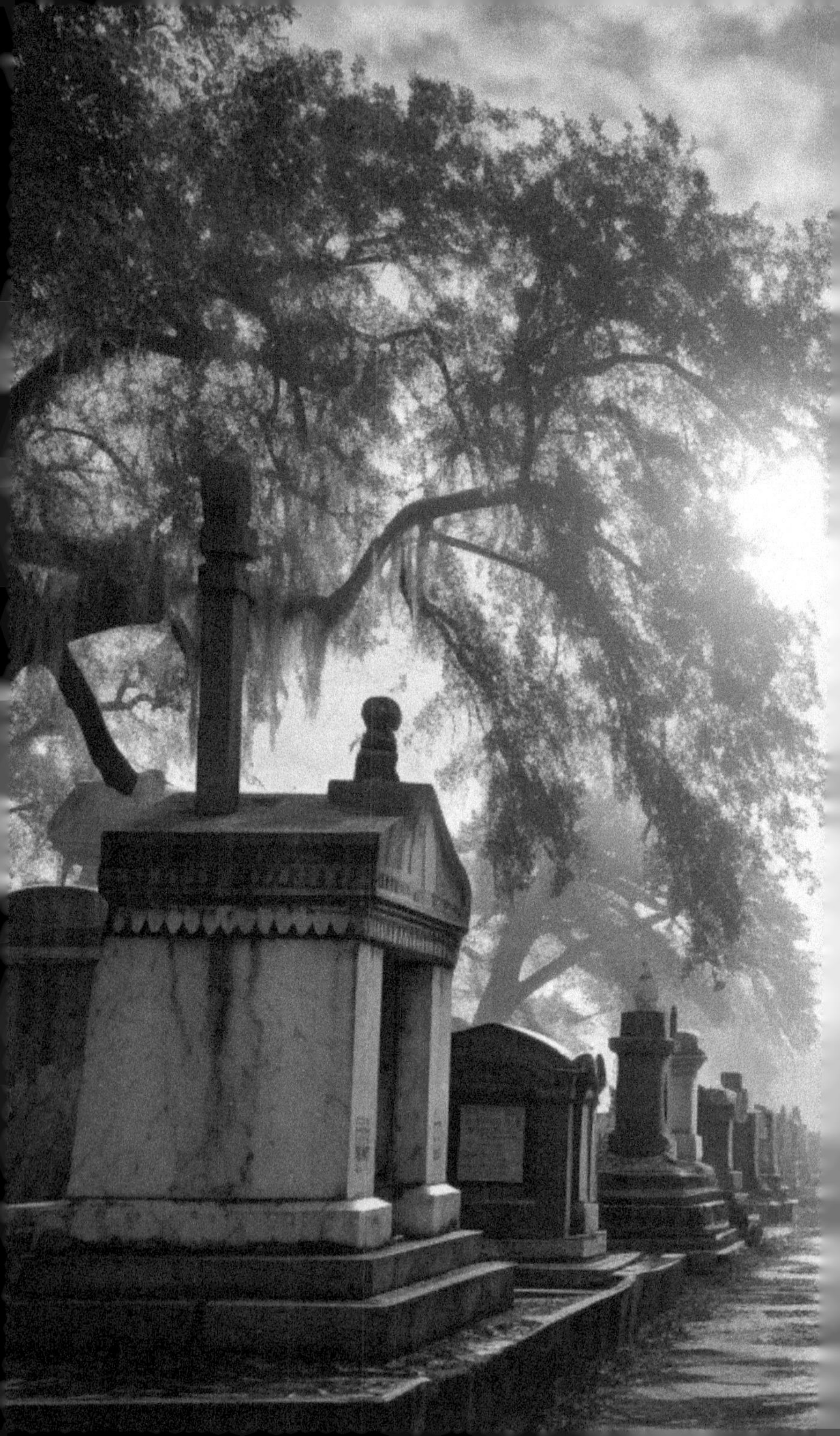

Chapter Twelve

The Transfer

Tate and Hazel spent one more night at the downtown hotel before returning to his house in the suburb of New Orleans. They had to stop at her apartment before heading out of town, so she could pack more of her belongings for what was looking to be an extended stay. She felt admittedly nervous about staying at his house for so long, mostly because she did not want to overstay her welcome, although he assured her it was a needless concern.

They ran into Candy at the apartment, and she and Hazel had made their plan to practice memory transfers. They did not know how to make it happen, but they intended to try. They agreed their first attempt would be on the following night, since Tate had an overnight shift. Tate, on the other hand, had been tasked with seeing what information about Jake's case would be able to be shared with her. She intended to make her own requests, once things with the storm had settled down, but, until then, she hoped Tate could get some kind of lead from Jake's case file.

When he got home from work later that night, he did not have much information to share, but he did have a list of names. The names included those individuals who were interviewed after Jake's murder. Although most of the names were standard, including Jake's family and a few friends, one name had never been mentioned to Hazel before. Harmony Richard.

According to the brief notes attached to the list, Harmony claimed to be Jake's girlfriend. Neither she nor Candy had realized Jake had a girlfriend, and she could not wait to tell Candy about the discovery. Jake had never mentioned a girlfriend, although Hazel did not think he was being intentionally secretive. He clearly lacked much of his memory, especially the memories from closer to the time of his death. Still unable to use the internet, Hazel did not have the ability to research the girl on social media, but she would do that as soon as she was able.

Candy appeared on Tate's sofa within thirty minutes of him leaving for work. Already dark outside, Hazel could feel herself growing sleepy, but her mind buzzed with the possibilities that could come about if they could succeed in transferring Candy's memories intentionally. Sitting down next to Candy, she told her about Harmony, bracing for a passionate reaction, but none came. It seemed that, although she loved Jake, Candy had already accepted the idea he had probably dated someone after her. She realized he would have eventually had to at least attempt to move on, because that was how life went.

Having already taken her shower as soon as Tate left the house, she and Candy moved to the bedroom for their attempt at a memory transfer. All Candy needed to do was what Angela had done, and climb into Hazel's brain, somehow, show her some memories, and try not to mess anything up in there. Easy as pie. Hopefully. The problem was they did not know how to do it. Hazel closed her eyes and hoped their plan would work.

Candy laid down next to her and placed a hand against Hazel's cheek. She shivered against the chill but pulled her blanket up to her chin to compensate. Neither of them knew how Angela had transferred her memories to her, and they had no way to ask her since Angela had crossed over to the other side, but they were going to try whatever they could to achieve the same result.

She was not sure how long she had laid there with Candy's hand against her cheek, but sleep eventually consumed her.

Walking up to the church that held Candy's body, Hazel could see that the church was a large pink building with pointy arched windows and doors that reminded her of the gothic style from Europe. The stained-glass windows were beautiful, but it made her curious if Candy was making her see the building as pink, or if it really was a pink church. It made her smile to think about Candy adding that level of detail to the memory, just in case she noticed. Standing outside on the sidewalk, she felt nervous about opening the odd shaped wooden doors. She was not sure if she was prepared to see Candy, lifeless in her casket, when she had only ever seen her as though she was still a living woman. Although a spirit, Candy had almost always appeared solid to Hazel. She had seen memories of Candy's death, as well as the moment in which Candy's spirit had separated from her body, both of which haunted Hazel's mind ever since.

Without warning, she noticed a change in the memory. Her vision rippled as though she were in a pond of water being hit by rain droplets. As suddenly as it started, it stopped again. Taking a deep, cleansing breath and blowing it out slowly, Hazel tugged on the large wooden doors and walked inside.

She felt a sense of awe at how cavernous the inside of the church was. The doors echoed as they closed behind her. The ceiling was covered in wood paneling, which gave it the appearance of a cabin. The walls were painted in a color between tan and gold, but the back wall, behind the altar, was painted in a deep red. She could hear the soft murmuring of voices; however, she could not make out the faces of the people. In the church's front, she could see a solo cellist playing a somber tune next to a beautiful white casket. She shuddered at the sight of it. The thought of approaching Candy's body made her sick. She was not ready for that, not that she ever would be. Instead, she wanted to find Jake. She wanted to see who was sitting near him and wanted to see if she could speak to him within the memory. Glancing around from the center aisle, she found him sitting at the back of the church and made her way towards him. Sitting by himself with his eyes closed, he looked as though he was trying to make sense of his surroundings, or maybe he was praying for peace.

"Jake," *she said, grabbing his hand gently.*

He didn't seem to notice her. He didn't even open his eyes. She felt her chest tighten as desperation crept in, unsure if her intention to communicate with him would actually work.

"Jake!"

She pleaded with him, shaking him harder, but he was still oblivious to her presence. Frustrated, she let go of him and began frantically looking around the church, hoping she could recognize anyone sitting in the nearby pews. She hoped someone could hear her, could see her, but her own eyes deceived her. She could not decipher any faces in the blur of people. They were unrecognizable, as though their faces had been erased, but the rest of their body remained. She tried to make a mental image of the rest of their features, at least for those who were sitting next to Jake, at least those who may be the mysterious Harmony. She didn't have any way to know how long he waited to date her after Candy's death, but it was possible he and Harmony were friends before they dated. It was possible she was there.

"Hazel," a whisper called out to her from the direction of the altar.

She turned her head from the crowd of people to see where the whisper was coming from, but she didn't see anyone who could have called out to her.

No figure stood alone in the crowd of people. She raced to the entrance of the church, desperate to escape the memory, but the door was gone. A solid wall stood in its place, preventing her escape and forcing her to go to the altar in the direction of Candy's body. Her heart raced, causing her to feel like a caged animal. Swallowing down the fear in her throat, she bolted towards the other side of the church, turning her eyes towards the door with the clear exit sign overhead.

As she approached the last couple of steps before the altar, when she could just almost see the mane of red hair peaking up over the side of the casket, her vision rippled, and her surroundings shifted. The church walls no longer surrounded her, and the altar no longer stood before her. Instead, she stood in a sea of white, in a white void. Her feet stumbled as she planted them on the white floor, no longer knowing what direction to run because every direction appeared the same. She called out for help, but her voice only echoed back to her. There was not even the sound of wind. She was surrounded by nothingness, lonely, horrifying nothingness. She rubbed her eyes vigorously, as though she could smudge her reality back into being. When her vision cleared, the blank canvas remained, but a form had appeared paces ahead of her, lying, unmoving, on the ground. She rubbed her eyes again, just in case the appearance was a trick of vision, but it wasn't.

Details of the form on the ground began to stand out among the white. Fiery red hair illuminated the nothingness and sent a jolt through her brain, causing her to run forward. She knew, instinctively, that it was Candy. When she approached Candy's body on the ground, Hazel dropped to her knees near Candy's face. Candy was unmoving, unbreathing, but she didn't look like a corpse. She looked like the Candy that Hazel had spent the last year of her life with, her best friend.

Did Candy interfere with her memory to spare me the trauma of seeing her dead?

Instead of having to see her in the church, in a casket, she was lying on sheets of white and pastels, in a beautiful, flowing, white dress, surrounded by delicate roses. She looked like a porcelain doll. Bending down to touch her face, Hazel relished in the warmth of her skin, a warmth that she had never felt when touching Candy. Although Candy's touch always filled her with calm, Candy was a spirit, therefore her touch was always like ice on her skin. In this beautiful vision, Candy's body was warm.

Tears filled Hazel's eyes as she grieved for the friend, the living friend, she never had the chance to know, but one she wanted to know so badly.

Her heart broke as Candy's warm body remained unresponsive to her desperate touch. It was almost as though, if only she had gotten there sooner, she could have saved her friend, seen her alive for just a moment. Laying down next to Candy, Hazel nuzzled her face in Candy's soft red curls, watching as her tears poured down the strands of hair like rain on blades of grass.

"Hazel."

Someone whispered from somewhere within the void. She felt desperate to know who they were and what they wanted, but she could not fathom leaving Candy. Not while she was still warm, maybe not ever.

"Hazel, come back to me."

Hazel awakened in Tate's bed, to Candy lightly shaking her and leaning over her with startled eyes.

"Hazel. Hazel. Are you okay?"

Candy frantically brushed the hair away from Hazel's face, looking for signs of consciousness. Hazel squinted, rubbed her eyes, and then turned her gaze in Candy's direction.

"Candy? What happened? What was that?"

"What do you mean? Did it work? What did you see? I couldn't wake you, so I got scared."

Candy looked drained.

"I think so. I walked into a church, and I saw Jake, but I couldn't really make out anyone else's face."

"Could you speak to him?"

"No. I tried though."

"And then what happened?"

Candy looked down and began picking at her fingernails.

"I started walking towards your casket, but the vision changed. Did you do something? Did you change the memory?"

Candy looked up at Hazel, opening her mouth to speak, but closing it back quickly before looking away.

"What? What did you do? Candy?"

Hazel pulled herself into a sitting position and reached out to Candy, trying to get Candy to look at her.

"Nothing that you wouldn't have done, love. I didn't want you to see me like that, so I tweaked the memory, just a little. Although I didn't expect it to work. I think I may know why you couldn't make out the faces of many of the people at my service. When I was at my funeral, I didn't pay attention to most of those people because I didn't even know most of them. I think most of those people showed up because of the media frenzy surrounding my murder. Maybe you couldn't see their faces because they weren't part of my memory?"

"Oh, that actually makes sense. Well, hopefully we can find out more from Jake about Harmony, if he can ever appear reliably. He hasn't been able to help much so far, but if she was dating him prior to his murder, maybe we can talk to her. It's the best lead we have. Maybe, after we get better at this memory transfer thing, we can even try it with him. He must have some memories of her."

"Possibly. I can't even stand thinking about him dating someone else. Ugh. It disgusts me. And then if she was possibly responsible for all of this? How would we even prove that if our only witness is dead? I feel terrible that Brad spent all of this time in prison for something he probably didn't do. Sure, he was a rotten boyfriend, but he wasn't a murderer. I just wish I had a way to talk to him so I could tell him I'm okay."

"We could probably figure something out,"

Hazel reached out and placed her hand on Candy's. She did not know if Brad would believe her, but she could try to pass on a message to him from Candy and take the chance he would believe her.

"Oh, and thank you for changing the vision from your memory. You looked beautiful."

"Well, of course I did!"

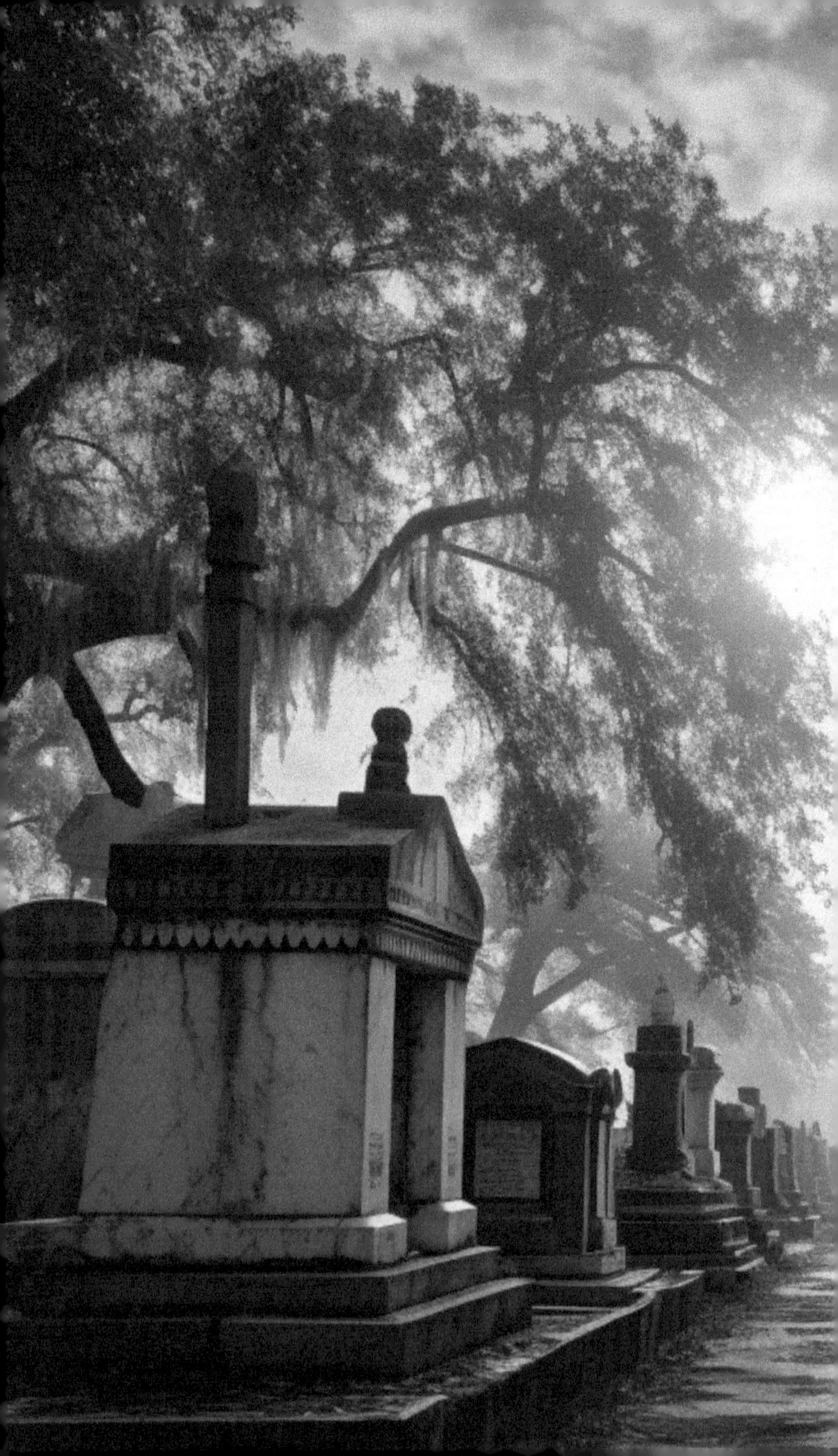

Chapter Thirteen
The Prison Visit

Hurricane Ida left a wide path of destruction across the eastern part of the state. Hundreds of thousands of residents were without power and many homes were destroyed or at least damaged. Trees and power lines lay twisted across several major roads and roofs were torn off. A storm surge of over fifteen feet barreled into the coast, flooding many areas with stagnant water that was slow to recede.

Emergency personnel were being worked to the bone, keeping Tate away from home for more hours per week than he was used to working. Hazel occupied herself by working through her case files, familiarizing herself with every facet of Brad's first case, as well as working on the paperwork needed to postpone his trial until more progress was made on Jake's case. Although she had not met with Brad yet, she knew it would be the wisest move.

Candy continued to visit her at Tate's house, practicing intentional memory transfers and spending time together when she could not be with Jake. After days of practice, Hazel was exhausted, but Candy had proven skilled at immersing Hazel into her memories, and even changing their contents. Although that was not quite the point of the exercise.

By the time a few days had passed since the storm, she could not put off visiting Brad in prison any longer. Begrudgingly, Hazel and Candy set off from Tate's house towards the facility where Brad was being kept.

She had taken the time, over the past few days, to go through the evidence within his case file and had discovered that his fate was not sealed with DNA evidence, but only with circumstantial evidence. Brad was the likely suspect, at least in the eyes of the prosecutors. He was Candy's boyfriend, and they had a history of turbulence in their relationship. It was also well known, in their group of friends, that she had been trying to break it off for some time and that she had become quite attached to Jake. All of those facts would have been seen as a motive to convict Brad. Plus, he lived alone and was in his apartment when she was murdered, or at least that was where the police found him when he was arrested. There was no one who could vouch for where he was. No one could provide a solid alibi for him. So, even though he was most likely innocent, a series of unfortunate circumstances had caused him to be convicted of murder. It was a miscarriage of justice for him, and for Candy.

Candy, who usually filled car rides with mindless chatter, usually about guys or sex, sat quietly in the passenger seat, gazing out of the window and fiddling with her fingernails. Every once in a while, she would turn to Hazel to ask her a random question, or comment on the hurricane destruction out of the window, but never in an effort to start a conversation. Candy's current state of being created an ache in Hazel's heart, one she did not know how to soothe without solving Jake's murder, and even that would still leave Candy to mourn his death. Her usually annoyingly joyful best friend was in pain, because her entire world had been turned upside down, and she was powerless to do anything about it, because she was dead. Usually, it was Hazel who relied on Candy for support while she fumbled through life, falling apart at almost every turn. She was not used to this new arrangement, having so much responsibility on her shoulders that made such a difference to Candy's happiness.

As they got closer to the prison, Candy's posture stiffened, and it became clear to Hazel that her friend was feeling nervous about seeing her ex again. Although he had not killed her, their history was not a positive one. Reaching across the cup holders, she threaded her fingers between Candy's spectral ones, ignoring the numbing sensation caused by their chill.

"You don't have to come in, Candy. I'll be okay to go in by myself. It's completely up to you. I know this can't be easy."

"I know, but I need to. I've been to his prison cell before... before I knew he was innocent. I used to try scaring him right after I died, but he never seemed to know I was there. I think I did it more to make me feel like I was getting back at him. Things are different now. You're right. It's not easy. It freaks me out to think about sitting across from him, even if he can't see me. But I feel like I need to hear what he has to say with my own ears. I'll leave if it becomes too much, and wait for you outside, but I do intend to stay. Thank you though. I know you can handle it without me, and I appreciate you trying to give me an out. We are in this together, like everything else."

Hazel squeezed her hand before nodding in acknowledgement.

"I'll support you no matter what. Love you."

"Love you too."

She held Candy's hand until they parked at the prison, forcing her to have to rub the sensation back into her fingers where the chill of Candy's touch had caused numbness. Grabbing her satchel and taking a deep breath that she forced herself to blow out slowly, she and Candy walked to the entrance of the prison. She approached the attendants, showing her credentials so she could be escorted to her new client. The one client on earth who she was dreading working with but had no choice.

An armed guard approached her from behind a barred door and offered to escort her to the meeting room. Swallowing back all of her hesitation, she threw her satchel back over her shoulder and followed him, as Candy followed closely behind. Opening the door to the meeting room, the guard went in first and checked Brad's restraints while Hazel waited in the hall, only entering once she was summoned.

Although she had seen pictures of Brad before, she did not know what she was expecting to see when she walked into the room. Part of her had imagined him as a villain, so she was not expecting a clean shaven, harmless looking guy to be handcuffed to the table, but that's what she found. Candy gasped when they entered the room, but Hazel did her best to ignore Candy's presence so she could at least appear to be a normal human being. The first thing she noticed about Brad was his eyes. They were bright hazel, and he actually looked fairly well rested. His face had been recently shaven. His hair had been recently cut and was brushed in a way to make him look like a regular guy she would see in the mall. He was actually an attractive guy, not that she could expect any less from one of Candy's exes. He looked up at her expectantly, as though she were someone who could deliver his future back to him. Although she did not feel so confident in her ability to do so.

Choosing the chair directly across from him, she attempted to sit up tall and appear more professional than she was.

"Brad Chiasson?"

His face fell as he nodded, as though hearing his name connected him with the crime he had been convicted of.

"Yes, and you are?"

"My name is Hazel Watson. I'm the public defender who has been assigned to your case. With the delay caused by the storm, I've gone through your case file, including the recordings, and..."

"Recordings?" he interrupted; a troubled look deepened on his face.

"Yes, the original interview you did with the police was recorded, but don't worry, the interview stopped when you asked for an attorney. I did not come across anything particularly damning in it."

She watched his face settle into a more relaxed state before continuing.

"However, it did not give me much to go on. I am glad you didn't continue talking to the police without an attorney, since people say things they shouldn't and incriminate themselves, even if they aren't guilty, but it left me, admittedly, without an understanding of your side of the story. I listened to the statement you made while being coached by your attorney, but I can only take it with a grain of salt, I'm afraid. I need to know what happened with no one telling you what to say. It's the only way I can prepare for what may become uncovered in trial. Whatever you tell me is confidential, so I need for you to trust me, and tell me what really happened. Can you do that?"

He hesitated and then nodded solemnly. She readied her notepad and pen, forcing an impassive expression onto her face and then nodding her head as a sign for him to begin.

"The first thing I want to say is I didn't kill Candy... I swear it. I know what they've said about me, the press, and the police. I wasn't the best boyfriend to her, but I loved her, and I would never have hurt her like that."

Hazel chanced a glance at Candy, who was staring at Brad intently, emotion etched across her face. She returned her eyes to Brad quickly, making notes on her pad.

"Do you have any idea who killed her?"

"No. I don't know how anyone could hurt her. She was a good person. A bit of a firecracker, but she had a good heart. She and I had our problems, and I realize I should have let her go long before I did, but I did love her. I still do."

Candy let out a sob, and it took everything in Hazel to keep her eyes on Brad and not console her. She desperately regretted the fact she would have to bring up Jake, knowing it would hurt Candy more, but she did not have a choice.

"Have you heard about Jake? What happened to him?"

Brad nodded, but his face revealed the guilt he felt.

"Yes. It's why I filed my appeal. I was not trying to capitalize on his death. Jake was my friend. Well, it was complicated. I cared about him, though. I do not know who killed him, but I know I did not. And I know I did not kill Candy. So, I thought, just maybe, that the same person killed them both. I hoped they would find the perpetrator and that would prove my innocence. I do not know. Maybe it was a long shot... but I had to try."

"It makes sense to me, but it is premature since Jake's murderer is still out there. I think it would help you the most if we delay this quest until more progress has been made on his case."

"What do you suggest?"

"I think it best if I get a continuation on your case for as long as we can, hoping they find Jake's killer. I can't delay it forever, but I already have some time since it is a high stakes case and I'm new to representing you."

"Okay. What do I do until then?"

"Wait... I'll be in touch, but probably not until you are returned to the city. I'll file paperwork and send it over for you to sign. I will update you if I hear anything new in Jake's case."

"I can't thank you enough."

"Don't thank me yet, but I'll do my best."

Packing her notepad back into her satchel, Hazel stood up from the table, and followed the guard back to the foyer of the prison, eyeing several spirits along the way. Most of them had clearly been prisoners of the facility, and still wore the wounds that had taken their life. One man, with a broken neck, turned to watch her as she walked past, eyeing her as though she were fresh meat. Wrapping her arms defensively around her chest, she looked away from him, hoping he would not follow her home.

Although she had seen spirits since she was a child, it still was not easy. And combined with prisons, it really gave her the creeps. Another spirit, that of a guard, smiled at her as she pushed open the metal door and exited the prison.

She had not realized how stagnant the air within the prison was until she took in her first breath once outside its walls. The outside air was hot and sticky with humidity, but it was fresh. It did not feel like it had been recycled in and out of the lungs of thousands of men without ever going through the trees. Even Candy, who no longer had the ability to breathe, seemed to notice the change. They walked to her car in silence, reeling from the experience of being in such proximity to Brad.

"How are you feeling?" she asked Candy as they settled back into the car.

"I'm okay. It wasn't as bad as I expected, actually. He seemed sincere. I guess sitting in prison has given him lots of time to think. He certainly never acted like he truly loved me. He always just seemed to want to control me. I think he's exaggerating on that topic, but I do believe him when he says he didn't do it. He was never a good liar."

"I believe that part was genuine as well. But I think, at least for some stuff, he was trying to convince me, and himself, of his feelings. At least he admitted why he filed the appeal, but I can't say I blame him. I'm assuming he did the paperwork himself. I guess he's keeping busy while he's in there."

"Ugh. Let's talk about something else. I feel like I've been doing nothing but dwelling, and it sucks. I don't feel like myself at all."

"Cut yourself some slack. You have been through so much and you always appear to take it in stride. It's okay to fall apart a little. You've seen me do it more than I had the right to."

"You're right. It's just unlike me to be so depressed. Anyway, how are you and Tate? I feel like I see little of you since Jake has been coming and going."

"We are perfect, and it's understandable that you've been preoccupied. I can't blame you."

"I'm proud of you, you know. With how you handled everything that happened with Raymond Waters, how you let it propel you instead of dragging you down. I'm just proud of you."

Hazel felt a warm sensation crawl over her as she internalized Candy's words, trying to let them sink into her psyche and improve her doomed self-esteem, even if only a little.

"Thank you. I'm still working on it."

She hesitated, unsure if she should tell Candy about her dreams of Raymond Waters. However, after a brief inner struggle, she decided she had to or risk upsetting Candy when she inevitably found out. She had promised Candy that she would tell her things like that from now on.

"I've dreamed about him. Raymond. Well, I've had nightmares about him, intense ones."

Candy looked at her with wide eyes. Hazel could feel Candy's concern roll off of her like a current, filling the car until the air became almost too thick to breathe.

"They are nightmares, right? He's not showing up in our house, is he?

It was not a question she had considered yet, and just the thought of Raymond in her house filled her with dread. She had never dared to consider him following her home after she was forced to kill him in self-defense, because just the thought of it was terrifying. Once Candy mentioned it, it sent her mind into a whirlwind, spinning through the nightmares for any clues that they were real experiences.

"Please don't even suggest that. Damn. That would be horrifying. I'm pretty sure they are nightmares. I mean, I haven't seen him when I've been awake, not since that day at his cabin."

She could tell that Candy was forcing back a comment for her sake, but she did not probe. Chances were, she would not want to know.

"I hope you're right. I will certainly keep my eyes peeled for him. Maybe you should burn that sage after all."

"The what?"

"The sage... that you got from the voodoo shop. She said it would get rid of evil, and his ass is evil. It couldn't hurt, well except if it triggered the smoke alarm."

"I guess we could try it, but I really think they were just dreams. I'm sure, if he was back, he'd have shown himself to me by now... while I'm awake, I mean. Just to rub it in my face."

"We can leave it at that, after you use the sage... just in case. It may be a bunch of hocus pocus, but it wouldn't hurt to try. I'll stand by that. Now, I want to hear all about your sex life because mine is dead."

She smirked, causing Hazel to nearly spit out her water.

"Did you really crack such a grim joke? That's terrible. My sex life is grand, but I'm not a kiss and tell kind of girl."

"You'd better tell me or I'm going to pop up unannounced."

The rest of the drive back to Tate's house comprised of Candy prying into Hazel's sex life, and Hazel's giggles and gasps at Candy's quips. Unlike the ride to the prison, the ride home felt like the real Candy had joined in, which cut the tension that had built up during the interview with Brad. They both needed a distraction, a subject change, so Hazel was grateful that Candy felt up to it.

By the time she had arrived back at Tate's house outside of the city, he was already home from work and cooking his famous grilled cheese for their dinner. Greeting her with a bear hug and a kiss, he was eager to hear about her meeting with Brad, which she was glad to get off of her chest. He poured a glass of pinot noir for her and then pulled out a chair for her to sit in. Setting her up to unleash the details of her day on him in comfort while he finished cooking. She pondered how lucky she was as she watched him showing more skill in making their sandwiches than she thought she probably put towards any activity she performed. Her self-esteem may have been dismal, but he was someone who did not have that problem, and it showed. Hopefully, with time, that could rub off on her.

After dinner that night, she and Tate played a game of cards and drank an entire bottle of wine. It did not take long for her to put the interview with Brad behind her, or at least the anxiety of the case. For the time being, Brad's appeal would be put on the back burner and the focus would be on solving Jake's murder. Although it seemed to be a tall order, Hazel had a secret weapon.

Memory transfers from Candy had proven to be successful. Now she just had to try it with Jake. She did not expect the initial attempts with him to be smooth, especially with his lack of energy control. But she hoped with Candy's coaching, he would catch on.

Jake knew who his killer was. Hazel knew that for sure. He just needed to bring that knowledge to the front of his mind, and share that memory with Hazel. She did not know how long that would take, or how many of Jake's memories she would have to endure, but she believed the truth would come to light, eventually.

When she closed her eyes that night, even with the swirl of the red wine in her head, she felt good about their chances of cracking the case.

The smell of mud filled her nose as her consciousness sprung to life. Gasping for air, she screamed, but air did not come. Instead, mud poured into her mouth, her nose, choking her. She desperately clawed at her surroundings, trying to get herself out, but it was no use. She was buried.

Panic set in as she dug her fingers through the mud in an effort to pull herself out of the grave, but the ground seemed endless. The more she dug, the more she screamed, the more earth poured into her mouth, muffling the sounds.

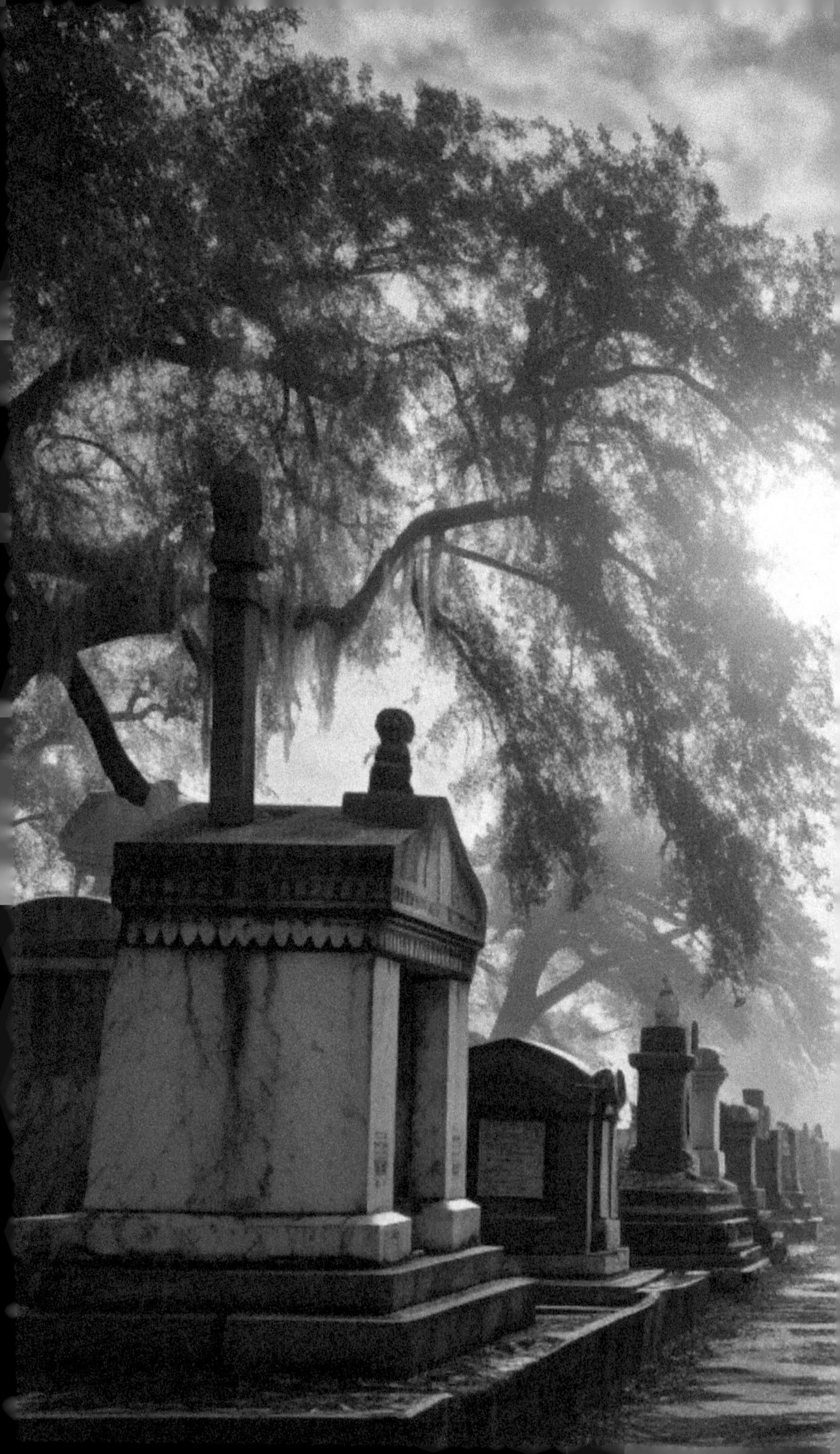

Chapter Fourteen

Glimpses

Waking from a nightmare of being buried alive, Hazel wondered what it would take to prevent her mind from seeing such horrible visions in her sleep. She did not know where the thoughts had come from, or why her subconscious was playing such tricks on her, but it had gotten out of hand. She realized it could have been a spirit memory, but whose? Neither Jake nor Candy was buried alive, and she was not actively helping any other spirits, so she had no idea who the memory could even belong to. She could not help them if they did not interact with her during the times when she was awake and lucid.

The more intense her nightmares were, the harder it was for her to move on from them. She spent her day in a dreadful rut, unable to shake the sinking feeling, or the taste of earth from her mouth. She moved through her office in a trance, completing all tasks simply from routine, and not in active participation. By the time she had completed all her paperwork and met with a few clients, she felt wound up enough to skip her car and run home on foot. If it was not storming outside.

She arrived home to find Candy already there. Seeing her best friend looking like herself again improved her mood, if only a little. Her disposition was dampened, however, when she thought about having to do a memory transfer with Jake that day, but at least the transfer had a goal in mind. Find her best friend's killer.

Hazel and Candy sat quietly on the sofa in her apartment, waiting patiently for Jake to manifest. His appearances were unreliable, not because he did not want to appear, but because his energy was still too unstable, having been murdered only recently. Hazel did not understand the science behind why Candy was so good at controlling her energy, yet Jake was so bad at it, but she had no choice but to roll with it.

"Have you talked to him about how to do it? Transfer the memory, I mean."

"I've told him what I do, but I don't know if the same will work for him... I mean, his energy control is a kind of mess. Oh, how I wish he'd figure out how to control his spectral body already... the things we could do."

Candy looked towards the window dreamily, and Hazel could almost imagine the salacious scene that was probably playing in Candy's head. She allowed her friend a moment to fantasize before clearing her throat.

"So... you guys can't..."

Candy rolled her eyes and sighed before responding, clearly agitated.

"Not yet, but I'm not giving up hope!"

"How would that even work? You know what... I don't want to know. I hope, for your sake, it gets better. I know how much you miss him."

"Am I interrupting?" said a male voice from behind them, causing them both to jump.

Jake stood behind the sofa, looking at them curiously. Hazel wondered how much of the conversation he had heard before speaking up. Candy jumped off of the sofa and threw her arms around him, although his form was not as solid as hers, so her arms nearly fell through him. She did not let it phase her.

"I'm going to go wait for you two love birds in my bedroom. Join me when you're ready to try, but don't wait too long. We don't know how long Jake will be able to hold this form."

They barely acknowledged her, as they were completely involved in their affections, but she figured they heard her, and left for her bedroom, anyway.

Her heart was sitting heavy in her chest as she laid down on her bed, although she tried to appear passive. She may have experienced spirit memories fairly often, but they usually felt like more of an assault than a welcomed event. She knew why she was doing it willingly, and she repeated the reason to herself to try to calm her mounting nerves, but it did not help all that much. Either way, she was seeing something she was not meant to see in another person's mind, and it made her uncomfortable.

Candy and Jake entered her bedroom only a few minutes after she had laid down on the bed, and her heart beat harder with every step they took towards her. Sitting down on the side of the bed, Candy scooted in close to her face, patting the bed next to her for Jake to sit down. He hesitated, looking at Hazel apologetically for invading her space, before taking his place beside her. She could tell he was uncomfortable with the arrangement, which made her feel slightly better. If she was going to be uncomfortable, the least they could do was be uncomfortable as well. He looked at her with his eyes lowered as he smoothed out the sheet next to his leg. He was stalling.

"Thank you for doing this. I can't imagine it's a fun experience... to be stuck in someone else's head. I haven't been able to talk to you much, but I just wanted to tell you thank you. It means a lot to me."

He looked at Candy adoringly, reaching out to hold her hand. Hazel could see her friend's eyes light up with his touch, which warmed her own sinking heart.

"It means a lot to both of us," he finished, smiling coyly at her.

"You're welcome. I'd do anything for Candy... and she would do anything for you."

Hazel pulled her blankets up to her chin to compensate for the drop in temperature that had accompanied the two spirits now sitting on her bed.

"Are you ready?" Candy asked, using her free hand to brush across Hazel's face. The touch sent a moment of calm into her, and she wished Candy had not pulled away so soon.

"Yes... I think."

"Okay."

Candy looked at Jake, her face set with determination. He mirrored her sentiments, focusing in on what she had to say.

"When I transferred memories to her... well, when I did it purposely... all I did was hold my hand against her cheek and concentrate on the memory in question. I don't know how, but she could see the memory in her mind, almost as though she were me and was experiencing it herself. For now, since this is the first time, focus on something you remember clearly. Trying to remember what happened to you... at the end... may not come out clearly if you don't remember it yourself. So maybe don't start there, but it's up to you."

Nodding, and giving Hazel one more apologetic look, Jake reached to her face and laid his hand across her cheek. At first, his hand on her face made her feel wrong, like it did not belong there. She did not know this man, and he was touching her. The only man who usually touched her was Tate, and his hand did not feel like this. Jake's hand was icy, and her teeth chattered against it. Closing her eyes and focusing all her energy on the task at hand, she allowed her mind to focus on sleep, although her body wanted to recoil against him. His hand was unyielding, and her skin grew numb. Eventually, after the endless silence, and then boredom, she fell asleep.

Dispersed visions filled Hazel's mind as she tried to focus in on one of them, but just as paper upon the wind, they were just out of her grasp, fluttering away as soon as she drew too close. Picking up her speed, she ran along the street, chasing the scattering pieces of memory that eluded her.

A spiraling flurry of energy drew her in one direction, making her powerless to go any other way. She knew, even without seeing another person, where she was being led. She followed the beckoning force, up the stairwell, and down the hallway, until a door was illuminated in the corridor.

Arriving at the door, she recognized it immediately. She was standing outside her apartment. Reaching out, she opened the door, finding Candy inside. For a moment, the scene looked as though it could be one of her own memories. Maybe Jake's attempt at a memory transfer hadn't worked? She thought it could be her memory until Candy approached her, throwing her arms around her neck and pulling her in for a long kiss. Jerking away, she looked at Candy in confusion, sputtering confusedly, before seeing the hurt look on Candy's face.

"Jake... what's wrong?"

She wanted to correct her, to tell her it was not Jake. It was Hazel. But she realized that would have been a bad idea. She realized if Jake and Candy were still alive, in the memory at least, Candy would have no idea who she was. She was not there to disturb the events. She was only there to witness them. Instead, she swallowed back her aversion to kissing her best friend and played the part she was meant to play. She wrapped Candy back into a hug.

"I'm sorry. Nothing is wrong."

Candy smiled hesitantly before falling into the embrace.

"I was thinking we could..."

The vision changed, sucking Hazel back out onto the street without warning, but the street had changed. She no longer looked at her apartment building. Instead, she stood in a place she did not recognize. She was not even sure if she was still in New Orleans. Spinning in place, she tried to get her bearings. The movement between the two visions had left her dizzy. With her palms on her knees, she took a moment to gather herself. She walked to the end of the street, trying to read the street sign, but it was too blurry to make out. Cursing out loud, she realized she could see nothing Jake had not seen with his own eyes. Re-centering herself right when she had appeared at the beginning of the vision, she studied the houses on the street, hoping one of them would stand out to her and give her some sign as to where she was supposed to be.

The houses were all old but had been well taken care of. The yards and shrubs were all freshly manicured, but it appeared to be a ghost town. She could not see another person anywhere on the street. She paced, hoping something would stand out in the vision's bleakness, but she never got the chance to discover her purpose in that location before she was pulled violently from her spot and dropped into another time and place.

The hallway was dark. Hazel scurried to the wall and leaned her back against it, breathing heavily and wishing she could leave the memory. She expected to experience one memory, to see one event in Jake's mind, not to be pulled through different scenarios and dropped into others without warning. The experience was getting to her, making her feel nauseated and disorientated. A voice rang out from the darkness, pulling her away from the wall and down the hallway to the right, in the sound's direction.

The voice came from a woman, but there was a door separating Hazel from her, and Hazel felt too afraid to open it. The door was generic. Nothing about it told her where she was, or what was inside. Leaning against the wall next to the door, she tried to hear what the woman was saying, but the woman quieted down as though she had heard Hazel's footsteps. Hazel braced for the door to open, to be caught eavesdropping, but the woman seemed to believe it as a false alarm and began chatting again.

She seemed to be talking to herself. Hazel could not hear any other voices.

"I love you," *the voice said, in almost a coo.*

"No, you don't. You love her," *the woman responded to herself, but in a sterner voice.*

What in the hell?

Stepping a few paces away from the door, Hazel stared back at it in shock, not understanding what she had heard. She knew both voices had come from the same person, but she didn't know why the woman would be having such a conversation with herself. Unwilling to chance meeting the woman in the hall, Hazel began walking briskly towards the direction she hoped to find the exit. Before she made it to the exit, she was pulled out of the memory altogether.

Hazel awoke to find Candy peering down at her, gently petting her head as she had done so many times before. She was surprised to find Jake no longer there. She still reeled from the dizziness of the memory transfer, but she closed her eyes again and tried to ground herself to her bed, where she was safe.

"Where's Jake?"

Candy looked around the room, as though she hadn't realized he was gone, returning her tearful gaze back to Hazel. Hazel watched a single tear cascade down Candy's cheek. It sparkled as it fell, creating a mesmerizing effect. Candy wiped her cheek before placing her hands back on Hazel's face, resuming the hair petting Hazel had grown so fond of.

"He's gone again. He dematerialized just before you woke up. I know he tried to stay, but he wasn't able to hold onto his energy any longer."

Candy let out a sob, suddenly making Hazel's worries and discomfort feel insignificant. Pulling her hand out of the blankets, she reached around Candy and pulled her in. Candy did not object.

She could not have been happier when Tate knocked on her door after his shift. Candy's grief over Jake had only made her appreciate her own love that much more. He was the greatest living part of her life. He and Candy were her whole life. She did not have family nearby, or even other friends. She had Tate and Candy, and she needed to do whatever she could for both of them. Tate only had simple needs, for her to love him and keep herself safe. Candy, on the other hand, needed her murder solved, and Hazel knew she was the only person who had the abilities to do it. That's why she had to press on with their plans of traversing Jake's memories, no matter how unpleasant the experience was.

The erratic movement of Jake's memories created an uneasy feeling in Hazel's stomach for the rest of the night. It was like she had spent the day at an amusement park riding those simulator rides that swish you around. She was all too ready to climb into bed that night and allow her body to rest from the day.

"Mommy! Mommy! Let's play!"

A little girl with long braided pigtails jumped up and down excitedly. Her blue eyes sparkled in the sunlight. She ran inside of a handmade playhouse that looked like a miniature castle and peeked through the window.

"Come on Mommy! I'll make tea!"

"I'm coming Bella. Tea sounds delicious."

The mother stood up from her place on the bench and strolled casually to the playhouse, admiring her handiwork in the flowerbeds that lined where the swamp met her yard. It was backbreaking work to replant all of her flowers after the winter killed them off, but it was worth it.

"Emily... Bella... I'm home," a man called out from somewhere inside of the house.

"We're out here, Joshua. Bella is making tea! Join us!"

She turned to see a ruggedly handsome face smiling at her through the screen of the back door.

"Did someone say tea?" he asked. "Count me in!"

For the first time in many days, Hazel did not wake up startled or traumatized from her dream the night before. She did not doubt there was some significance to it, but she was grateful for the pleasant scene that played out before her. She had not recognized any of the people in it, but she hoped the swamp in the background was not an omen for what was to come to the beautiful family who lived on its bank. If they appeared in her dreams, it was not a bet she was willing to make.

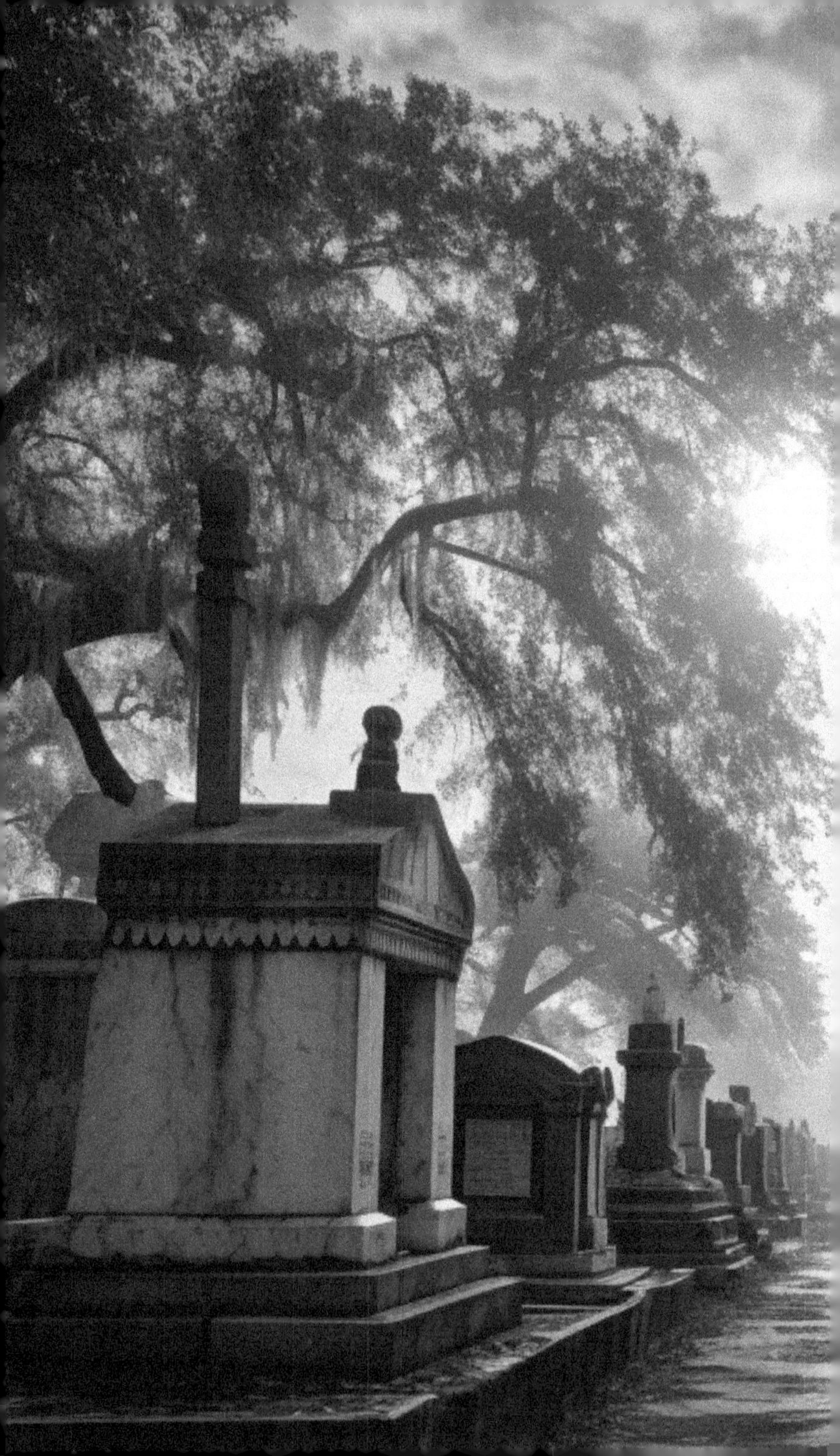

Chapter Fifteen

The Girl in the Memory

The next few days went in much the same way. After leaving her office, Hazel returned to her apartment, where she expected to find Candy and Jake waiting for another attempted memory transfer. Jake's irregular appearances proved to be a challenge, because there were some days where he did not appear at all.

They used their time wisely, however, and practiced transfers between the two of them when he was not there. Hazel much preferred the memory transfer experiences with Candy because Candy had more control over her energy and selected what memories to share based on what she thought Hazel could handle. She never had to worry about being yanked out of one vision and thrust into another one when she was memory surfing with Candy, and that was something she was thankful for.

On the third day, she had finished her case with the hit-and-run driver, Ms. Babin, and had received her new set of cases that were all less demanding than Brad's appeal, which loomed over her like a dark cloud. She had successfully gotten a continuance on his case, hopefully pending new evidence in the murder of Jake, so she was able to stay dry, although that cloud loomed just behind her, trailing her every thought.

Arriving at her apartment that afternoon, she was surprised to find Candy and Jake, already there and cuddling on the sofa. Her chest tightened when she realized she had to enter Jake's memories again that day, which was sure to give her whiplash and nausea, but she was happy for Candy to be once again in his arms. She knew how much Candy loved and missed him. She had never seen her friend as emotional as she had become since his spirit first appeared. She did, admittedly, worry about what would happen if Jake ever decided to cross over, but that was a problem for another day. Most people would have hoped the same for Candy, to be able to cross over the veil and be where spirits were said to belong, but Hazel was too attached to her for thoughts like that.

"Hey!" Candy shrieked, hopping off of the sofa and running over the Hazel with more spunk than Hazel had the energy for. Jake smiled warmly at her, chuckling as Candy almost toppled her onto the floor.

"Hey to you... how are you two?"

Giving her one last squeeze, Candy returned to the sofa, plopping energetically onto it.

"We are as good as could be expected and hoping that today's memory transfer will show you something helpful."

"Me too."

Hazel placed her bag on the table and kicked her shoes off by the door.

"I'm going to head in there and get ready. Are you feeling okay today?"

She looked at Jake, who met her gaze and smiled apologetically, as though he knew his memory transfers were near torture for her, although she never told him so.

"I feel like I'm getting stronger, but I guess you'll be the judge of how much."

He looked sheepish, but Hazel smiled at him warmly, trying to encourage his continued struggle for strength.

"I understand it's hard for you, although I can never claim to understand how that feels. I'm patient, so don't worry about me. Just keep doing what you're doing. Things will not come easily, but I'm sure you'll get there. Just keep hanging out with Candy... she can do all sorts of stuff."

Candy blushed, then wiggled her eyebrows comically as though Hazel had made a dirty joke, which she had not intended. Abandoning the two lovers, Hazel walked into her bedroom, grabbing a pair of comfortable pajamas and making her way to the bathroom to change. Taking naps after work would have normally been a welcomed event, but memory transfers were anything but restful. The least she could do was dress the part of comfort. Jake and Candy entered her room only a few minutes after her, taking their position by her side and readying themselves for the task at hand. She could only hope that this would be the memory transfer that would solve their murder, or at least give her some sort of clue to go on, so she would not have to dip into Jake's consciousness again. She pulled her blanket to her chin, but still shivered because of her proximity to the two spirits.

"It's freezing."

Candy tossed another blanket on top of her, tucking the edges around her body.

"You know that there are people who live in huts... who only have blankets made of animal skins and their only heater is a fire. Acclimate, doll. We've got more blankets where that came from."

Hazel stuck out her tongue, which Candy attempted to poke with her finger. They both giggled before she resigned to the reality of the situation. There was no escaping the cold, so she had to just grin and bear it.

"Okay... I guess I'm ready."

Jake nodded, flashing her a familiar rueful smile before placing his frigid hand against her cheek. Her shivers increased intensity, but she fought back the urge to shrink against his hand, closing her eyes instead. Candy played with her hair as she focused on slowing her breathing, exhaling out the stress of the day, and welcoming unconsciousness to fall over her.

Although her discomfort was palpable, her exhaustion won the battle of wills, pulling her into blackness once again.

Dropping into a dark hallway, Hazel immediately recognized it as a location she had been thrust into once before, in her very first memory transfer with Jake. Her fear caught in her throat as a bitter lump when she realized it was the same hallway housing the door beyond which was the woman who had been having a two person, two voice conversation with herself. She began feeling slightly ill at the thought of running into the woman, although she knew the location was relevant enough for her to have been placed in it twice, so she had to forge on. She kept repeating in her mind that nothing in the memory could hurt her, although with the physical symptoms that had often plagued her during and after such experiences, she believed being injured was relative.

Forcing back her hesitation, although it felt counterintuitive, she pulled herself away from the wall and in the door's direction she knew would be ominously stationed towards the other end of the corridor. The walk towards the door was foreboding, and she felt like her feet had to be forced to take each step, like she was walking towards the end of a plank, and she would ultimately arrive at the end and plunge into the depths of the ocean, never to be seen again. This time, when arriving at the door, she could hear no voices coming from inside, but that did not reassure her. Instead, she worried that the silence may be a trap. Unwilling to give up the opportunity, and be forced into Jake's memories again, instead of turning around and running, she grabbed the handle and forced the door open.

As soon as the door opened only a few inches, she immediately regretted her decision, falling against the wall opposite of it and dropping her hands to her knees as her breath quickened into panic. She recognized the room immediately, because she had seen it in a memory transfer once before, and it had haunted her own memory ever since. Before her laid a small room, lacking much furniture other than a queen bed and a few other items. Last time she had seen the room, there had been a morbid collage scattered on the backside of the door, filled with pictures of Candy, with her face marked out, and even a lock of Candy's hair. This time, however, the room was not empty. A young woman stood near the foot of the bed, looking at her in horror, as though she had been caught in the act of something.

The fact that she was in Jake's memory told her that Jake knew the girl, but Hazel did not recognize her. The young woman looked unassuming. She did not look like the psychopath who would have made the infamous collection that hung on the back of the door. Standing only about as tall as Hazel, she looked young, maybe mid-twenties. Her large doe eyes were stretched to capacity and her dirty blonde hair hung unkept to her shoulders.

"What are you doing here?" she demanded, her voice tiny enough to have come from a child.

Not knowing how to answer, Hazel turned and ran as fast as she could towards the bright red exit sign, only chancing a single glance over her shoulder to see if she was being followed. Skidding to a halt in front of the exit, she screamed and banged on the door urgently before being violently pulled from her vision and back into her waiting bed.

Screaming herself awake, Hazel's eyes shot open to see Candy and Jake both staring down at her, concern etched across both of their faces. She jolted back, creating more distance between her face and theirs, which was only a few inches from her. Jake's hand no longer rested against her face, which she was happy about, leaving an opening for Candy to reach out and caress her to calm her down. Candy did not push her but allowed her to come out of the memory slowly.

"You're okay, doll. You're safe."

Candy cooed at her, but Jake looked horrified and guilty. She wanted to assure him, but she did not know what to say, so she said nothing to him, and spoke to the room at large instead. Both he and Candy would want to know what she saw.

"I think I saw her."

"Her? Who?" Candy asked, taken aback by the statement. Jake's eyes grew in size as he looked at her curiously.

"The woman who created the stalker collage of you. I think I saw her."

"It was a woman?" Candy asked, looking at Jake for his response, only to find his eyes blank, portraying neither confirmation nor rejection of the idea. Returning her gaze to Hazel, Candy's voice rose as her anxiety undoubtedly had.

"Who was she?"

"I'm not sure. Jake, do you have any idea who she could have been? She was young... oh and petite... no taller than me. She had enormous eyes; dark green, I believe."

Jake met her stare, but his face fell as his own memory failed him and his eyes looked to the floor. He brushed his fingers through his hair before settling his hand on his beard, scratching at it in concentration.

"I'm trying to remember. It's just hard to collect my thoughts. Maybe she was a girlfriend?"

He looked at Candy guiltily, but she reached out and grabbed his hand.

"It's okay," she assured him. "I understand if you had a girlfriend. You can say it. I was gone."

He nodded, returning his eyes to Hazel.

"I think she may have been a girlfriend, someone I dated after Candy left me. That feels like the truth, although I can't remember anything about her. Do you think it's possible for Tate to find out more about any girlfriend I may have had?"

Hazel thought about it briefly before returning a nod.

"I do think it's possible. A woman claimed to be your girlfriend in a police interview. I can certainly ask him for more information on her."

For the first time since she had seen him, Jake looked hopeful. Grabbing her cellular phone off the bedside table, she sent a text message to Tate asking that he dig into the girlfriend angle, before setting her cell back down by her side. After the stress of her visions, she felt more exhausted than when they began the memory transfer. She yawned sleepily, unsuccessfully stifling it with her hand.

Climbing off the bed, Candy grabbed Jake by the hand, leading him to the door.

"We'll leave you to rest. Is Tate coming over tonight?"

Hazel nodded her head, curling into her blankets and closing her eyes yet again.

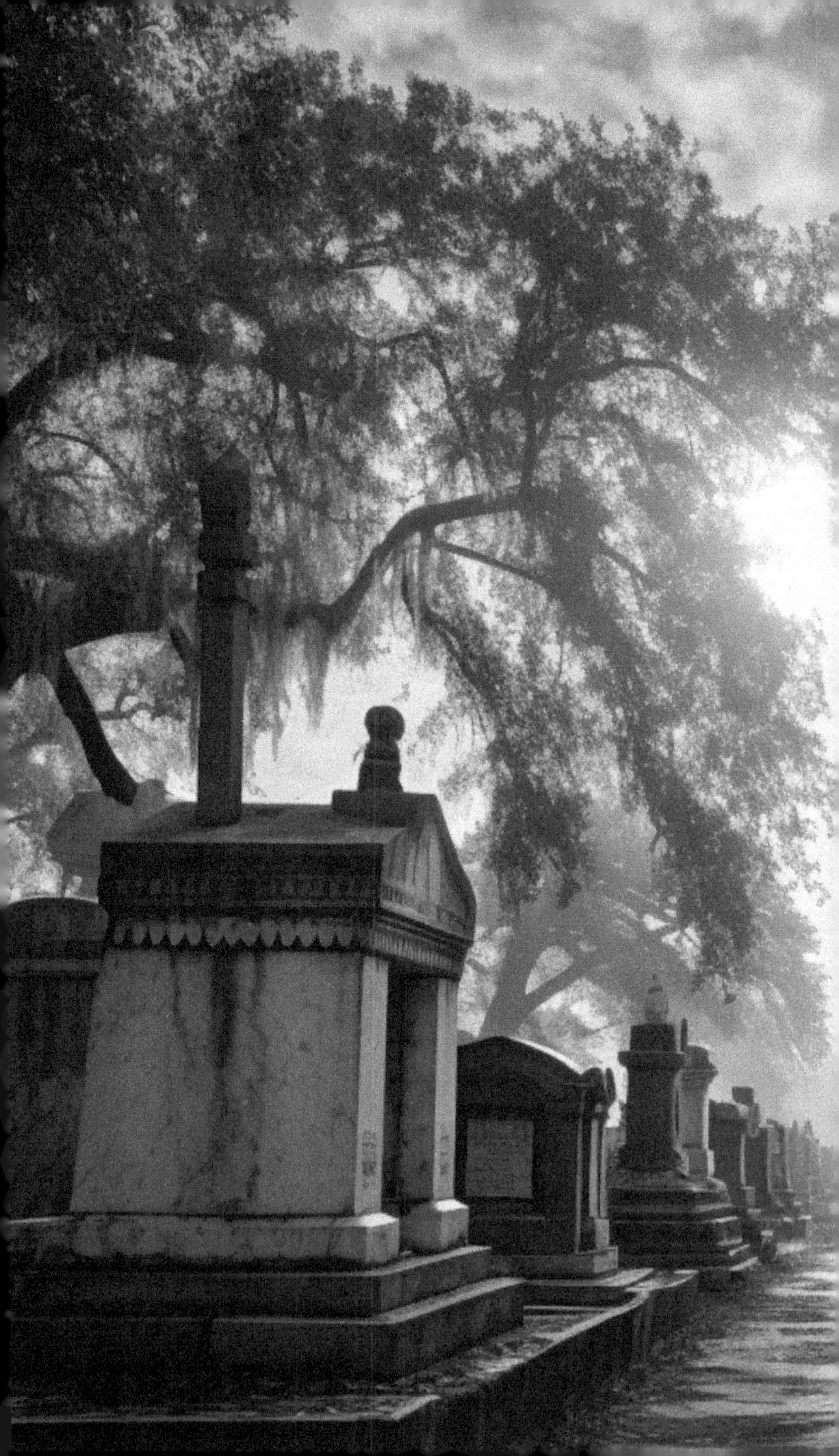

Chapter Sixteen

Shadow from the Past

Although Hazel tried to sleep after her trek into Jake's memories, she could not cross the barrier into unconsciousness. Instead, she got out of the bed, deciding that taking a shower would at least further wake her, since sleeping was not an option.

Standing below the falling hot water, she closed her eyes and imagined the stress of the day falling away, and swirling down the pull of the drain. Feeling somewhat refreshed, she climbed out of the shower, got dressed, and made her way into the living room to wait for Tate's knock on the door.

By the time she went into the main living area, Candy and Jake were gone. Jake had probably vanished against his will, but Candy was probably conserving her energy for the time being, either that or venturing somewhere outside of the apartment.

No sooner she had sat on the sofa with a bowl of ramen noodles, Tate was knocking on her door. Setting her bowl gently down onto the coffee table, she jumped off the sofa and ran to the door. Not bothering to look through the peephole, she threw the door open to find the other side of the door empty. Tate was not there.

She glanced around the corridor, but it was vacant. A familiar sinking feeling filled her belly. A breeze drifted by her, although there were no windows for it to have come from. A fluttering piece of paper caught her attention as it flapped just in front of her feet. Bending over, she grabbed the single sheet of paper, eyeing it warily. Getting only an initial glance at the document, Hazel dropped it back to the ground as though it had bitten her, gasping loudly. Dread filled every available space within her.

The document was one she had seen before. A copy of it lived in a box of her belongings. She could not imagine how it had gotten on her front stoop, and just thinking about it caused her blood to chill. Scanning the empty corridor again, she scooped the document off the ground, retreated into her apartment, and slapped the page down onto her kitchen table. Standing several feet away from it, she eyed it like it was the villain in a story, because it was. The words and numbers blurred together as the stress of the moment caused her heart rate to ascend to an obscene level. The name, Aberdeen Trucking Company, was highlighted on the bank statement, as it was on her own copy of the document, the bank statement from Waters Financial Firm.

Waters Financial Firm was a shell of the company it had been, only months prior. The previous owner, Raymond Waters, had turned out to be a sociopath, who murdered four women, and Hazel was almost the fifth. The incident ended with Raymond dead, by Hazel's hand, and her unfortunate case of post-traumatic stress disorder that was only starting to rear its ugly head. The idea of being a murderer weighed on her daily. Sure, she had killed him in self-defense. He had given her no choice. It was kill or be killed, and he had nearly succeeded in his endeavor. She only survived, thanks to the help of his victims. Three of the four women he had murdered put their spectral powers together and fought him valiantly, slowing him down as they battered and bruised him. By the time he had made it to her, in the bathroom where she and Candy hid, his violent energy was depleted enough for her to have a chance at fighting him off, and she fought as hard as she could, although it was a close call.

The bank statement in front of her was one of the many pieces of evidence that were hidden away by his last victim, Angela Spencer. She had been his secretary and had realized he was embezzling from his company. She had been murdered because of it, but not before collecting tons of evidence against him and hiding it away at her mother's house. Angela had attached herself to Hazel when Hazel represented another employee from the firm and had led her on the quest that not only discovered the hidden evidence but also found the bodies of four victims. Hazel had turned the evidence over to the authorities, after storing a copy for herself, just in case anything happened to the originals.

She stared at the single page of the bank statement for what seemed like hours, almost as though she were waiting for it to reveal its secrets to her like the Marauder's Map, but it only laid there, taunting her.

The sound of knocking thumped in Hazel's head. Although she hadn't moved, she found herself lying on the sofa.

Had I fallen asleep?

She was confused, not knowing how she got to the sofa, and completely ignoring the now frantic knocking on the door. How long had she been asleep? She scanned her mind for some memory of a dream, thinking only of the bank statement on her kitchen table. She jumped off of the sofa with more energy than she could normally muster, scurrying to the kitchen table to find the document gone.

It was a dream.

By the time she acknowledged the knocking, Tate had called out to her, clearly worried. Stumbling to the door, still staring back at the space on the table where the paper had been only moments before, she quickly opened the door and fell into Tate's arms as he rushed forward to grab her. Checking to see that she was okay, his eyes had softened from their previous state of alarm.

"Are you okay? Why didn't you come to the door?"

"I'm sorry... I had fallen asleep."

"Oh. I was so worried."

Wrapping his arm around her waist, he escorted her back into the living room to sit on the sofa and pull her onto his lap. He had not yet changed out of his police uniform, so he pulled off his cumbersome belt and placed it on the coffee table.

"Was it a nightmare?"

The concern in his voice was clear, but she quietly debated whether she wanted to burden him with the contents of her dream. Instead, she shrugged noncommittally. Tate, however, knew what the response meant.

"You can tell me about it, love. It may help to get it out."

She hesitated, shifting on his lap.

"I didn't even realize I was asleep... in the dream, I mean. I thought I was awake the entire time until I woke up on the sofa."

"That explains why you didn't answer the door. What happened? Did it involve a spirit?"

She shrugged again, unsure of the answer herself.

"It was really strange. Basically, I heard a knock at the door, and I thought it was you, so I opened the door, but no one was outside."

Tate watched her, maintaining his silence so she could continue.

"I noticed a piece of paper on the floor outside of my door. It was..."

She shuttered. Tate, realizing she had arrived at the hard part of her story, squeezed her lovingly.

"What was the paper? It's okay... the dream is over... nothing in it can hurt you. It would have to go through me, and I'm not bad in a fight."

She giggled, poking at his bicep as he flexed it playfully, before leaning back against his chest and arranging the next thoughts in her head.

"It was a page from the Waters Financial Firm bank statements..."

Tate's body tensed up in response to her words.

"What do you mean? It just appeared at your door in your dream?"

"Yes. It was an exact page that I have hiding in a box in my closet. I didn't see who dropped it off. It just appeared."

Pulling his arm from around her stomach, he pinched the bridge of his nose, taking a moment to think before responding.

"Maybe it was just PTSD causing the nightmare. Maybe it had nothing to do with him."

He sounded as though he was trying to convince himself as much as he was trying to convince her. She did not want to think about it anymore.

Refusing to sacrifice one more second to Raymond Waters, or his memory, she opted to wrap her arms around Tate, kissing him instead. He was all too ready to forget Raymond Waters as well, because he melted into her kiss, holding back nothing.

Unable to resist his touch, they moved to her bedroom and forgot about everything else, at least for a while. When he made love to her, it was like he was making up for all the years they wanted each other but didn't say it. By the time she fell asleep, she was no longer thinking about Raymond Waters, or his company's bank records.

The hallway loomed before her, as it had twice before. Except this time, she was not Jake, but was watching him as he walked towards the door at the other end of the hall. Although he was walking towards the door where the creepy photo collage hung, he seemed completely unaware of what he was walking into. She wanted to call out to him, but she already knew he would not hear her, so she tiptoed behind him, hoping to understand more about what caused his death.

He walked without worry, knocking on the door as though he expected a warm reception from the girl on the other side, the girl who had killed the woman he loved. He did not know that fact, but Hazel did. She stood just behind him as the door opened, revealing the doe-eyed blond girl she had seen when navigating his memories before.

The girl looked harmless. She was pretty, although she looked like she could almost pass for thirteen. Unlike Candy, who was an actual bombshell, with flowing red hair and a body that could bring some women to tears, this girl packed none of the same pizzazz. Still, Jake appeared to like her. He smiled when he saw her and pulled her in for a kiss.

When they entered the room, Hazel realized it was not the same room that had appeared behind the door before. This time, they entered a living area. The room had a sofa, a television, and a few other furnishings to make the room comfortable. Unknown to them, Hazel had walked in behind them. She stood a few feet away and hoped the visit would not include sex. It was one thing she had no interest in seeing. Thankfully, the couple moved to the sofa, flipping on the television instead. At least for the moment.

For hours, she sat in a chair across the room, watching the two of them, as they watched a movie, until she was close to falling asleep. As the movie drew to a close, Jake pulled out his cell phone to check a text message, and Hazel glimpsed Candy's picture as he scrolled through an app on his phone. She hoped his girlfriend had not noticed the picture, but the look on her face proved that was not the case. The girl's face twisted.

"Why is she on your phone?"

Jake, not expecting the accusatory tone in her voice, stuck his phone back into his pocket.

"Who? Why are you mad?"

"Because your ex-girlfriend's picture is still on your phone!"

"My ex-girlfriend? You're mad I still have Candy's picture on my phone? She's dead. You shouldn't be mad about that."

"I don't care if she's dead. That doesn't matter."

Something within Jake shifted when her insensitive words landed in his ears. His jaw clenched and his eyes narrowed.

"It doesn't matter? She was murdered! I loved her! Of course, it matters! I will always keep a picture of her, no matter who I'm with! What in the fuck is wrong with you?"

Furious, Jake rose from the sofa and marched to the door. Hazel, shocked by the turn of events, took a moment before she rose from her chair as well, intending to follow him out of the door.

The girl, seeming to realize her behavior was repelling her boyfriend, jumped off the sofa and ran after him, grasping at his shirt to get his attention. She did not get the attention she wanted, however. Jake turned to look at her, a look of fury burned on his face, before turning away and reaching for the door.

"Wait! Don't go!"

He ignored her, opening the door and storming out into the hall, not stopping until after he reached the exit and stomped out onto the street. The girl did not chase after him.

Hazel followed him but stopped once he got into his car. Instead of getting in his vehicle with him, she spun in a circle in the middle of the street, committing the neighborhood to memory. Her heart dropped as she scanned the houses. She had seen them before. She had seen the neighborhood only once, when she first entered Jake's fragmented memory. She still did not recognize the location, however. She did not even know if it was in New Orleans. All she was sure of was that she had seen the scene before.

Knowing it was a dream, she sat on the porch of a nearby house and waited to wake up.

Waking up before the sun had a chance to shine light into her bedroom window, Hazel watched the peaceful rise and fall of Tate's chest as he slept. His face was gentle, even with the layer of stubble that had begun to line his chin. She could not help but smile as she lay there next to him, and she wished things could always be so simple. At some point, she did not know how long it took, but she fell back asleep.

"Good morning."

Tate smiled at her just as her eyes opened, instantly improving her usual morning grumpiness. She scooted closer to him, curling up into his waiting arm.

"Morning. You're in a good mood this morning."

"Because I woke up next to you."

He leaned over and kissed her, sending warmth throughout her body, but before she could lose herself in his affection, Candy materialized at the foot of her bed.

"Candy! You scared the shit out of me!"

Tate's eyes widened, and he instinctually checked that he was fully covered by the blankets. Candy noticed his struggle and raised an eyebrow, smirking mischievously.

"Is he naked under there?"

"Oh, hush. What's going on? You don't usually just pop up at the foot of my bed."

"Oh… sorry about that. I was curious if Tate ever got back to you about the girlfriend thing."

"And that couldn't wait until we came out there?"

Hazel motioned towards the living area, which stood just on the other side of the bedroom wall.

"Hey… I do not keep myself as busy as you do." She wriggled her eyebrows. "Fewer things to occupy me means that I have more time to dwell on the few things that are left."

Hazel looked over at Tate. His thick brown hair was longer than usual, and disheveled, while his blue-gray eyes darted around the room, trying to get a glimpse of the invisible woman Hazel was speaking to. She gave him an apologetic glance.

"Candy is asking about the girl I texted you about yesterday, Jake's ex-girlfriend. Did you find out any more about her?"

Tate's face relaxed.

"Not much. Her name is Harmony Richard. She was interviewed after he died. She claimed to be his girlfriend, but they were unable to confirm it."

Candy floated further into the room, sitting on the edge of the bed.

"How are we going to prove she did it? There has to be a way... there has to be something the police missed."

"I don't know. We will figure something out. I promise."

Hazel's eyes widened.

"I can take a hint. I'll wait out front for you... no rush."

Candy snapped her fingers, disappearing on the spot. It only took a moment before Hazel heard the television turn on. Tate heard it also and, realizing their unexpected guest was no longer in the bedroom, reached onto the floor for his boxer shorts. Hazel stifled a chuckle.

"You were naked under there."

"Huh?"

"Candy asked if you were naked under there... and you were. I didn't realize you hadn't gotten dressed during the night."

His cheeks flushed.

"Do you think she saw anything?"

"Nah. She asked. It wasn't a statement. I think your modesty has been preserved for another day."

He laughed, throwing the blankets off.

"Modesty, you say?"

"Okay. Okay. I stand corrected."

They both fell into a fit of giggles before climbing out of bed, getting dressed and heading into the living room.

Hazel brewed coffee while Tate made an omelet. Candy was still positioned on the sofa, watching her usual true crime television shows. Setting Tate's coffee in front of him, and giving him a peck on the cheek, Hazel walked over to the sofa and sat next to Candy.

"So... do you have any ideas about how to find out more about Harmony?"

Candy turned the tv off and then turned to face Hazel.

"I think you should try to get to know her... maybe try to be her friend."

"Candy... no way. She's a psychopath and I'm no good at making friends, anyway."

Candy's face fell with defeat. She started fiddling with the hem of her skirt.

"Just look her up, doll. That's all I'm asking. If she is accessible, and close by, then maybe you can fabricate an accidental meeting."

Hazel knew she was the only person who could realistically help her best friend, so she was backed into a corner. She turned to Tate, who had since sat on the chair across from them, and relayed Candy's idea. His eyebrows furrowed as he listened. He had already made it clear he did not want her to go on anymore spirit-led wild goose chases that could end up getting her killed. But this task was not led by just any spirit. Candy was her best friend, her murdered best friend, and Candy's murderer was still out there masquerading as a normal person and getting away with it. He realized that, too. So, although he was probably against Candy's plan, he gave his approval with ground rules.

"I don't want you getting caught up in something that's going to get you hurt, but I understand why you have to go about it this way. But... I don't want you going anywhere near this girl without Candy by your side.

That way, she can find me if things get hairy. I will pay close attention to any disturbances on my scanner. Also, I want to know where you are when, or if, you meet up with Harmony. Just please send me a text with your location. Oh, and stick to public places. As of now, she is not a suspect, so any information could help the case. But don't go getting yourself into another Raymond Waters situation. Deal?"

Hazel glanced at Candy, whose face had become more hopeful. She nodded approvingly.

"Candy agrees with your plan."

"Perfect. Well... I've got to head in to work."

Tate stood up from the sofa, gave Hazel a lingering kiss, and then left the apartment. Just as the door clicked shut, she realized how hungry she was. Tate had left a plate of eggs on the table for her. She smiled to herself as she reheated her breakfast and sat back down with Candy.

"Can you try to look her up? I'm dying to see what she looks like... pun intended."

Hazel shot a side-eye glance at Candy and then pulled open her laptop and searched Harmony by her full name. To her surprise, the youthful face with the doe-eyes showed up in scattered images across her screen from a public social media page. She clicked on the first one, expanding the profile onto the screen.

"This is her. I'd recognize her anywhere."

"How old is she? Twelve?"

Candy's mouth was hanging dramatically open as she gawked at the profile picture of Jake's ex. She appeared to be looking at Harmony more as her competition, than as their murderer.

"I think she's in her mid-twenties, but yea, she looks super young. Her voice is mousy too. She is nothing like you. Plus... she's crazy... so there's that."

Candy made a satisfied grin. Hazel scrolled through the profile, surprised by how much of their lives people plaster online.

"Look, it says here she's a hairdresser. There are these pictures from the shop."

"There's our answer!"

Candy reached out to touch Hazel's hair and grimaced.

"You dreadfully need a haircut, anyway, doll. It's a win-win."

Hazel pretended to be offended, gasping loudly, before shrugging in resignation.

"It's true. I know. It's been like six months. But that doesn't mean I want a psycho near my throat with a pair of sharp scissors."

Candy waved her hand dismissively.

"Oh, please."

"She's not going to slay you in front of everyone in the shop. It's the perfect setting to get to know her. Even Tate would approve."

Candy wanted her to approach Harmony soon, but the entire situation made her uncomfortable. Even in a public setting, Harmony was a killer and meeting her would put Hazel on her radar. She would prefer to not be on the radar of another killer. It had almost gotten her killed last time. She wondered how many times normal people came face to face with serial killers. She felt like she was probably above average in that regard, and chuckled at the thought, but it was not funny. Dealing with spirits for her entire life usually put her in touch with more murder victims than she liked. And where there were murder victims, there were murderers.

Giving into Candy's pressure, she called and made a hair appointment with Harmony for the next day. She was admittedly nervous about it, but she did not see any other way to accomplish what she needed to accomplish. Knowing Harmony was probably Candy and Jake's murderer, and realizing how far away the police were from making that connection, she felt it her obligation to guide them to the young woman. She could not do that if she did not get any evidence to prove it.

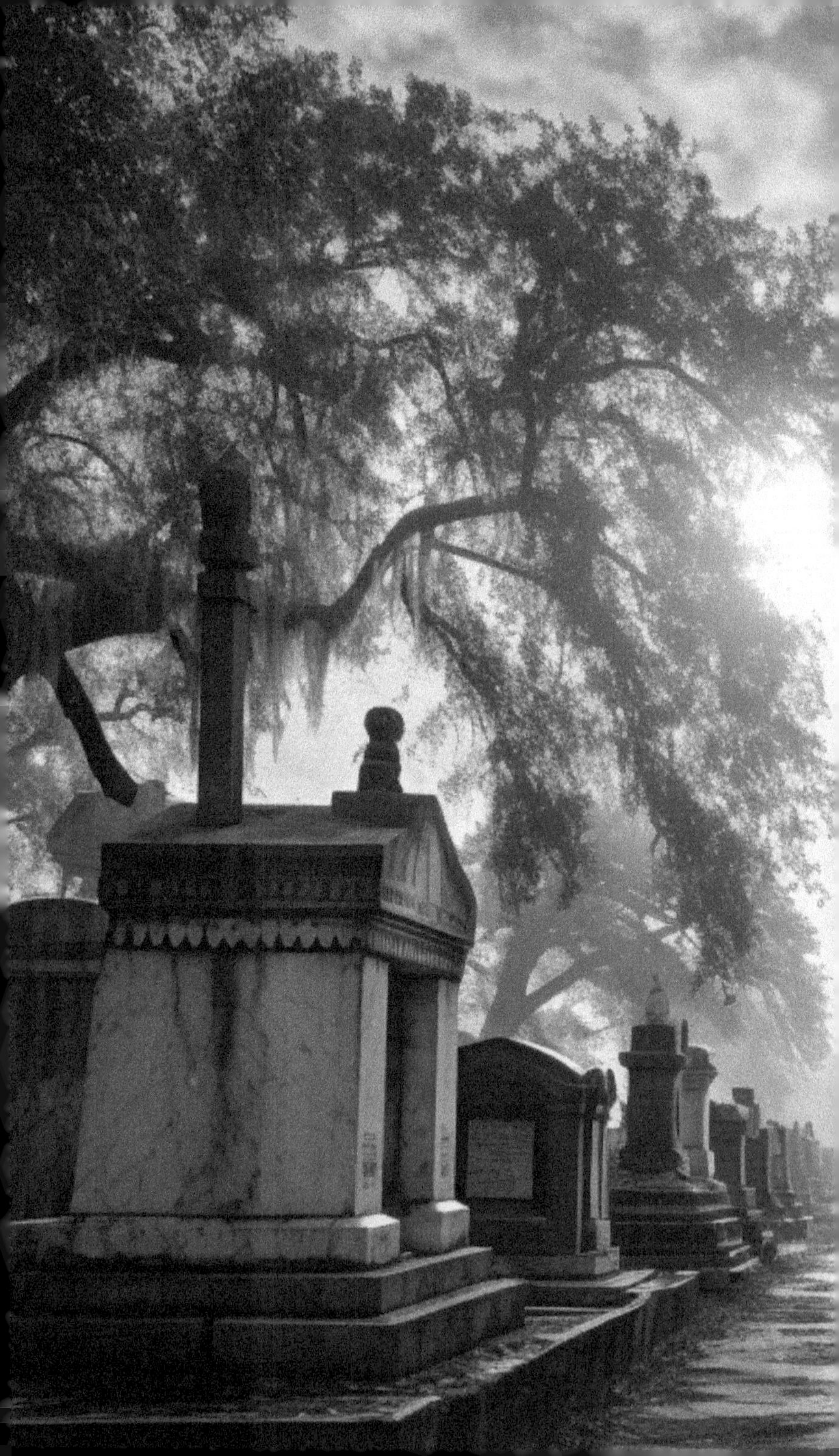

Chapter Seventeen

Harmony

Walking into the hair salon where Harmony worked, Hazel immediately regretted her decision to try to get to know her, even if it was to prove her role in Candy and Jake's murder. Checking into the front desk, she was escorted to the back of the salon where a petite, doe-eyed woman stood waiting for her.

Harmony looked no older than her teens, but Tate had verified through his records that she was actually twenty-five. Standing no taller than Hazel, Harmony had dirty blond hair that hung straight to just past her shoulders, and her eyes were dark green. Her look was disarming. If Hazel had not seen Harmony's erratic outburst in Jake's memories, she would never believe the girl capable of such behavior.

"Hazel?" Harmony asked, her voice just as tiny as she was. Hazel, who was lost in her assessment of the girl's appearance, startled to reality at her name being called.

"Yes!" Hazel responded with more vigor than the situation warranted, feeling slightly awkward as she shuffled into the chair for her scheduled haircut.

"How much do you want to cut off?"

"Sorry? Oh, only two inches. I think it's time to freshen it up. Thank you."

She had to admit, even though she was getting a haircut by a psychopath, she was excited to not have to wash her hair that night. Candy, who had accompanied her to the salon, stood scowling only a foot away from Harmony. It took everything in Hazel not to show her reaction to Candy on her face. They had an entire game plan, for Hazel to pretend to be new to the city, and try to befriend Harmony, but she was slowly losing her nerve. Candy, however, would not let that happen, and was gesturing at her with fervor to expand the conversation, but Hazel was an introvert, so conversations were not her strong point. Gritting her teeth, she debated what to say next.

"So... are there any good places to get coffee around here? I'm not familiar with this area."

Her first lie had escaped her mouth and flowed into the universe. She braced herself to be caught in it, and called out for her deception, but Harmony took the bait.

"Absolutely! I go on my lunch break after your cut, if you want me to walk you over. I didn't bring lunch today, anyway, and I could really go for one of their soups."

Candy, clearly pleased with the turn of events, was flashing a gleaming smile and two thumbs up. Hazel dared to roll her eyes before correcting her face and pointing her eyes back into the mirror, hoping Harmony hadn't caught the gesture. The last thing she wanted to do was make Harmony think she was crazy before she even got her hair washed.

"Okay. Sounds good. I'm getting hungry as well."

Taking her to the wash station, Harmony did the one thing Hazel hated doing, washed her hair. She closed her eyes and tried to pretend that Harmony was not crazy, before reopening them and hoping Harmony would not take a snip of her hair and add it to her macabre collection of stalker paraphernalia. She watched her like a hawk until every piece of hair was cut and thrown in the trash before relaxing her mind into a passive state.

They left the salon and headed towards the coffee shop Harmony had in mind. Hazel actually knew the place well. Leaving with Harmony was unnerving, but she sent a message to Tate and flashed a cautionary smile to Candy. She was glad that Candy was with her. Not that she was expecting Harmony to snap and murder her, unprovoked, in an alley, but she still enjoyed knowing Candy was there, with all of her spectral power, just in case she was needed.

Just as they approached the café, Hazel had a moment of hesitation. She hoped no one in the café recognized her and blew her cover. But, realizing she rarely spoke to anyone in public, she suspected her cover would be safe. She moved towards the most isolated table in the back, just in case.

"I'm going to order some lunch, but hang out here and hold our table. This place gets pretty busy. Do you want anything?" Harmony asked as she dropped her bag at the table and turned towards the counter.

"Just coffee. Thanks."

Hazel watched as Harmony approached the line, puzzled how this tiny young woman could become the monster she had seen in Jake's memory. The woman was a chameleon for sure. It was no wonder she had eluded police and had only appeared to be the grieving girlfriend when Jake was murdered.

Hazel sent a quick text to Tate, updating him on her location and status, as Candy leaned over her shoulder to read the correspondence. By the time Harmony returned to the table with her soup and Hazel's coffee, Hazel had closed out her text app and was browsing mindlessly, trying to appear like every other person in the café. Setting Hazel's coffee in front of her, Harmony sat across from her, smiling warmly, appearing as disarming as a person possibly could.

"I just chose their regular brew. I hope that's okay."

"It is. Thank you."

"Your hair looks great, and I'm not just saying that because I cut it."

"Oh, I appreciate it. It's been a while since I've had it cut."

"So, what do you do for a living?"

Hazel thought for a moment, unsure if she wanted to give her true identity away. Believing it to be too dangerous to tell Harmony the whole truth, she opted for a half truth.

"I just finished law school."

Harmony looked impressed. She nodded as she chewed her food.

"That's awesome! That's quite an accomplishment."

"Thank you. It was a lot of work, so I'm glad to be done."

"I can imagine. Do you know where you're going to work yet? I don't know exactly how the lawyer world works, but are you opening your own office or something?"

"I don't know yet. I'm thinking of working for the government."

Hazel was glad she did not have any social media accounts, because her cover would have certainly been blown if she posted her business online. Harmony would have to do more research to discover she already worked for the public defender's office, and had for a year, so she hoped it would remain a secret for the time being.

Although Harmony did most of the talking, she must have appreciated Hazel's listening abilities, because she unexpectedly gave Hazel her cell phone number before leaving the café, just in case Hazel ever wanted another coffee date. Hazel waited until Harmony was long gone before venturing out of the café herself. Making sure the coast was clear, she walked to her car, so she and Candy could make their way back to her apartment.

Returning to her apartment, she still wondered how someone like Harmony could do something so heinous, like murdering two people in cold blood. Her appearance and demeanor were so disarming. Hazel was not surprised that the police had never narrowed in on her, and she was not sure how she would create that connection for them. The thought of spending any more time with Harmony made her skin crawl. It only took one time for the girl to snap and put her into a precarious situation, and she did not want to end up there again. Unexpectedly, she received a text from Harmony on the very next day inviting her for another coffee. She wanted to decline, but she knew she could not.

She spent the rest of the night in a grumpier mood than usual. She knew why she was meeting with Harmony, but she did not have to like it. Tate came to her apartment after his shift, and even brought her flowers, but it did not release much of the tangle that had developed in her stomach. It squeezed and pulsed like a living being.

When turning into bed that night, she was grateful to have Tate lying beside her. His presence was the one thing that calmed her, at least a little. She was not a fool, though. Whether she felt calm or in turmoil, she knew it would not make a difference once she closed her eyes. Her feelings while awake seemed to have no bearing on what happened in her sleep. So, when she closed her eyes that night, she braced for the onslaught of nightmares, or hellacious memories, that would undoubtedly assault her.

The swampland was roaring with the sounds of life. She sat with her fishing pole bobbing in the water, hoping to catch dinner before too long. The sun was setting, and the mosquitos were only going to get worse with every hour she was still out there. The cricket on the end of her line was fresh, so it should hook something edible, eventually. Hopefully not an alligator gar fish. She hated having to deal with those.

A week alone in her father's fishing cabin was a much-needed break from everyday life. Some people would have found it isolating. No television or cell signal, but she reveled in the privacy. She had a stack of novels to flip through, and she intended to read at least a few of them. If she could ever catch a fish.

A flock of birds scattered in the distance, causing the echoing sound of flapping wings. She glanced up to see them fly away, only to catch the glimpse of something in the distance. She squinted into the sunset, trying to make sense of what she was seeing.

The form looked to be human, walking on two legs, but it seemed to stand over seven feet tall. She was too afraid to move, so she slouched her body down in her chair, watching the creature quietly. The frame was covered in a thick coat of matted, grayish brown hair, but there were swamp weeds tangled within the strands. Its movement was cautious, silent even. It was hunting.

She clinched her eyes shut, hoping the form would be gone when she opened them again, but it did not work. When she reopened her eyes, he was still there, but now his yellow eyes were looking towards her. They reflected the sun's light, almost causing them to glow. He grunted loudly. He had seen her.

Terrified, she dropped her fishing pole in the water and ran into the cabin, bolting the lock behind her.

"Swamp monsters," Hazel said as she discussed her nightmare with Candy. "Actual swamp monsters."

Candy arched her eyebrow playfully. "Like the Rougarou or the Honey Island swamp monster? Like those swamp monsters?"

Hazel shrugged.

"I guess. How am I supposed to know? I'm not from here. I'm just glad it wasn't another spirit memory. I'm tired of them. No offense."

Candy smirked, reaching out to smooth Hazel's flyaway hair.

"None taken, doll. But how do you know it wasn't a spirit memory? People see swamp monsters all the time."

Hazel snorted.

"Yeah... I'm going to call bullshit on that and file this one under unrealistic nightmares from my sadistically creative mind."

Candy flourished her hand dramatically.

"Suit yourself, but don't cry to me when the Rougarou gets you."

"Deal," Hazel responded as she parked her car around the block from the coffee shop.

Her stomach had begun to swirl. Candy sat nervously beside her, fidgeting with her fingernails. They had discussed getting to know Harmony, so they could try to find evidence of her crimes, but the reality of the task was becoming more unnerving the closer they got.

Harmony was already seated when they walked into the café, so Hazel went to the counter to get her coffee before approaching the table. Her heart rate was already elevated, so she opted for a cup of decaf instead. She would not do herself any favors by adding lightheadedness to her list of nervous-induced symptoms. Harmony looked as harmless as always, but Hazel was not fooled. She pasted a fake smile on her face and tried to act happy to be there, although it could not have been further from the truth.

"Hey, Harmony!"

She took the seat across from Harmony while Candy stood at her side.

"Hey, Hazel. Thanks for coming."

"No problem. Was there a particular reason you wanted to meet?"

"No. Not particularly. I just really loved their soup today and thought about you, since I was going to come back here. I don't have a large circle of friends in the city. Are you hungry?"

"I am, actually. I'll have to grab a bowl. I'll be right back."

She rose from the table. She was not actually hungry, but she intended to play the part, so she returned to the counter and got a bowl of shrimp and corn bisque before returning to the table and dropping back into her seat. The soup smelled delicious. She did not really know how to start a conversation with Harmony and keep the disdain she felt from being evident. Conversation starting was not one of Hazel's top skill sets, as it was. Thankfully, Harmony seemed much better at it.

"So..., tell me a little about yourself. I know you just finished law school, but that's it. Where are you from? Do you have a boyfriend?"

The question caught Hazel off guard. She thought about lying but did not want to create so many false narratives that she started to lose track of them, so she opted for the truth with this question.

"I'm from out west. I do have a boyfriend."

"Ooh. What's his name? What does he do? Spill!"

"His name is Tate. He's a police officer. You?"

Harmony's eyes shot to the floor, and the conversation went quiet. It was as though she had hoped to keep the attention on Hazel only. The silence created an uncomfortable situation more unbearable. Hazel shifted in her chair. Finally, Harmony answered, although she still looked at the floor.

"I did... He died... recently."

This was it, Hazel thought, but she did not know how to respond.

"Oh... I'm so sorry. What happened?"

Harmony looked at her cell phone. Her face the definition of detachment.

"He was murdered. I've got to go."

Before Hazel could respond, Harmony had risen from the table and run out of the café. She did not know if she should run after her, because the last thing she wanted to do was ruin her chances of getting close enough to get evidence against her, but she ended up doing nothing but letting her go. She thought about maybe texting her later, and apologizing for upsetting her, or making up some other excuse to talk, but chasing after her was not an option. It was Saturday, and she had dinner plans with Tate that night, so she needed to get back home to get ready.

She and Candy made it back to her apartment about an hour before Tate was due to arrive after his shift, which did not give her much time to get ready. Candy had begged to dress her, fix her hair, and makeup during their entire drive home from the café, and she had finally agreed, sort of. She had agreed with limits. As long as Candy did not make her look over the top, she promised to be open to the makeover. Candy insisted that the new look would "blow Tate's mind," but he'd never seen Hazel in any way other than her way, so she did not even know if he would like Hazel 2.0.

Since she did not own any clothes Candy found acceptable, Candy had insisted on stopping at a boutique, while on their way home, to get a sexy black dress and a pair of heels for Hazel to wear. She was not even sure if she could walk in heels, and was borderline afraid that she would fall flat on her face and knock out a tooth. Which would not be sexy at all.

As soon as she got out of the shower, Candy got to work, supervising her to make sure she used the hairdryer properly so she would not make her hair frizzy. After her hair was fixed, Candy used her spectral powers to operate the curling iron, with Hazel's help, which was admittedly terrifying. Not only had Hazel worn her hair in a ponytail almost every day, for most of her life, but a hot curling iron free-floating near her face was dangerous. However, the task went down without incident, and her date night hairdo looked, according to Candy, sexy as fuck. Hazel was no help when it came to doing her makeup, because she could count on two hands how many times she had worn makeup in her life, but Candy insisted on finding a way to get makeup on her face, so they worked together to make it happen. Candy put her spectral powers to work, through Hazel's hands, and guided her through putting on a flawless face, with only a few bumps along the way. When it was all completed, Hazel thought she was overdone, but Candy thought it was just perfect. They both agreed it would be Tate's opinion that would matter the most, so they waited for his response before pulling out the makeup remover.

The dress was, by far, the sexiest item Hazel had ever worn, and she felt ridiculous. It was a black dress with a deep v-neckline, spaghetti straps, and it wrapped into an asymmetrical shape. It was backless and quite short. She tried to cover it with a jacket, but Candy refused to let her. She did not even know where they were going for dinner, so she hoped she was not overdressed.

When Tate's knock sounded at the door, her stomach felt like it was filled with buzzing bees. She answered the door with her face already burning with embarrassment, before she even knew what his reaction would be. To her surprise, his face lit up when she opened the door.

"Wow! Hazel... you look incredible!"

He took her by the hand and pulled her close to him, spinning her around and then giving her a passionate kiss. Her own face exploded with heat, but she let herself become lost in his affection.

He pulled her away so he could get a better look at her, before lifting her up off of her feet and giving her a long kiss. She was glad he was holding her because it made her legs weak.

"Is it my birthday or something? I mean... you always look beautiful to me, but I've never seen you so dressed up. I don't know what the occasion is, but you look stunning. Did I mention I love you?"

She giggled, wrapping her arms around him.

"Thank you and I love you too. There's no special occasion. Candy just wanted to dress me up."

"Is Candy still here?"

"Yeah. She's in the living room."

Tate looked towards the living room and yelled out, thanking Candy, before carrying Hazel through the threshold of her apartment and into her bedroom.

"Hey! But aren't we going to dinner?"

She was still giggling as Tate carried her in his arms set her down on the bed.

"Yes, but later."

Running his hands gently over her shoulders and down her back, her dress slid down to her waist, where it easily slid the rest of the way off. He guided her back against the bed as he started kissing her all over her body, making her forget about dinner altogether, as her back arched with pleasure. There was only one thing that she needed at that moment, and he was lying on top of her.

By the time they left the bedroom to go to the restaurant nearly an hour later, Jake had joined Candy on the sofa. Candy congratulated them on the damage they had done to her job on both Hazel's hair and makeup. She was adequately embarrassed as they walked out of the door.

Tate had asked her to go on dates with him for years before she agreed, but she only held out because she did not want to complicate their friendship. Also, she had never felt she was good enough for him, and those doubts still sometimes plagued her thoughts. Although they had finally made the leap into a romantic relationship, with everything that had happened in her life over the past few months, they had only enjoyed a few out-on-the-town dates. Most of their time together had been spent in her apartment, not that she was complaining. She was a homebody, after all.

Although fancy dinners had never been Hazel's thing, once she was sitting across from Tate, she did her best to tune everyone else out and focus her attention solely on him. On this night, however, it was harder to do, because she recognized a woman sitting at a nearby table. Harmony Richard was sitting alone, three tables away from them, eating a soup and salad, and there was no way for Hazel to avoid being seen. Harmony stared at them for several awkward minutes before cracking an enormous grin, rising from her seat, and approaching their table.

"Harmony's here," she whispered.

Hazel tried to warn Tate, but he did not understand her whispered message before Harmony got close.

"Hey, Hazel!"

Harmony's voice caught Tate by surprise, causing him to jump. His eyes darted in her direction. She looked at him and smiled.

"Hi. You must be Tate."

She reached out to shake his hand. He hesitated, but complied, shaking her hand lightly.

"Yes, and you are?"

Tate was trying to be polite, but Hazel could tell he was fighting to hide his confusion about why this random girl was standing only inches from him.

"Oh, sorry. My name is Harmony."

Hazel could see a slight change in Tate's face, but she hoped Harmony hadn't noticed. He glanced at Hazel, who forced a smile before looking back at Harmony.

"Nice to meet you, Harmony."

Harmony's eyes lit up as though Tate's response made her day. Hazel felt instantly uncomfortable, so she decided to interrupt the moment.

"I'm starving, love. Are you ready to order?"

"Yes! Let's do that."

He turned to Harmony, whose smile had turned sheepish.

"Nice to meet you again, Harmony. Have a good night."

He turned his gaze down to his menu. His tone had been kind, and she was receptive. Smiling and nodding, she said goodbye and returned to her table.

"You weren't lying when you said she looked like a kid," Tate said over his bowl of soup. "Those eyes though... deer in the headlights."

"I think she thinks you're cute."

"What?"

"I could just tell. I don't know. Something about the way she looked at you made me uncomfortable."

"Sweetie, obviously you don't have to worry about another woman… but she's a killer… so you definitely don't have to worry about her."

"No… no… I didn't mean it that way. I just hope she doesn't start getting any ideas."

"I wouldn't worry about that, but I will be sure to stay away from her, and so should you. We should probably just let the cops do their job. I know waiting sucks, but I don't want you getting hurt."

"I don't want that either."

Tate reached across the table and held her hand, drawing sweet circles in her palm.

"Then let's make sure that doesn't happen."

She smiled, but she could not help but notice Harmony watching them from the corner of her eye.

"Ready to go?"

"I was thinking the same thing."

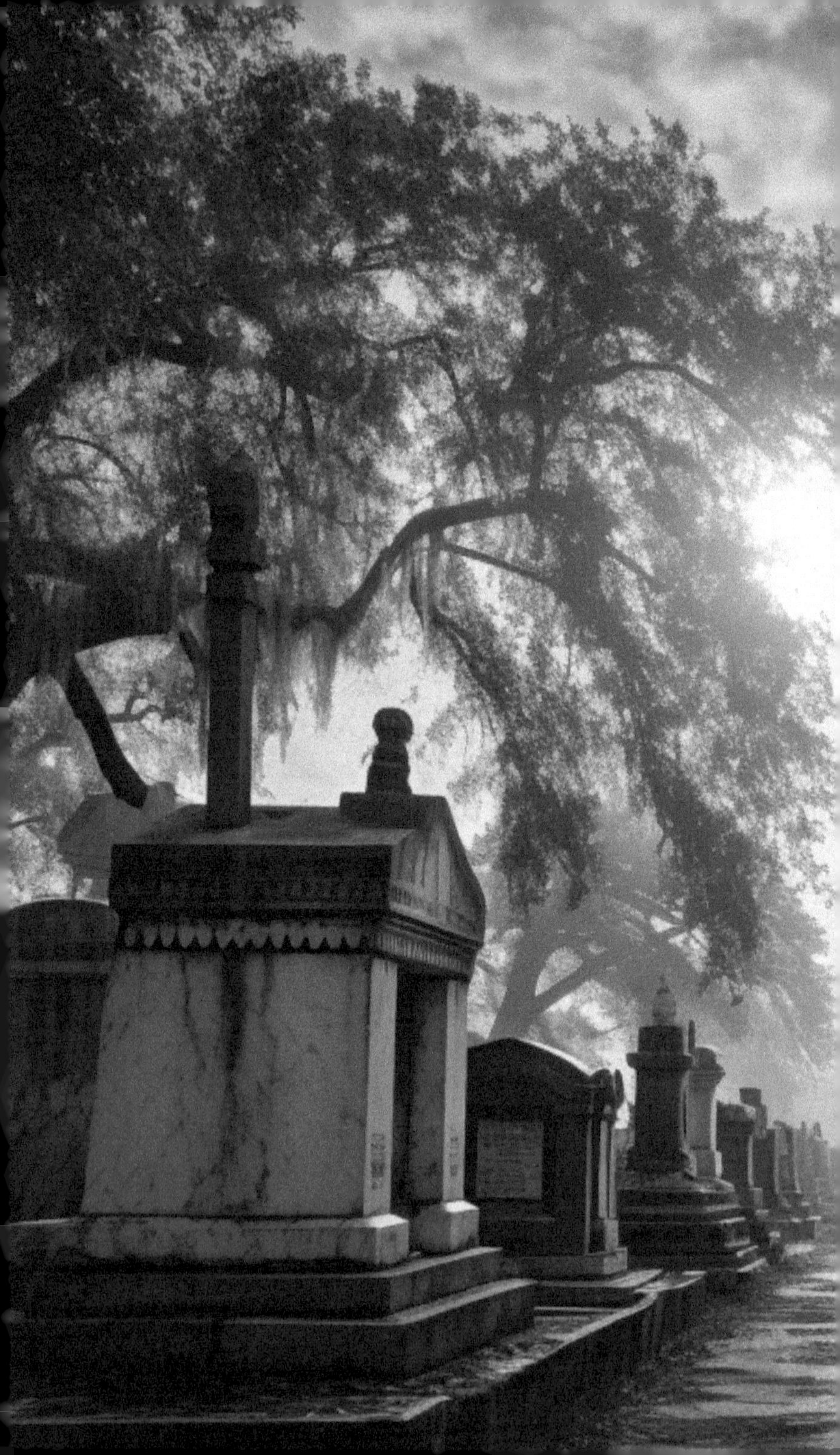

Chapter Eighteen
The Stalker

Cowering in the corner of the dilapidated shed, she trembled with fear. She had lost track of the sunsets and sunrises since she had been taken prisoner. He came to her almost every day, to use her for what he could, but she did not even know his name. She did not know if, or when, he would throw her away like garbage.

The tears had dried up days before, leaving a shell of who she once was. She begged for death every time his face loomed over her. Death or freedom. Either would release her from the hell she was in. Until then, she no longer had any fight left in her. She had resigned herself to whatever fate lay before her.

The rain pelted the bedroom window, pulling Hazel out of a scene she was all too happy to leave. Her consciousness rescued her, as it had done so many times before. Her heart pumped violently as she tried to force the visions in her head away. She had experienced similar nightmares and spirit induced memories, when Angela was haunting her, but Angela was gone.

She saw these visions through the eyes of the person who was held captive, so she had no idea who the person was. All she knew was that it was not her. She had been held captive before, but not in the building she had now seen twice in her unconscious mind. She shivered. The trauma she felt in her chest was almost unbearable. Raymond had abducted her, but he had not sexually assaulted her. This was a reality she was grateful for every day since. He had raped some of his other victims, but the circumstances had spared her. This woman, however, the woman in the nightmare she was now reeling from, had not been so lucky.

She did not know who this woman was, but she was afraid she would eventually find out.

The thought of Harmony developing a crush on Tate plagued Hazel's thoughts during her entire day of work. She did not know why, but she had a strong feeling about it, about the way Harmony looked at him. It was not jealousy Hazel felt. It was dread. When added to the residual emotions from her nightmare, the anxiety was debilitating.

Walking into her apartment building, Hazel had never been so ready to get home in her life. She had met with two new clients that day, both with misdemeanor charges, but the paperwork had run her ragged. She aimed her eyes towards the glass doors of the entrance, but a flicker of motion caught her attention. She stopped and turned in its direction, expecting to see Jim, the recently deceased maintenance man for her building who was always up for a chat, but she saw a woman instead.

The woman's dark hair flowed down her back, and her amber eyes gave her an exotic look. Hazel did not recognize her, but she did recognize one thing. The woman was dead. The bruises around her neck, where she had clearly been strangled, were unmistakable.

The spirit reached out a haunting hand in Hazel's direction, desperate for help, but Hazel panicked. She had enough on her plate and could not imagine throwing herself into another murder investigation. She could not fathom being responsible for the justice of another victim, at least not until Candy's case was solved. Candy was her best friend. They were like sisters, and Candy needed her to be one hundred percent invested. So, instead of approaching the strangled woman, as she was raised to do, she looked away, turned on her heel, and darted inside.

Throwing her keys and satchel on the table, she leaned her back against the backside of the door, as though sheer will would keep the strangled spirit from following her inside. She knew the door was merely false security. It did nothing to keep spirits out. If they wanted in, they simply walked right through it. Regardless, she braced herself against it as her breathing came in short bursts. She knew it was only a matter of time before that spirit refused to allow her to ignore its needs. She just hoped it gave her a little time.

Her phone, sitting on the kitchen table, vibrated loudly against the wood, startling her. Leaving the support of the door, she reached for her phone to see a text from Tate. He asked if she was home because he needed to talk to her about something important. Nervously, she replied she was home, but the uncertainty of what he wanted to talk to her about only made her heart beat faster. Pocketing her cell phone, she walked around the apartment looking for Candy, but did not see her.

Though she and Candy were technically roommates, and Candy was a spirit, they still tried to give each other space. Which Hazel usually appreciated. She wished she had a way to contact Candy when she needed to talk to her, but it was not like spirits could carry cell phones. She had grown so accustomed to Candy always being around that she could not help but miss her when she was not. Even though she worried about what Tate needed to tell her, his knock at the door promised to end her nervous anticipation.

A knot developed in her chest when she opened the door. The look on his face only made her heart drop more. Her mind swirled with the endless possibilities of what plagued him. The only thing that brought her comfort was he still gave her a hug and a kiss, as he always did. Closing the door behind them, he took her hand and walked her to the sofa where they sat together.

"Tate, what's wrong? You're scaring me."

"It's Harmony."

He hesitated, reaching up to scratch his chin.

"I think she's following me."

Hazel's heart fell further into her stomach and her blood ran cold. She knew something was off in how

Harmony looked at Tate at the restaurant. She was just hoping she was wrong.

"What... what do you mean she's following you?"

"Where is the salon where she works?"

"By Tulane Medical Center."

"Okay. I thought so. That's nowhere near the precinct. I saw a strange car parked right outside the building when I arrived for my shift this morning. It wouldn't have been unusual, except the car was running with a woman inside. She had on large sunglasses, although the sun wasn't bright, so I couldn't make out her face. But later, when I left and went to the café near work to grab a sandwich, she showed up and tried to make small talk with me. It was just really... strange. She wasn't there by accident."

Hazel felt the panic creep in as he explained. The image of the psycho-collage flashed through her head. Taunting her. Threatening her.

"I knew it. I could tell she was into you at the restaurant. I should've never met with her."

He grabbed her hand and pulled her in closer, resting his head on top of hers.

"You did it for Candy. Don't worry. I can take care of myself. I'm just worried about you. If she's as dangerous as you suspect, I don't want you to get in her crosshairs again. I made an excuse to leave the café, and I'll do the same thing if she comes around me again. I just don't want her around you."

"We need her to be caught. She can't just get away with this. What if she turns her psycho-obsessive bullshit on you?"

She felt her tears bubbling just below the surface, begging to be let out, but she fought them to stay inside.

"They will catch her. And let her try that shit on me. It would only get her caught faster."

She knew he was trying to reassure her, but it did not help. She knew if any guy could defend himself; it was him, but it did not make her worry any less. She did not want him to be the object of a crazy person's affection, no matter how capable he was. Her tendency to get mixed up in cases that could get her killed had officially gotten out of hand. She could feel her cynicism growing. Tate's hand brushed her cheek, pulling her out of her pessimistic spiral, and into his arms.

"I want you to come and stay at my house when I'm not here. I know it's a far drive, but I don't like you being here alone. Just in case she finds out where you live. That could be bad. She knows Candy lived here. And

I know you have Candy, but she's not always here, and there's only so much she can do when she is."

Hazel nodded in resignation. Not that she did not want to stay at Tate's house, she just did not want to be forced to under such circumstances. She longed for her life to be normal, or at least normal for her. Less life threatening would be a start. She needed Harmony to be arrested.

"We need to find her house."

She did not know if the morbid collage remained on the bedroom door, but she thought it was a good place to start if they were going to help put Harmony in prison. She pulled back just enough so she could look Tate in the eyes. His face looked serious, but he was listening.

"What are you thinking? What do you think she's hiding in there?"

"In my visions, there was that collage of Candy and Jake's pictures and random sheets of paper with writing. She even had a lock of Candy's hair. Maybe it's still there. If it is, maybe we'd have a chance at probable cause for a search warrant... as long as no one enters the location without permission."

"I doubt she lets anyone in there if it's still there, not in that room anyway."

Hazel thought for a moment. He was right, of course, but there had to be a way.

"I don't know... maybe it can be an accidental, on purpose type of thing. Like accidentally stumble in when visiting the rest of the house."

Just saying it sounded ridiculous, even to her. She sighed.

"That would put you in her house, so I don't like that idea."

"Yea... it probably wouldn't work, anyway."

"Let's worry about this later. I don't want to give her the pleasure of consuming any more of our day. Deal?"

"Deal."

Wrapping his arm around her back, he pulled her into him, into a kiss that melted at least some of her worries. No matter how she tried, however, the thought of them ending up on Harmony's sick wall plagued her. She knew where Tate stood on her staying away from Harmony, but she had to protect him.

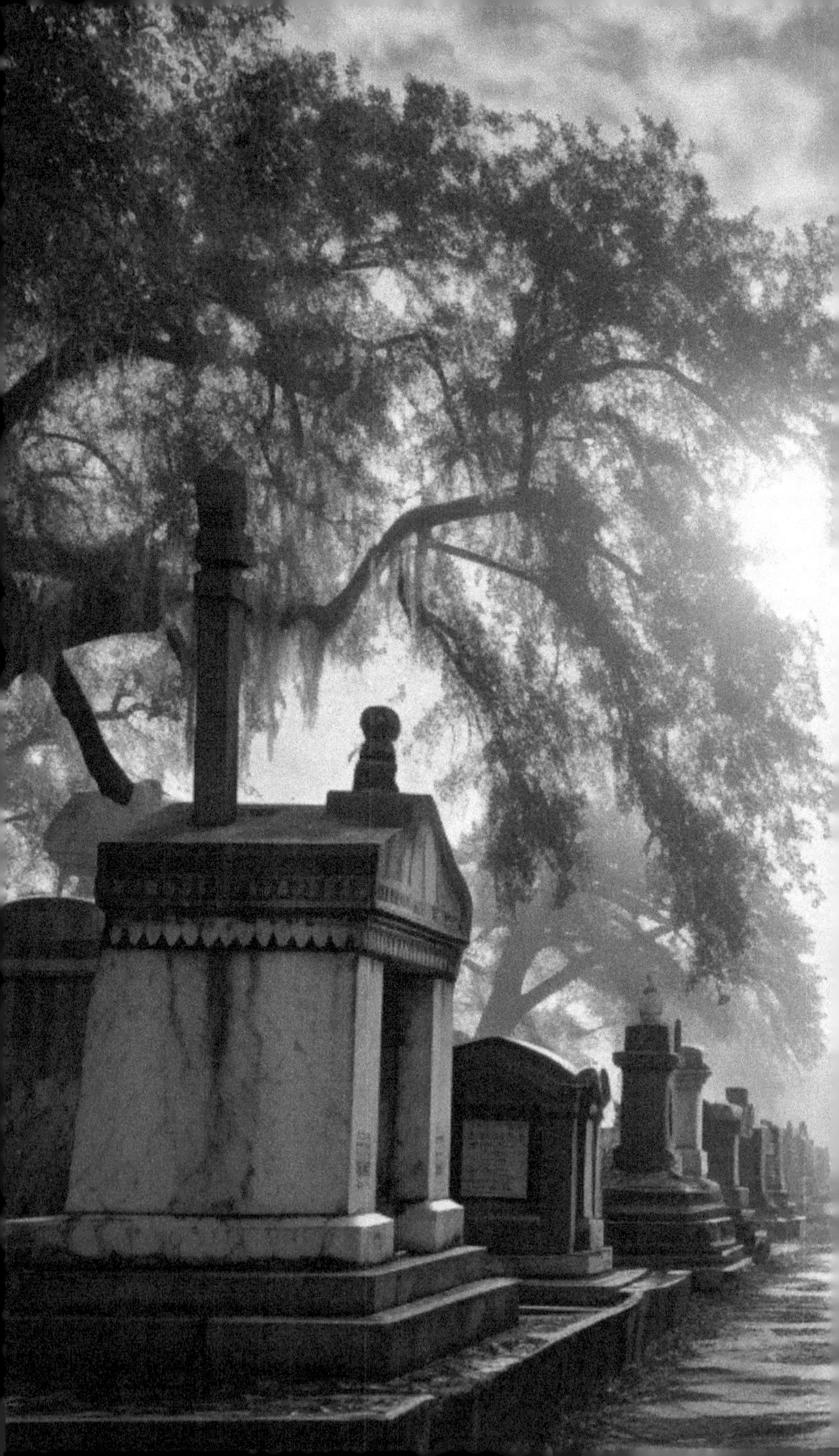

Chapter Nineteen
The Stakeout

When Tate left her apartment the next morning, she knew what she needed to do, although she was not feeling confident about it. She needed to continue getting close to Harmony, but with Candy by her side, for some protection. There was only so much protection Candy could offer, but it was better than none at all. She knew it was a risk, and she knew Tate did not approve, but she had to do something. She could not just sit idly by while Candy and Jake's killer remained free and moved in on her man.

She hoped to send Candy in secretly for the riskier stuff, at least to get proof of the photo collage, before entering and putting herself in unnecessary danger. But before she could do that, she needed to figure out where Harmony lived. For that, she would need to pull a page out of Harmony's book and follow her.

Climbing out of an empty bed, she already felt Tate's absence. She had grown used to waking up beside him, but his early shift had pulled him from her bed well before she had opened her eyes. Trudging into the living room, she found Candy in her usual spot on the sofa. She was watching television, but Hazel could tell that her mind was somewhere else.

"You're such a couch potato."

Candy powered off the television and turned to look at her with a forced scowl.

"And you look like a potato. Just kidding... you're actually really cute. Good morning."

Hazel smiled before turning to start the pot of coffee.

"Good morning to you. What's on your agenda for the day? Are you going to see Jake?"

Candy rose from the sofa and floated to join her in the kitchen. She sat down on the kitchen counter with her legs swinging side to side below her. She looked like an oversized kid.

"Maybe... you know how unpredictable that whole situation is. I could come with you to work today."

She looked at Hazel expectantly, waiting for a reply. Hazel used to never allow Candy to join her at the office because Candy could be incredibly distracting, to say the least. But, under the current circumstances, having extra backup was not a bad idea. Plus, she had a plan that involved Candy for after work.

"Actually, I wanted to talk to you about that."

Candy's smile faltered slightly, revealing a bit of nervousness.

"What's going on? What happened?"

"Tate and I ran into Harmony at the restaurant a few nights ago. I would have told you, but we haven't spent much time together since then. Well, now Tate thinks she's following him. I just found out last night."

Candy's already enormous eyes widened further.

"And... he's sure?"

"Yeah. He's pretty sure. She knew he was with the police department, so he thinks she waited for him outside of the precinct. Later, she popped into the same deli where he was grabbing a sandwich and tried to make small talk with him. He's never been one to embellish, so I think he's probably on to something. I mean... you should've seen how she looked at him at the restaurant. It made me uncomfortable."

Candy's mouth morphed into a sardonic smile as she cupped her mouth with one hand to censor the line of obscenities that fought to spill out.

"That crazy bitch! I know he's hot, but damn. Is this just her thing now... to get obsessed with other people's men and then stalk them? What is Tate going to do? What are you going to do?"

"He wants me to stay away from her, but you know I can't completely do that. She needs to be caught and arrested. I know he can defend himself, but she has been free long enough."

Candy shook her head in disbelief before dropping her head into her hands. She spoke through splayed fingers, muffling her voice.

"Do you have a plan... one that won't get you killed? You can't keep putting yourself into dangerous situations, Hazel. I know you didn't choose to be mixed up in this... being my friend at all... but I'd rather you'd step back than get hurt. I'm sure Tate would agree. You know how that affected your parents."

Hazel's heart dropped. Her mother's gift had driven a rift between her parents. They were still together, but more because of their codependency to each other, than because of love. It was one of the main reasons she had fought her feelings for Tate for so long. She did not want the same thing to happen to them. There was only so much worry and stress she could put him through before he moved onto someone with less drama. She pulled in a deep breath and let it out slowly, trying to calm her worsening nerves.

"I know. I think about that all the time. That's why I've figured you into this equation. If you're willing."

"You know I'll help you. You're the most important person in the world to me."

Candy hopped off of the counter and wrapped an icy arm around Hazel's shoulders.

"What do you need for me to do?"

Hazel thought for a moment, leaning her head on Candy's shoulder.

"We need to find out if her psycho collage is still on the back of that door, but I don't even know where the house is. If we could find any evidence of what she's done... I think we need to follow her. We need to find out where she lives."

Candy nodded, but her face revealed her hesitation.

"I will not let you break into the house of another killer."

"I know... that's where you can help me. If I can find the house, maybe you can go inside and look around. All I'm able to see otherwise is what Jake saw... what I see in his memories, but it's not enough. It never shows me the name of the street. I can't even tell if it's in the city."

Candy nodded again, but Hazel could tell she still was not sold on the plan. She moved to sit on the sofa. Hazel followed.

"But what will you do if it is there? Is my word enough of a reason to start an investigation into her? I mean... that's not how the law works."

"I know, but I need to know if it's there before I can plan my next move. At least, if we know there's evidence that can put her away, we can plan for how to expose her."

"I'm not saying it can't work, and you know I'm your ride-or-die, but I'm only going to go along with this if you promise to stay out of her house. You need to stay alive, and that bitch is crazy. Okay?"

"Okay."

Candy's face relaxed, becoming less stern. She patted Hazel on the knee.

"So, when does this sleuthing begin? And can I dress like Sherlock Holmes, minus the cocaine in my pocket?"

Hazel broke out into a laugh, but Candy tried to keep her face serious. It did not last. Before she knew it, they were both giggling on the sofa.

"Okay... I would pay to see you dress like Sherlock Holmes, but you have to wear the hat. Will you wear the hat?"

Candy rolled her eyes, as though the answer was obvious.

"Uh... the outfit wouldn't be complete without one."

Hazel nodded her head, letting out one more giggle.

"Indeed. And to answer your question... I think we should try to follow her today. I only have to meet with a few clients and show up in court today. I should be done before she gets of work."

"Okay. How long until we leave?"

Hazel glanced at her cell phone and gasped.

Why can't I ever be on time?

"Ten minutes!"

Jumping off the sofa, Hazel ran to the bedroom, not even waiting for a response from Candy. All Candy had to do was snap her fingers to get ready. It was not that easy for the living to get ready. Grabbing the first clean suit she could find, she looked anything but stylish. Candy, on the other hand, had taken their conversation about dressing like the super sleuth, Mr. Holmes, seriously. Dressed in a tan plaid suit, complete with an overcoat, scarf, pocket watch, and deerstalker hat, she looked the part perfectly. Albeit sexier than Sherlock could have ever been.

Stifling back laughter, Hazel closed the door behind them as they headed to her car.

"Okay... be honest. Did you already own that outfit somewhere in your ghostly closet, or do you just snap your fingers, and the outfits just appear?"

"It's closer to the second option."

"I thought so."

Hazel's workday was rather uneventful, at least after shooing Candy out of her office when she pulled a magnifying glass out of her pocket and started magnifying the dust that covered every surface. She and her detective gear found other ways to keep themselves busy in the historic building, probably chatting with the resident ghosts haunting the halls. They reconvened just as Hazel finished her final meeting for the day.

Motioning for Candy to follow her out of the building and to her car, she refrained from speaking to her until they were away from other people. She did not need to develop a reputation at work as the crazy person who walks down the hallway talking to herself. The closer they got to the car, however, the more Candy laughed, making it nearly impossible for Hazel to keep her composure. All bets were off when they got to her car and she finally started laughing as well, although she had missed the joke completely.

"Candy! What is so funny?"

"Some old spook just called me 'sugar tits.' Who in the hell says that?"

Hazel rolled her eyes. She knew exactly who still used misogynistic terms like that.

"Ugh! That would be Judge Boudreaux. Old perve. But why are you laughing?"

"Oh... more from discomfort than anything else. The entire thing was super awkward. But he was so old and dumpy... I couldn't really get mad about it. I mean... I think he was trying to flirt with me. It was just kind of funny. His eyes got as big as saucers when he saw me, almost like a cartoon character."

"Yeah, well, you are the hottest thing he's probably seen in a while. Anyway... are you ready to go?"

Candy's laugh halted as her face tensed. Hazel felt the energy in the car shift.

"As ready as I'm going to be. Are we just going to park outside and wait for her to leave?"

"That's the plan. I won't park too close but hopefully I can park close enough to see the door."

Putting her car into drive, Hazel pulled her car onto the street. Her heart beat louder within her ears, the closer she got to the salon where Harmony worked. She still had no plan for how to get access to Harmony, even if Candy found something within her house. Not without going against Tate's wishes and putting herself in danger.

Arriving at the salon, she was able to park across the street, but about halfway down the block. It was farther away than she had intended, but at least Harmony would not see her, but she could still see the door.

Waiting patiently in the car for close to two hours, Hazel listened as Candy chattered on about everything under the sun. Candy's nervousness was more apparent the faster she spoke. Hazel's nervousness had yet to hit her, but she knew it would the minute she saw Harmony.

Just as their stakeout had crossed the one hour and forty-five-minute mark, a familiar, doe-eyed face exited the salon and climbed into a black sedan parked outside. Hazel and Candy shared an uneasy glance before she pulled her car away from the curve and followed stealthily behind Harmony. She did not think Harmony knew what her car looked like, but she was not willing to take any chances, so she made sure to leave some distance between them.

The drive took them just east of the city, to the city of Chalmette. The traffic increased to near chaos as they left the downtown area, making it nearly impossible to keep Harmony's car in view. Just as Jim, the deceased maintenance man for Hazel's building, always told her, people in New Orleans did drive like they were crazy. The last thing she could deal with was an accident, so she ignored Candy and did her best to drive like a good driver, although she was just as crazy as the rest of them. Relief washed over her as they exited the freeway, although the relief was replaced with a knot in her chest as they pulled into a neighborhood.

Hazel had never spent any time in Chalmette, but she recognized the scene from her time in Jake's memories, causing a strange sense of déjà vu.

"This is it."

She chanced a glance at Candy, who's posture had changed with her words. Candy had been casually gazing out of the window, but she now sat stiffly, facing forward with her eyes alert.

Hazel pulled to the side of the street and put her car in park as she watched Harmony, a few blocks ahead, pull into a familiar driveway. She did not want to pull up too close and blow her cover, but she did not need to. Returning to the street while awake pulled the image of the mystery house to the front of her mind. She knew exactly which house Harmony would be walking into.

She and Candy sat for a few minutes in silence. Although she would not be able to see Candy, Candy was still nervous. Hazel could see it in her eyes.

"Do you want to back out? It's okay to change your mind. It can't be easy to face someone who's done what she's done, even if she can't see you."

Pulling her hands to her face, Candy rested her eyes on her palms, but only for a moment.

"No. I'm not going to back out. She needs to be caught. It's just hard to even consider seeing those pictures of me... and Jake. I don't want to see them. I think it would make it too real."

Hazel did not know how to respond.

Shit. I'm an awful friend. I hadn't even thought about Candy's reaction to seeing the collage... and her lock of hair. Shit. Shit. Shit.

"Candy... I'm so sorry. I was so wrapped up in the idea of catching her. I didn't even consider how you would feel if you saw it. I'm a terrible friend."

Candy pulled her face from her hands, shaking her head and staring into Hazel's eyes.

"Don't call yourself a bad friend. You're the best friend. I know you're doing this for me. You're putting yourself at risk. We both have to sacrifice to catch this bitch. None of this is your fault. You didn't hang that morbid shit. I may not want to see it, but I have to. I understand that. It's not your fault."

Hazel nodded, but she did not feel much better. She knew Candy had a point, but she still felt like she had some control over the situation, even if she did not.

With nothing more than a smile and a quick squeeze on her hand, Candy disappeared from the seat next to her, and reappeared just ahead of the car on the empty street.

Hazel's guilt became almost toxic as she watched her best friend walk down the street and into the house of her murderer. Thankfully, Candy was not gone long, reappearing in the passenger seat only ten minutes later.

"Well... what happened? What did you see?"

Candy did not reply at first, almost as though she was lost in her thoughts.

"Sorry. There are still pictures behind the door, but she's added a new one."

Hazel's heart dropped.

"What do you mean?"

Candy looked at her with a grim expression.

"Tate."

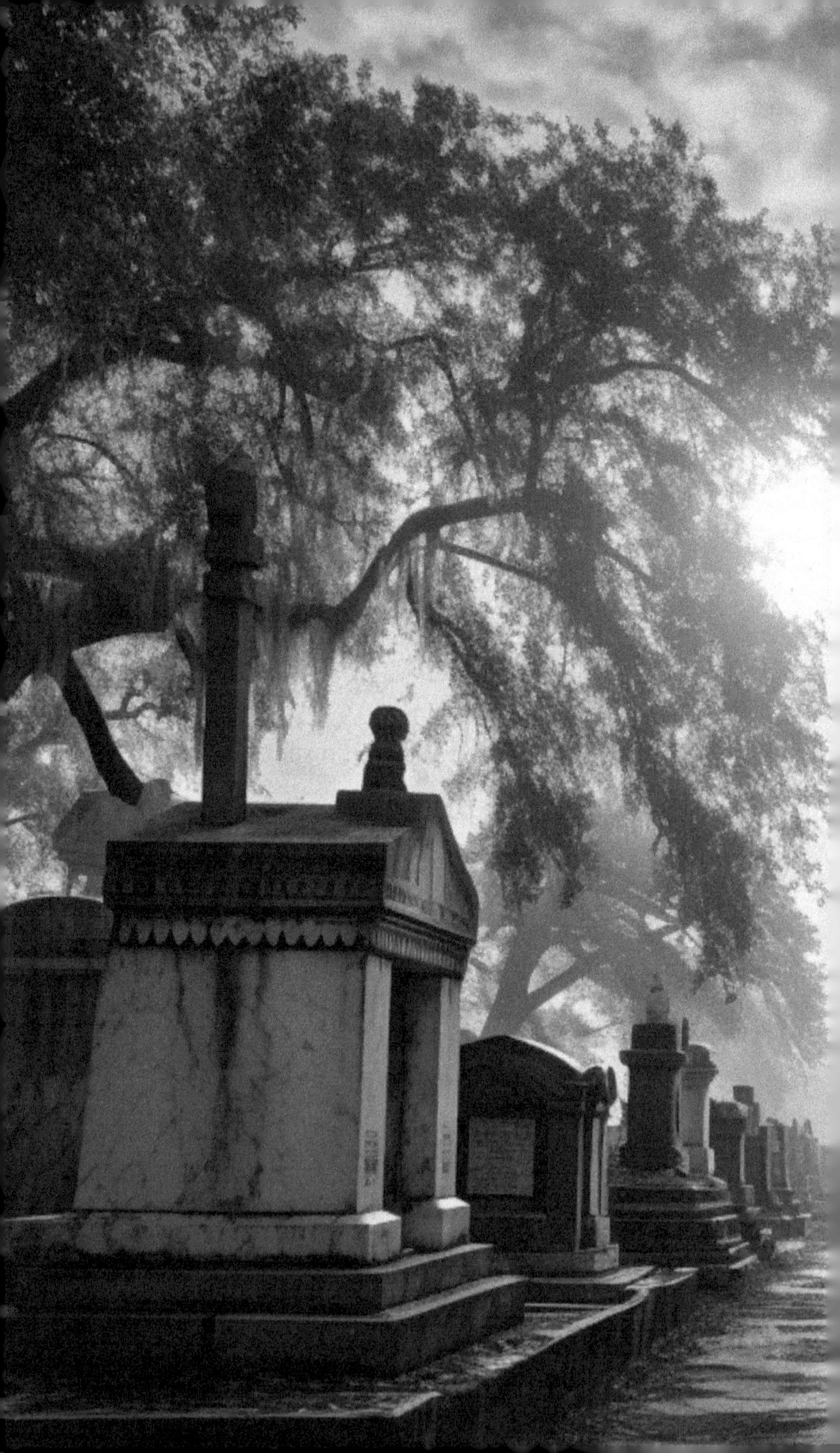

Chapter Twenty
The New Target

The sounds of the road filled her ears as her eyes saw only blackness. The cloth against her tongue tasted of sweat and dust, but she could not push it away, forcing her to gag against it. The car jerked along the road as it hit ruts and potholes, telling her it was not paved. Something about the moment felt familiar, like she had experienced it once before, but had somehow survived the ordeal. The air in the trunk thinned, causing her breath to come in short bursts and her head to spin. She tried to remain stoic, to fight her emotions as much as she planned to fight her captor, but her eyes betrayed her, allowing her backstabbing tears to reveal her fear.

As the car slowed to a stop, she wiped at her tears, attempting to harden her look before the trunk opened and revealed her as a weak, sobbing mess. She needed to fight.

Trying to shift her weight, to stretch her legs before fighting for her life, she kicked something large on the other side of the space. The mass budged only slightly against her feet, but she could not see what she was touching. Panic swelled in her chest as though a hand squeezed her heart.

The brakes squeaked as the car pulled to a stop, and the driver only took a second to climb out of the car and slam the driver's side door. She started to hyperventilate. The footsteps were nearly silent as they approached the trunk, making her think they were parked on a soft surface, like mud or dirt.

The setting sun barely lit the interior of the trunk as the door flung open, leaving her captor in shadow. She knew it was a man, but she could not make out his face.

Chancing a glance at her feet, she stifled a scream when she saw what she had been trying to kick. A woman, long dark hair and amber eyes staring sightlessly at the darkening sky, laid dead by her feet. Struggling to scoot her body away from the corpse, she expected the man to grab her, to kill her, but he only grabbed the dead woman and slammed the trunk door shut above her head, shutting her back into darkness.

Jolting awake, Hazel flung herself into a sitting position in the bed, feeling around herself to ensure her hands and feet were not bound. She closed her eyes, trying to make sense of her nightmare.

Another memory. The dead woman who was outside the building... it was her. But she wasn't one of Raymond's victims... was she?

Reaching her hands to her head, she gripped at her temples, trying to find the opening that allowed spirits to input their memories into her mind. She wanted to close it once and for all. She was tired of them taking over her sleep, tired of not being able to control her own mind. Feeling as though she was losing control, Tate's gentle touch to her arm calmed her.

"Hey, are you okay?"

His hand was placed sweetly on her for support. She allowed herself to fall back into the bed, landing in the crook of his shoulder. Although he would want to know, she held off on telling him about the new female spirit haunting her dreams, the one she had seen outside of her building. She did not like feeling like a burden. It seemed like something new was always popping up in her life, and she did not want to pile anything else on his plate. So, instead of telling him about her memory-induced nightmare, she curled up in his arms and tried to enjoy his affection.

She did, however, still need to tell him about Harmony's photo collage, and his presence on it, but she did not know how. Realizing that putting it off would only make it worse, she swallowed back the bitter taste of fear in her throat and resolved to tell him.

"I have to tell you something, but I don't want you to be mad at me..."

She chanced a glance into his eyes and found him looking at her. He wrapped his arm tighter around her shoulders, kissing her forehead. She continued.

"Just please understand my reasons."

"Okay... now you've just got me worried. What happened?"

His eyes narrowed, but his hold on her remained snug.

"Candy and I followed Harmony yesterday, so I could see where she lives."

Slightly pulling away from her, so he could look into her eyes, she could see he was worried. It made her heart squeeze in a way that made it hard to breathe.

"Hazel..."

"I didn't get close to her. I promise."

The look in his eyes caused her tears to well up. She could not fight it. Gently wiping her cheeks, he pulled her head back close, nodding his head.

"Please don't be mad. I needed to protect you, and to help Candy... but I was safe. I promise."

"So, Candy was with you?"

"Yes."

He stroked his hand against her back. It soothed her, but it only made her cry more. He was so good to her and her obligation to the spirits kept causing her to hurt him. She did not know how to resolve the continuous conflict of her priorities.

"I understand why you are doing this, but I need you to be safe."

"I know, but I was. I promise."

"Well, at least tell me what the two of you found. What happened?"

"We trailed her after she left the salon because, although I've seen the inside of her house in Jake's memories, I had no idea where it was."

"Is it here in the city?"

"No. She lives in Chalmette."

"Are you sure she didn't see you? That's a long drive."

"There was a lot of traffic, and I stayed a good bit behind her. I really don't think she saw me."

"Good. Did you just follow her?"

"Not exactly."

She felt him stiffen, but he let her continue.

"Well, I only followed her, but Candy went into her house."

"Where were you when Candy went in?"

"Parked down the street."

His body relaxed again, allowing her heart to do the same.

"Lead with that next time. You scared me. I understand that this is a huge part of your life, and you may not be able to ignore the spirits, but you can't let it put you in danger. I don't want to lose you.

Wrapping her arms around him, she squeezed him tightly. She had never had a man care about her so much, and it meant everything to her.

"Thank you."

He looked at her and smiled.

"For what?"

"For loving me. It means more than you know."

Pulling her lips to his, he kissed her deeply, making the weight of the morning melt off of her.

"You don't have to thank me for that. It came naturally a long time ago, and it's here to stay."

"I feel the same way. I'm sorry for worrying you... and I don't want to spoil the mood more... but I have one more thing to tell you. I feel like I need to tell you now."

He looked at her attentively. His face was always so kind, but she had become a ball of nerves again. It seemed to be her default setting. Just thinking about Harmony did that to her.

"Okay. I'm listening."

"Candy saw the photo collage in Harmony's house."

His eyes widened, but he remained quiet, hanging on her every word.

"Your picture was there... one of you on a traffic stop."

His face tensed. She could see a muscle tighten in his jaw. He continued to caress her back, but he did not respond for several agonizing minutes.

She laid patiently next to him, allowing him to process the onslaught of information. She wanted to ease his mind, but she did not know how. Just when she thought she could not take the silence any longer, his hands stopped running across her back. Instead, he wrapped his arm around her shoulders.

"I wasn't expecting that. Sorry I was quiet for so long. I'm just trying to figure out what we can conceivably do to turn the police in her direction without involving us."

Rolling onto her side, she faced him, intertwining her leg with his. He glanced down at her leg before looking back up at her.

"Maybe we can talk about this later?"

Nodding her head, she slid on top of him, not willing to let thoughts of Harmony take away any more moments with Tate. At least not that morning.

Upon exiting the bedroom suite later that morning, she found Candy staring out of the window. Tate left her side to make coffee, but she approached Candy, startling her. Candy shrieked and turned to look at her as though she had been the one to see a ghost.

"I'm sorry I scared you. What are you looking at?"

Hazel peered out of the window as well, locking her eyes on the exact item of Candy's interest... Harmony's car. The car was parked in a way making it impossible to see if she was inside.

"Do you see it?"

"Yes."

"What are you going to do?"

"One second."

Hazel walked into the kitchen, whispering in Tate's ear. She told him what was outside but did so quietly, just in case Harmony was outside her apartment door.

Tate nodded, grabbing his cell phone and following her to the window. Stealthily, he peeked around the sill, taking a few pictures of the car, before sending a text to someone, although Hazel was not sure who. Grabbing Tate and Candy by the hand, she pulled them into the bedroom so they could speak without worry of their voices traveling outside the apartment.

"What do we do?" she asked.

Candy shrugged as Tate returned his phone to his pocket.

"I'm going to let those at my office, those who I trust, know she is following me. She hasn't really done much yet, but I also don't want to give her the chance. I need to let someone who can do something know about this. I'm going to let them know about her being Jake's girlfriend so they can make the connections... hopefully. We may have to continue nudging them along, but they clearly need help."

The weight on Hazel's shoulders lifted ever so slightly at the thought of turning the police onto Harmony's trail. There was nothing special about her for her to be so good at evading them. It needed to end.

"That sounds like a promising plan. I don't understand how she's gotten away with this so far."

"I just want this to be over," Candy sighed. "That bitch has caused me enough trauma. I want to be done with her."

Relaying Candy's words to Tate, she wrapped her arm around her friend's shoulders to comfort her. She could not imagine what Candy was going through. Losing her own life at only twenty-three years old, and then to find out that the same person killed the man she loved. The scenario must have been more than most people could bear, but Candy was the strongest person she knew. If anyone could see justice for themselves and the people they loved, it was her.

"Can Candy check to see if Harmony is still out there? Maybe see where she is hiding?"

Before Tate finished his statement, Candy had already left their sides and had floated through the front door and into the hall.

"She left. She'll figure out what Harmony is up to out there."

Tate nodded and then pulled her into a hug, the one thing that promised to temporarily melt away her stress. She would stay there forever, if she could.

Returning after only a few moments, Candy rejoined them in the bedroom to report her findings. Her face was almost amused.

"What's with the look? Did you see her?"

Hazel shared an incredulous look with Tate, shrugging her shoulders before she returned her glare to Candy, who was now giggling.

"What?"

"She's out there… in her car, I mean… but she's asleep."

Candy's giggles increased because of her amusement at the situation, but Hazel did not catch the joke.

"What?" Tate asked. "What happened?"

"Oh, sorry. I forgot you can't hear her. She said Harmony is asleep in her car. She's laughing. I'm not sure why."

Tate's lips curled into a half smile before tiptoeing to the window and peeking around the sill. Without saying a word, he pulled out his cell phone, sent a text, then returned to her side.

"This is perfect," he said.

"What is perfect? I don't understand."

Cupping her face in his hands, he placed a tender kiss on her lips.

"I just let another officer, one I trust, know not only is she stalking me, but she can be caught red-handed sleeping outside of my girlfriend's apartment. She has no reason to be here, no excuse at all. They're on their way now. They will catch her, and it will create suspicion against her. This one decision of hers could unravel this facade of innocence she's maintained until this point."

"What if she doesn't stop?"

"I don't expect her to. Actually, if she is who we think she is, she'll probably just become more desperate, so we will have to be more careful. I just want her to be on their radar, and I think this could do it."

"They're here," Candy said, unable to hide the anticipation in her voice.

Scurrying to the window, the three of them discreetly watched as an officer woke Harmony up, had a stern discussion with her, and wrote out a ticket. Hazel was not sure what the ticket was for, but it did not matter. She was caught outside of Hazel's apartment, a place she had no business being, and now there was proof. The officer waited until Harmony drove away before placing her cruiser into drive and doing the same.

Hazel worried about what a desperate Harmony would look like. She did not want to see it. She just hoped the police got to Harmony before she became violent against them. She no longer knew how she would get evidence on her with the events of the morning. There was no way she could get close to her again, not with Harmony going after her boyfriend.

With Harmony being willing to wait outside her apartment, Tate insisted on them abandoning her place and moving to his house, which was outside of the city. Harmony could have just as easily sat outside of his house, but his house made it more inconvenient for her, and it was an easier place to defend. They packed her things quickly, loaded into their vehicles and headed towards the outskirts of the city.

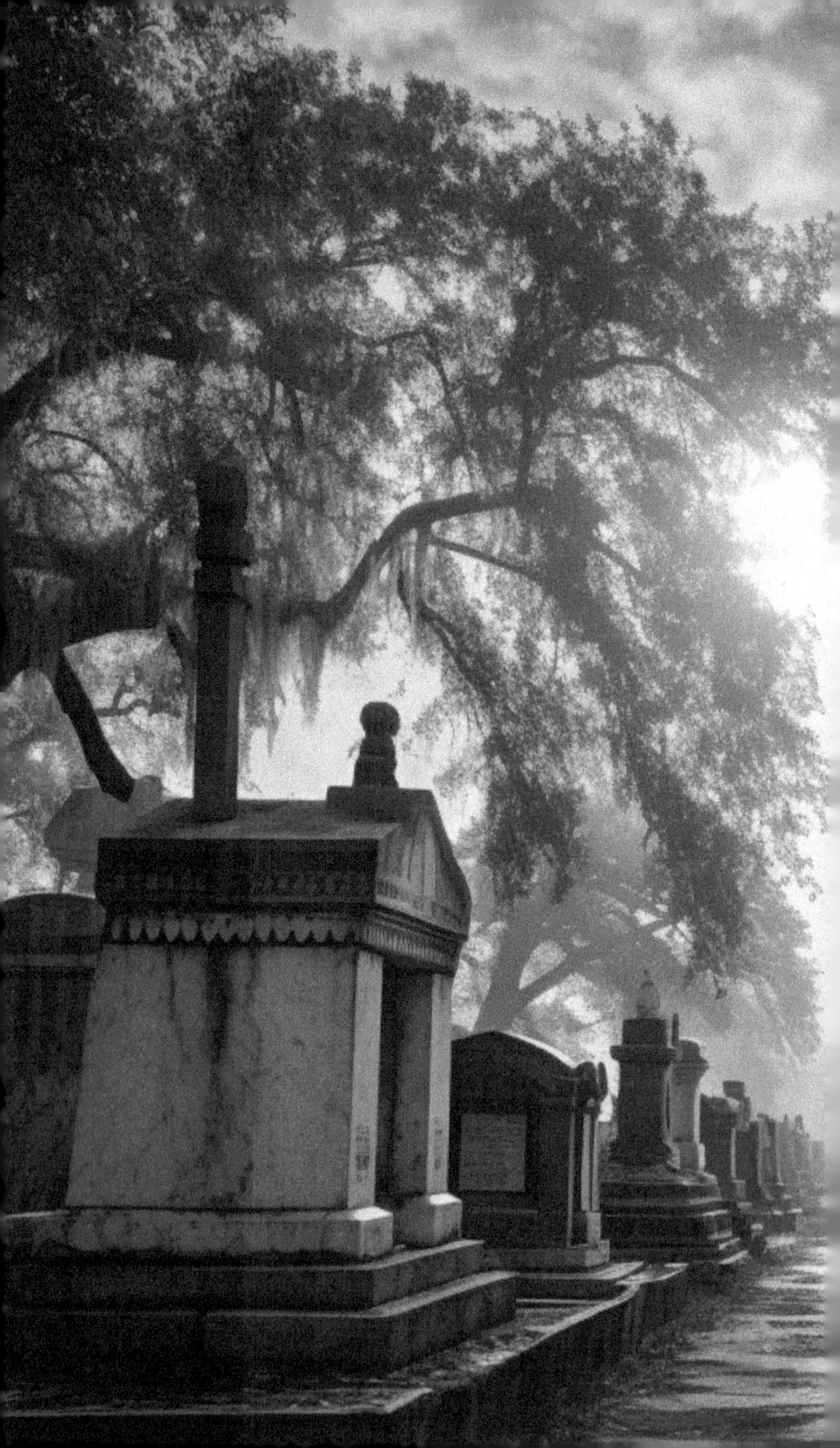

Chapter Twenty-One
Over the Edge

A little girl with brown braids sat on her bed, crying and fiddling with the clothes on her baby doll. Watching from the corner of the room, my heart broke for her.

"Bella... do you want me to read a story to you?" a man asked from the doorway. I recognized him. Joshua. Her father. "Why are you crying, sweetheart? Do you want me to lie down with you until you fall asleep?"

Bella looked up at her dad with a tear-stained face. Her blue eyes were glassy and mournful. She could not have been older than seven, but her eyes appeared to be wiser than her age. Her line of sight shot towards the corner where they locked in on me. I froze. Could she see me?

Her eyes flicked back to her father.

"I miss Mommy."

Her dad approached her bed gingerly and then reached out his arms to hold her. She hopped onto his lap happily, snuggling against him as he rubbed her hair.

"I miss her too, pumpkin. They'll find her. You and me, we're a team, and we will get through this together. I promise you."

His own eyes had become glassy as well, but he held his emotions in. It was clear he was trying to hold it together for his daughter. She nodded her head as she tucked her tiny face into his chest.

"Emily...," Hazel choked out as eyes opened.

"What's that?" Tate asked as he rolled over to look at her. "Emily?"

Hazel took a moment to respond. She tried to connect the pieces of information that floated around in her brain.

"Hazel... are you okay?"

She turned to meet his gaze.

"Oh, yea. Sorry. My dream had my mind for a second."

His eyebrows lowered, as they always did when he was concerned.

"Spirit-induced? Should I be worried?"

She bit her lip.

"I'm not sure yet. Could you check into something for me?"

"Of course."

"A woman named Emily, who has a husband named Joshua and a young daughter named Bella. Can you check to see if someone who fits that description is missing?"

His eyes had grown wide. She already knew what that meant but waited for him to say it.

"You astonish me, Hazel. You really are amazing. The things you know... it's just incredible."

He leaned over and kissed her.

"Uh... thanks. You're incredible too. Have you heard of her or something?"

"You hit the nail on the head, love. I do recognize that description and she is missing. She's only been missing for about a week, though. She disappeared from her backyard in the Honey Island area. The police don't have any suspects yet. Her husband has been cleared."

Hazel's heart sank. Bella's mother was dead, and she would be forced to live without her. Hazel had never seen Emily's spirit, but Emily was close enough to send those memories to her.

Two new spirits had attached to her now, the dark-haired woman from outside of her apartment, and now Emily. She could not fathom helping them until Harmony was dealt with, but she could not turn them away either. She had to find a way to help them. She just hoped the task did not prove perilous for her, too. She had wondered if the dark-haired woman could have been a victim of Raymond Waters, but Emily could not be, because Raymond was dead.

Even if she hadn't intended to, Tate insisted Hazel bring Candy with her to work the next day. He wanted to make sure there was someone looking out for her at all times. He had also put his fellow police officer, Christine, on high alert, and asked her to make passes outside of Hazel's apartment. Even if no one was home, he wanted to know if Harmony was parked outside of the building. Hazel may have been one to take risky chances, but Tate was not.

With them both working the next day, Tate agreed with them staying the night in Hazel's apartment.

Unfortunately, she got off a few hours before Tate. It was a bit unsettling, but Hazel was exhausted. So, with a few hours to spare until Tate arrived, she laid down on the sofa for a nap.

A knock at the door startled her awake. She was not expecting anyone until Tate got home two hours later. Candy, who also heard the knocking, joined her from the bedroom. Rising from the sofa, Hazel tiptoed to the door and looked out of the peephole. Harmony Richard was just outside. She instinctively backed away from the door and sat back down on the sofa.

Intermittent knocking sounded over the next hour, but Hazel remained deathly still. She knew Harmony stood outside. She could see the shadows under the door and hear the shuffling of Harmony's feet as she paced. She hoped Harmony would eventually leave, but she did not seem to be giving up. Instead, the knocking became more desperate, as did the pacing.

"Hazel... I know you're in there."

Harmony's voice pierced the silence like a knife. Candy had settled in next to Hazel on the sofa, motioning for her to contact Tate. She had been hoping Harmony would give up, that she would move on to something else. She did not want to summon Tate into a dangerous situation. She did not know what Harmony was capable of, or if she had a weapon. Realizing Harmony was not going to leave, Hazel texted Tate, filling him in on the situation. He and fellow police officer, Christine, were on their way. She only needed Harmony to remain outside for a little longer. With any luck, she would get arrested.

"How do you know Candy, Hazel? I don't think it's a coincidence for you to live in the same apartment as the whore who my boyfriend was in love with."

A steady pounding alternated with Harmony's words. It sounded like she was leaning against the door. Her words were muffled. Hazel's heart pounded in her chest, but she remained quiet, cowering on the sofa.

"How do you know her!"

Harmony's screams made Hazel's body tremble. Harmony's voice had changed, just as it had in Hazel's first spirit memory of her. Hazel tried to fight back tears, but she had been unsuccessful. She struggled to text Tate. Her hands shook as she updated him on how the knocking had escalated. He responded for her to stay away from the door, and they'd be there soon. He told her not to worry, but that was proving to be impossible.

The banging on the door gave way to scratching, causing the hair on the back of Hazel's neck to stand on end. She could imagine Harmony sitting on the floor, leaning against the door, with her fingernails bloody from the friction.

The scrabbling at the door stopped abruptly as Hazel heard footsteps approaching the door. She rushed to her front door, but only dared to listen through the wood. Her tears had halted as she strained to hear what they were saying. She still did not know if Harmony had a weapon. She shuddered at the thought. She knew Tate and Christine would have guns, but Harmony could, too.

"Don't make any sudden movements, Ms. Richard. Keep your hands where I can see them. I just want to talk."

Christine's voice had come out sternly.

"I don't understand what all the fuss is about," Harmony responded with an air of innocence.

Hazel wondered if Tate was standing back so he would not escalate the situation with his presence. She wished he was in the apartment with her because she needed to keep him safe. She did not hear his voice, but she knew he was there.

"Why are you outside this residence, Ms. Richard?"

"I was just here to see my friend Hazel. I believe she lives here... does she not?"

"You need to leave this apartment building and not return, Ms. Richard. You have no business here. You are scaring the residents, causing a commotion with all of your banging. Clearly the person in that unit does not want to speak to you."

"So, I can go then? I can go home?"

"Yes, ma'am, but please do not return to this building."

Hazel heard footsteps moving away from her door before a frantic four knocks sounded.

"Hazel, it's me. Open up."

Her heart leapt while she fumbled with the lock, throwing the door open and pulling Tate into a hug.

"I was so scared!"

She started to cry on his shoulder but held on to him while he slowly backed her into the apartment.

"It's okay. You're okay. She's gone."

Tate saluted Christine, and she returned the gesture before opening the door to the stairwell and disappearing inside. Hazel and Tate made their way to the window to peer outside and see to it that Harmony was indeed leaving. They did not trust her to follow the instructions of the police. They could see her vehicle, but they did not see her. Tate narrowed his eyes and pulled his lips into a thin line, scanning the surrounding area for the petite woman who had left the building only moments before. They did not see Christine either.

"Do you think she ran into Christine in the stairwell? Oh god... do you think she attacked her?"

Tate did not respond. Instead, he took off out of the door, yelling for Hazel to lock the door before leaving the room.

"Follow him!" she told Candy before locking the door and sliding down in front of it.

Moments ticked by slowly. She wondered what could happen on the other side of the door, but she knew better than to open it.

Tate's trained for this. Tate's trained for this. Candy will protect him.

Wrapping her arms defensively around herself, she squeezed her eyes shut and began counting. It was the only way she could stop her mind from flashing through the worst-case scenarios.

A gunshot rang out in the distance. It had come from outside. Leaving her spot by the front door, she bolted to the window. She watched as Tate ran down the street, trailing Harmony by only a few feet. Candy, dressed in an outfit that appeared to be all black in the setting sun, followed behind them like an angel of death.

Grabbing her car keys, she ignored Tate's demands and left for her car. She would not let Harmony get away, and she would not let her hurt Tate. Taking the stairs two at a time, she got to her vehicle faster than she thought possible. She pulled out of the parking lot and turned to face the direction they had been running only moments before, but she no longer saw them in the distance.

They must have turned off of the main road. Shit. Where did they go?

She continued on the same path they were on, but paused when she got to the stop sign to look both ways. She could see the faint flutter of movement to the right, towards the direction of the Carrolton cemetery. Candy. Hitting the gas with a heavy foot, her sedan jolted back to life, and she took the right turn that would lead her in their direction.

She arrived at the gates of the cemetery just as she watched Candy float through them and out of sight. She left her car halfway on the street and halfway on the sidewalk before heading in after them. Once inside, she slowed her pace, although her heart wanted her to run, to get to Tate as soon as she could. She had to believe he had it under control. She did not want her interference to get either of them killed. She maneuvered around tombs quietly, being careful not to stay in a straight line. Thankfully, the large tombs were mostly above the ground, and shielded her from view and from gunfire. She had heard no gunshots since getting out of her car, but that did not mean Harmony's gun was out of bullets, if Harmony had been the one who was shooting. As she crept around one of the large clusters of weathered tombs, she could see Candy's fiery red hair just ahead of her. She stopped in her spot, trying to see if Tate had the situation under control.

Harmony stood with her back to her. She held a pistol in her hands and had it pointed at Tate. However, Tate had most of his body shielded by a large statue of an angel. His own gun was pointed at Harmony.

"Harmony, put your gun down and we can talk about this."

His voice came out calm, although Hazel knew his heart could not have been. Candy stood between their guns, ready to act but clearly unsure of her best move.

"Talk about what!" Harmony sobbed. "I killed that cop! No one is going to want to talk to me!"

"You can still help yourself Harmony. Let me help you."

"Help me? Why would you want to help me? You can help me by telling me how you and Hazel knew about Candy!"

Harmony's arms flailed with the gun still in her hand. Tate flinched, ducking behind the statue before raising his head to look back into her eyes. Candy, braced for attack, held out her arms at her sides, as though her form could deflect bullets. Hazel maintained her hiding spot, but she reached into her pocket and sent a text to Tate's boss. The police needed to get there before someone got killed.

Tate's face looked strong, determined, not afraid. Hazel's own fear, however, coursed through her veins. She could not cry anymore. Numbness had set in as she was forced to watch the scene from the sidelines. She could only hope the police would not take long to get there.

"Hazel didn't know Candy. I didn't either. I only know of her because I was called to the scene when she died. Why, Harmony? Why are you asking questions about Candy?"

Harmony remained quiet, clearly not knowing how to respond to Tate's question, but she did not lower her weapon. Candy caught sight of Hazel from the corner of her eye, shook her head and mouthed for Hazel to stay where she was, before returning to her watch over the escalating situation. Hazel wished she knew what Candy had planned, but she had no way to call out to her without risking her hiding spot. She could see Harmony's body stiffen as Harmony grabbed her gun with both hands, pointing it at Tate's head.

"You know both of us can't leave here, Tate... but I didn't want to hurt you. I want you to know that. I wanted to know you. We could have been good together. You should have chosen me."

Tate's eyes grew wide, but he did not move from his position. Candy stood sentinel between them. Her hair blew in the wind, giving her a celestial appearance.

"I didn't know how you felt, Harmony... but this isn't the way."

Harmony let out a cynical chuckle. "It's the only way."

Before Harmony finished her statement, a shot rang out, echoing in the air. Birds scattered as Tate toppled to the ground. Hazel instinctively screamed, causing Harmony to turn in her direction.

Harmony's previously innocent eyes were wild. She looked like a rabid animal. She raised her gun, pointing it at Hazel. Candy shot forward, moving in between the two women. With one flick of her wrist, Candy used spectral energy to fling Harmony's gun from her hand and onto the ground. Harmony stared at the gun in stunned silence. Her hands began to tremble. Instead of picking up the gun, she turned to stare daggers at Hazel. Hazel shuddered.

"How?" she snarled. Hazel hesitated.

"Candy. She here, and the police are on their way."

Just as Harmony was about to respond, sirens sounded in the distance, and they were getting closer. She tried to run, but Tate had risen from the ground and had his gun raised to meet her eyes. He held his shoulder with one arm. It was bleeding. He was hurt.

Harmony glanced from his gun to her own that was lying on the ground a few feet from her. Before she had a chance to make any decisions, four police officers brushed past Hazel, grabbing Harmony and forcing her to the ground.

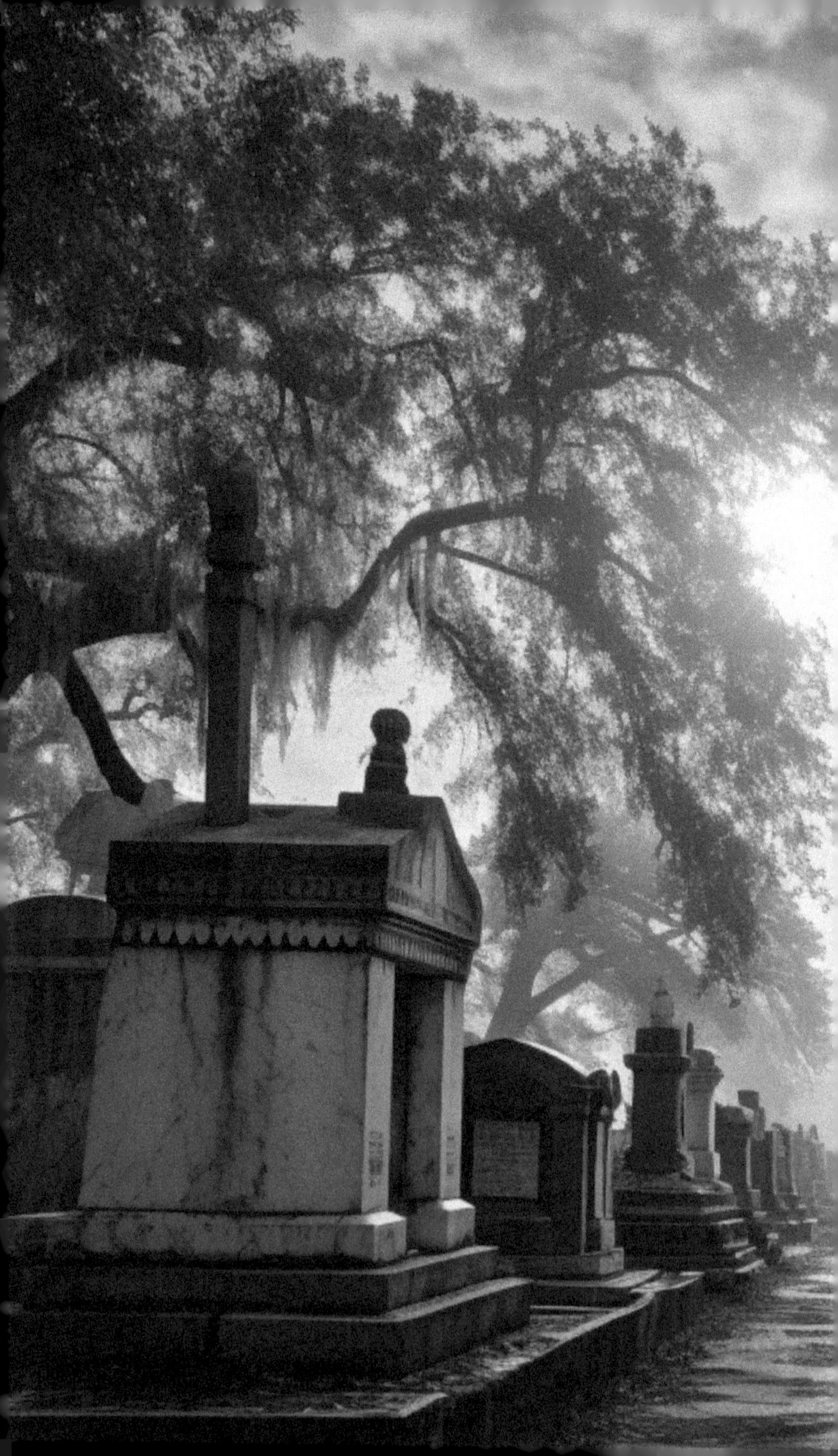

Chapter Twenty-Two

Moving On

"Are you going to dance with me?"

Hazel drove her car with one hand and held Tate's hand in the other. She did not usually drive them places, but his gunshot wound to the shoulder put her on driving duty. She rolled her eyes.

"I do not dance. You'd be leaving with your feet matching the bandages on your shoulder."

Tate chuckled. His shoulder was wrapped from the gunshot wound Harmony had given him, but he was healing well and was no longer in any serious pain. He was strong, only spending a few hours in the hospital before going home with her. He could have probably taken care of himself, but he let her fuss over him. She did not mind.

Harmony was in prison, waiting for her trial. Her arrest and admission of crimes to Tate in the graveyard was enough to get Brad out of prison. She had been formally charged with the murders of Christine and Jake, and then fingerprint evidence found from Candy's murder linked her to that crime as well. Hazel no longer had to worry about working Brad's appeal, a fact that released so much pressure from her shoulders.

After another harrowing ordeal, she and Tate both took some time off work to recover. Unlike Tate, she was not physically hurt, but her mental health had taken yet another hit, a hit she did not need after what she went through with Raymond Waters.

Candy giggled from the back seat. She sat with her head tucked into Jake's chest. He had gotten better at controlling his manifestations over the last few weeks, so he and Candy were enjoying their time together. Hazel worried he would eventually cross over, leaving Candy with the tough decision of whether she would cross as well, but Hazel put that thought in the back of her mind. It was too painful to consider.

They were going on their first double date, although Hazel was the only one who could see the ghostly couple. Tate was taking them to a food festival. Evidently it was a Cajun tradition, but Hazel had never been to one. The fair was more than thirty minutes outside of the city, but the traffic made it longer. Her stomach grumbled, but Tate had promised her jambalaya and crawfish pies at the fair. She had skipped lunch, so she had lots of space in her stomach for all the fattening Cajun food that awaited her. Arriving at the festival after nearly an hour's drive, she bolted to the food tent and suffered through the long lines to sample all the foods she could.

She had never listened to zydeco music before, but it was lively and upbeat. The man playing the fiddle never lowered his smile as he moved his bow across the strings at an expert level. The dance floor was filled with couples who danced hand in hand, most in conversation with each other, and smiles beaming across their face. Tate kept asking Hazel to dance, but the concept terrified her. She meant it when she said she was not a dancer. She had not only two left feet, she had one left foot and a crab claw.

The night was a fun respite from the traumatizing past few months. After eating her fill of food that was sure to upset her stomach later, Hazel gave in and let Tate push her around the dance floor. She stumbled more than danced, so they spent more time giggling than anything. She reveled in watching the elderly couples dance to the zydeco music as though they had done so for their entire lives, because they had. Her New Mexico family did not have any such traditions, which made her appreciate the Cajun traditions even more. In some ways, life was simpler on the bayou, and she would take a simpler life any day. It made her ponder her own life.

Maybe being an attorney was not the best career for her. The pressure was immense, and she seemed to always struggle with keeping safe. Her last year as an attorney had been the most challenging year of her life, but she did not feel better about it. She knew she would further disappoint her father if she gave up on the career, but a little more parental disappointment would not change her daily life. She did not know what she could do instead, how she would pay her bills, but it was a decision she intended to at least consider.

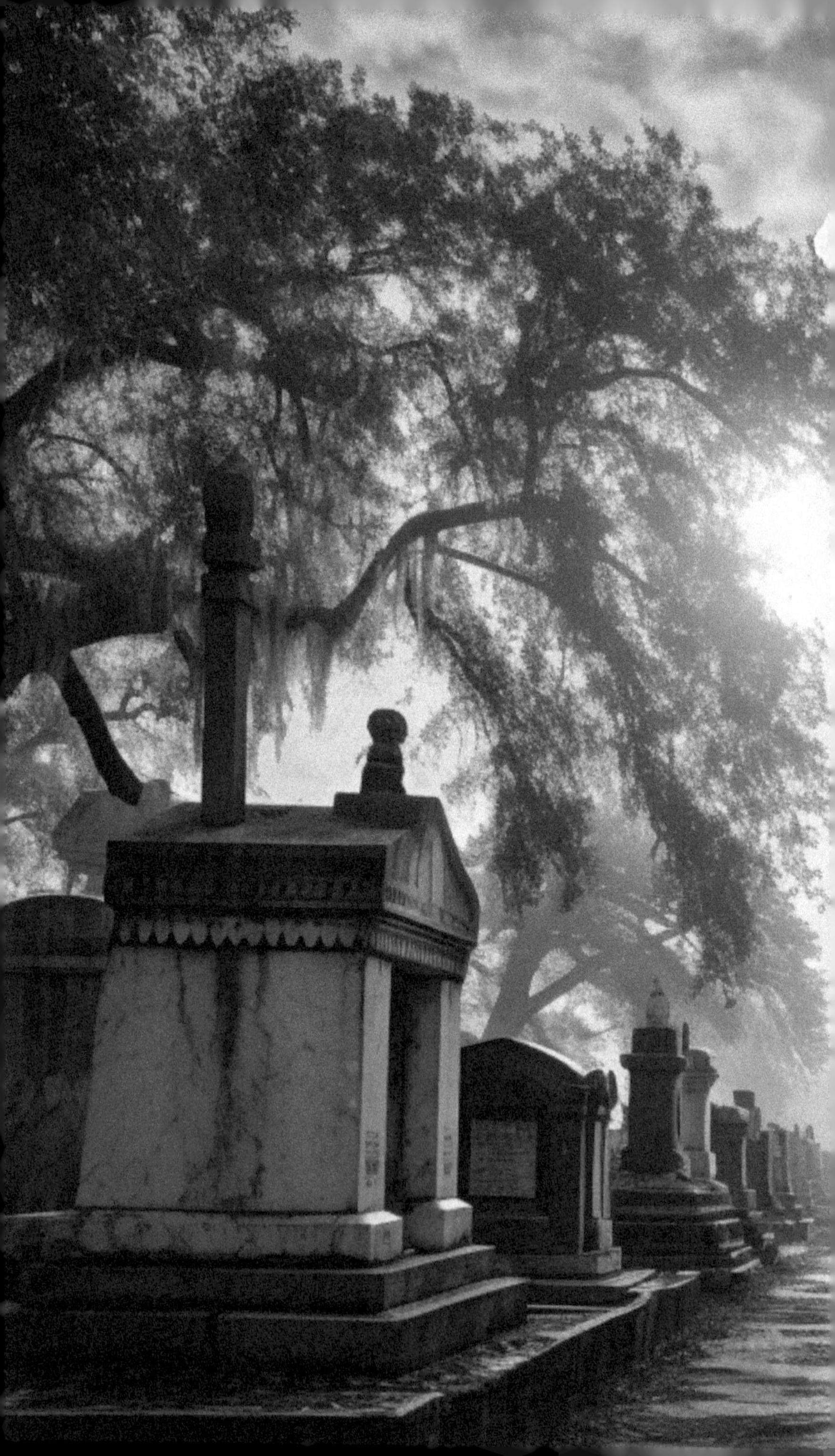

CHAPTER TWENTY-THREE

Epilogue

HONEY ISLAND SWAMP MURDERS

Hazel and Candy sat on the sofa, watching the local news. She was still leaning towards leaving her career at the Public Defender's Office, but she scanned through her case files to prepare for court on the following morning. Until she decided to leave, she had to carry on with her career as expected. The news played, but she had practically zoned out to focus on her paperwork and was no longer paying attention to the broadcast.

Breaking news pulled her away from the documents on her lap.

"The bodies of two women were found in the Honey Island swamp area. One body has been identified as Malerie Ledet. Authorities have not released the identity of the second victim. The police have no suspects. If you have any tips, please contact the number on your screen," said the female news broadcaster.

Hazel's heart dropped as dread washed over her. The woman's face on the television was the same face she had seen in her dream, the same ghostly face she had seen reaching out for her outside of her apartment. She did not need to see the face of the second victim. She already knew her name. Emily. The crime reeked of Raymond Waters, but it was not Raymond Waters who she saw in her dream. She could not make out the face, but she could tell that much, and Raymond was dead before Emily's disappearance.

Did Raymond have a partner?

The thought sickened her. She had to find the dead women. She had to know.

To be continued.

Candy Townsend
Born June 17, 1996
Died September 28, 2019

My heart was an inferno,
a raging fire that couldn't be
contained.
A flame that lit up the world
burning with fierce intensity.
A passion that could never be
quenched.
a spirit that could never be
broken.
A reminder to all that life is
too short
to not make the most of it.

Enjoyed Justice for the Slain?

If you enjoyed Justice for the Slain, please leave a review! I really appreciate it!

https://books2read.com/u/mqBPne

Follow C.A. Varian

Sign up for C. A. Varian's newsletter to receive current updates on her new and upcoming releases, sales, and giveaways:

You can also find all stories, books, and social media pages and follow her here:

https://linktr.ee/cavarian

https://cavarian.com

Also By

Hazel Watson Mystery Series

Kindred Spirits: Prequel

The Sapphire Necklace

Justice for the Slain

Whispers from the Swamp

Crossroads of Death

The Spirit Collector (coming October 2023)

Crown of the Phoenix Series

Crown of the Phoenix

Crown of the Exiled

Crown of the Prophecy (Coming Soon)

Mate of the Phoenix

Supernatural Savior Series

Song of Death

Goddess of Death

An Other World Series

The Other World

The Other Key

The Other Fate (coming January 2024)

My Alien Mate Series

My Alien Protector

Saving Scarlett (coming January 2024)

Second Chance with Santa (coming December 2024)

About the Author

Raised in a small town in the heart of Louisiana's Cajun Country, C. A. Varian spent most of her childhood fishing, crabbing, and getting sunburnt at the beach. Her love of reading began very young, and she would often compete at school to read enough books to earn prizes.

Graduating with the first of her college degrees as a mother of two in her late twenties, she became a public-school teacher. As of the release of this book, she was finally able to resign from teaching to write full time!

Writing became a passion project, and she put out her first novel in 2021, and has continued to publish new novels every few months since then, not slowing down for even a minute.

Married to a retired military officer, she spent many years moving around for his career, but they now live in central Alabama, with her youngest daughter, Arianna. Her oldest daughter, Brianna, is enjoying her happily ever after with her new husband and several pups. C. A. Varian has two Shih Tzus that she considers her children. Boy, Charlie, and girl, Luna, are their mommy's shadows. She also has three cats named Ramses, Simba, and Cookie.